"Just what do you think you're looking at?"

Jaime asked.

"The real Jaime Mitchell," Karl told her. "The one who's capable of feeling anger and passion. I always knew she was there, somewhere deep inside you, shouting to be let out. I've been waiting to meet her. Waiting and wanting..."

Mesmerized by his softly spoken words and the strangely compelling expression in his eyes, she watched his mouth draw closer to her own. His big, calloused hands gently cupped her face. Then his lips took possession of hers.

But when he pressed her back against the bed, she tore her mouth away from his in a last attempt to hold on to her sanity. "We have to stop this," she whispered. "It's—it's a conflict of interest."

He smiled down into her flushed face, murmuring between seductive forays, "I know what... I'm interested in... and it's pretty obvious... you're interested in... the same thing.... I don't think there's... any conflict at all...."

Dear Reader,

Welcome to the Silhouette **Special Edition**
experience! With your search for consistently
satisfying reading in mind, every month the authors
and editors of Silhouette **Special Edition** aim to offer
you a stimulating blend of deep emotions and high
romance.

The name Silhouette **Special Edition** and the
distinctive arch on the cover represent a
commitment—a commitment to bring you six
sensitive, substantial novels each month. In the
pages of a Silhouette **Special Edition**, compelling
true-to-life characters face riveting emotional
issues—and come out winners. All the authors in the
series strive for depth, vividness and warmth in
writing these stories of living and loving in today's
world.

The result, we hope, is romance you can believe in.
Deeply emotional, richly romantic, infinitely
rewarding—that's the Silhouette **Special Edition**
experience. Come share it with us—six times
a month!

From all the authors and editors of Silhouette
Special Edition,

Best wishes.

JOLEEN DANIELS
Against All Odds

Silhouette Special Edition

Published by Silhouette Books New York

America's Publisher of Contemporary Romance

To Clint Collins, Karen Hedenstrom Rois,
Maritza Ejenbaum, William O. Yates, Esq.,
and Eddie M. Schimek, Lt. (Ret.) N.M.B.P.D.,
who were so generous in answering my questions;

To Dr. Stephen Koncsol, who helped me understand;

To the alumni and current staff
of Units 01, 318 and 601;

And to Colleen, who always gives her best.

SILHOUETTE BOOKS
300 East 42nd St., New York, N.Y. 10017

AGAINST ALL ODDS

ISBN: 0-373-09645-3

First Silhouette Books printing January 1991

Printed in the U.S.A.

Books by Joleen Daniels

Silhouette Special Edition

The Reckoning #507
Against All Odds #645

JOLEEN DANIELS

lives in Miami, Florida, where she tries to juggle a full-time job, a part-time writing career, an unmanageable husband and two demanding children. Her hobbies include housework and complaining to her friends.

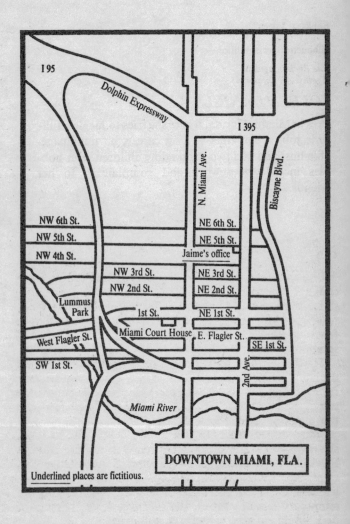

DOWNTOWN MIAMI, FLA.

Underlined places are fictitious.

Chapter One

"I want to see Jaime Mitchell, and I mean *now*!"

The sound of a deep, masculine voice raised in anger caused Jaime to look up in alarm, the case-record narrative she'd been writing temporarily forgotten. Hearing heavy footsteps approaching from the hallway, she pushed away from her cluttered desk and stood up, her wooden chair scraping against the floor tiles.

The six-foot-high wall that separated her small office from the hallway blocked most of her view, but she could see dark red eyebrows and even darker red hair projecting above the top of the partition. She was nearly six feet tall herself, but this man had to be at least six foot five!

Jaime forced herself to take a deep breath and let it out slowly. She was a social worker representing the State of Florida's Department of Health and Rehabilitative Services. She was a professional. Whatever this man's problem was, she would find a way to deal with it. Resenting her temporary loss of control, she sat back down, hoping the desk would enhance her aura of authority.

Then the owner of the loud voice and heavy footsteps strode into her office, and Jaime knew that all the authority that she could muster wasn't going to be sufficient to hold this man in check if he didn't choose to be held. He was the largest, most imposing human being she had ever encountered.

He paused briefly just inside the doorway, and Jaime had time to register a fleeting impression of a thick mass of dark red hair, a neatly trimmed beard, and eyes as blue and cold as a Scandinavian fiord. Then he came toward her desk looking for all the world like a bloodthirsty Viking warrior charging into combat. And from the look on his face he had no intention of taking any prisoners.

Jaime folded her hands on top of her desk, her features as composed and expressionless as she could make them. "*I'm* Jaime Mitchell. How can I help you?"

"I'm Karl Hallstrom, and you can start by explaining this!"

A white, legal-size piece of paper skidded across her desk, coming to rest in front of her. Jaime only had to glance at it to recognize what it was. Lord knew, she'd seen enough of these forms in the past five years to be able to recite one from memory.

"It's a notice that a hearing's been scheduled to evaluate the competency of—" She examined the document more closely. "—Ivar Hallstrom."

Jaime raised her eyes from the paper only to have them encounter a pair of muscular, blue-denim clad thighs separated from her by a scant three-foot expanse of desk. Slowly she let her gaze travel up to a thick leather belt and to the green-and-yellow plaid work shirt above it. She noticed the crisp red-brown curls lurking above the top button then tried to absorb the impossible width of his shoulders—shoulders so massive that they actually made his waist and hips appear slender in comparison.

She had anticipated a craggy, rough-hewn face, so, his handsome, finely carved features came as something of a shock. His skin was lightly tanned—darker than she would have thought possible, considering that red hair. But then no freckle would dare appear on *that* fiercely expressive face.

Her heart seemed to skip a beat when, without warning, her visitor planted the palms of his hands on her desktop and leaned forward until the face she'd just been examining was only inches from her own. She was immediately conscious of the fresh scent of pine and the musky fragrance of his cologne. In her peripheral vision, she could see the bulging muscles of his forearms below rolled-up shirtsleeves.

"Is the inspection over, lady, or is there something else you'd like to see?"

Jaime felt herself blushing for the first time in years. But she was determined to retain her composure.

Looking directly into his incredibly blue eyes, she projected every ounce of professionalism she possessed. "If you wish to continue this conversation, sir, you will have to take a seat."

The blue eyes widened in surprise, then narrowed in speculation. The big man remained motionless for a few heart-stopping seconds before he backed away. His gaze still locked with hers, he sank onto the nearest chair and folded his arms across his chest.

Karl Hallstrom felt as sullen and resentful as he had in the third grade when his teacher had reprimanded him for speaking out of turn. He was also just as powerless in this situation, and he didn't like that one damned bit. His grandfather, the only person he was able to call family, was being threatened. He was willing to fight to the limits of his strength to protect him, but he didn't even have enough information to know which weapons to use. To find that out, he had to learn more about the enemy.

He openly assessed the woman in front of him as she had assessed him only a moment before. At first glance she seemed as unremarkable as her office, with its gray walls and government-issued furniture. She was tall, thin and pale, her brown hair pulled back into an unflattering bun, her brown eyes innocent of makeup.

But those eyes had sparkled when she'd let her gaze trail over him. And her cheeks had flushed with color at his angry reaction. She'd looked attractive enough then. He'd even been tempted to apologize for his harsh words. But before he'd had a chance, she'd regrouped her forces and launched an attack of her own. She'd put him in his place with a voice that was anything but ordinary. It was as sensual as a caress and as cold as winter, like satin over steel. Wary now, he remembered the old warning about underestimating one's opponent, and wondered what other surprises she might have in store for him.

Breathing a heartfelt sigh of relief, Jaime began sifting through a tall pile of manila folders stacked on one corner of her desk. "Perhaps, Mr. Hallstrom, you'd like to begin by telling me how you're related to Ivar Hallstrom."

Karl shifted in his chair and grudgingly handed her a business card. "I'm his grandson. I own and operate a lumber company in Washington."

Jaime glanced at the card in her hand.

HALLSTROM LUMBER COMPANY
Complete On-Site Milling Facility
Serving the Seattle Area
Since 1908

For the first time Jaime noticed her visitor's heavy work boots with their liberal sprinkling of sawdust. All at once she realized where the pine scent had originated. "Is your grandfather a native of Seattle?"

"He lived there all his life until about five years ago. That's when he came out to Miami on vacation. He fell in love with the place, and he's been living here ever since."

Jaime opened her mouth to ask another question, but Karl cut her off impatiently. "Look, I came here to talk about the hearing notice. My grandfather called me when he got it in the mail." The blue eyes were filled with condemnation. "He was so upset that I flew down here myself to see what was going on."

Jaime finally located the appropriate folder and, flipping it open, began reading over her notes. Now she remembered. Ivar Hallstrom was the client that her neighbor, Wilma Woodruff, had brought to her attention. The last thing she had needed was another referral—especially one on a man who lived right across the street from her own home. But she knew Wilma well enough to be sure that her concern was genuine and well-founded. The woman might be a busybody at times, but she knew where to draw the line. And she was nobody's fool.

"Don't you even remember him?"

Jaime looked up from the file. "Yes, I remember him very well."

"Then how can you say that he's incompetent, that he's not able to handle things on his own anymore?"

"Three of us—three State social workers—went out to ask your grandfather some basic questions. For example, we asked him to name the President of the United States."

"But my grandfather's memory is better than mine," Karl asserted with a frown. "He can even tell you stories his father passed onto *him* about growing up in Sweden."

"There's a difference between long-term and short-term memory," Jaime said as gently as she could. "I'm not saying that your grandfather is a mental vegetable, Mr. Hallstrom. He's obviously an intelligent man. He can carry on a casual conversation as well as you or I. But once we got down to specific questions, he didn't know all of the correct answers." She glanced down at her notes. "He had to look at his newspaper to give us the date. He gave us an incorrect name for president, and—"

"Maybe you made my granddad nervous. If you were his age—or even the same age you are now—how would you like some stranger to come barging into your home uninvited, confronting you with questions like that?"

"I wouldn't like it one bit, but unfortunately it's part of my job. And it isn't simply a matter of his not answering the

questions correctly. Your grandfather has gotten too confused to pay his own bills, his doctor doubts that he's taking his medication properly, and then there's the matter
of—"

The phone rang, interrupting Jaime as she was about to
bring up the subject of the check that Wilma had told her
about. The five-thousand-dollar check that Ivar Hallstrom
had written out, but refused to explain. "Excuse me," she
murmured before turning her attention to her caller.

"Hello, Mr. Gonzalez. Yes, I'll be out there in a little
while. I know I'm running late, but someone just walked
into my office and . ..."

She spent the next ten minutes reassuring Mr. Gonzalez
before hanging up with an apologetic smile. "I'm sorry, but
that call concerned a woman who's very sick, but refusing
to go to the hospital. I'm due out there—"

The shrilling of the phone interrupted her in mid-
sentence. It was the niece of one of her Home Care for the
Elderly clients. The State was paying a small amount every
month as an incentive to the niece to keep her aunt at home
instead of placing the elderly woman in a nursing home. For
some reason, this month's check was late. Jaime pulled out
the woman's case and confirmed that she had processed the
necessary papers to issue the check. The man in her office
continued to stare at her with obvious impatience.

"If you still haven't received the check in two weeks, call
me back," Jaime instructed the niece before hanging up.

"Now, Mr. Hallstrom," she continued in a softer tone,
"I understand why you're upset. Sometimes it's hard to accept the fact that a loved one is getting to the point where he
just can't do all he used to."

"There's nothing wrong with my grandfather's mind, Ms.
Mitchell. And there's nothing wrong with mine either, so
don't patronize me. I know my grandfather better than
anyone. That old man raised me from the time I was eight
years old. He's the only family I've got left, and I'm not
going to let—"

The phone rang again, and Jaime automatically reached out to grasp the receiver. She was startled when her visitor's arm shot toward her. She hastily jerked her hand back and narrowly avoided having it pinned beneath his as he clamped down on the receiver, effectively preventing her from answering the phone. It rang on, a shrill counterpoint to Jaime's leaping pulse.

"Tell your secretary to hold your calls, Ms. Mitchell."

It was an order, not a request, and inwardly Jaime's temper flared. "I don't have a secretary," she told him, her words clipped, her tone frigid. "Our unit has a clerk—one clerk to cover six counselors, two aides and a supervisor. She doesn't usually have the time to hold anyone's calls, and today she's out sick. So I'm afraid that you'll just have to share my attention."

The phone stopped ringing. Jaime felt tension radiating across her shoulders and all the way up the back of her neck. She understood why this man was acting as he was, but that didn't necessarily make him any easier to deal with.

"I know that you're trying to protect your grandfather, Mr. Hallstrom," she said softly. "That's what I'm trying to do, too."

Karl couldn't believe what he was hearing. "By having him declared incompetent? By taking away his right to vote, his right to sign his own name to a contract, his right to make any kind of meaningful decision about his own life? I found out about the consequences of being declared incompetent before I came down here. I'm telling you, lady, he's a proud man. If you take all that away from him, it'll kill him! What right do you have to sit behind your desk and make that kind of decision?"

"No right at all, Mr. Hallstrom. I don't make that decision, the judge does." She glanced at the hearing notice. "In this case, Judge Harrison. In the next week or so, two psychiatrists and a layperson appointed by the court will be visiting your grandfather to evaluate him. They'll file their reports with the judge. At the hearing, the judge listens to testimony—yours and mine included—studies those reports, and may also question your grandfather personally before making a decision."

Karl looked at her suspiciously. "It sounds like I need to hire a lawyer to represent my grandfather's interests."

"An attorney has already been appointed by the court to do that. He'll also be stopping by to interview your grandfather, and he'll be filing his own report with the judge. But I have to warn you, if he feels that your grandfather is unable to handle his own affairs, that attorney will recommend that a guardian be appointed."

The possibility of things going that far chilled Karl to the bone. "And this guardian would be the one to take care of my grandfather's money?"

"And handle his personal affairs as well. Of course, the guardian is required to file a report with the court every year, detailing what he's done."

"If this Judge Harrison decides my grandfather needs a guardian, do I qualify for the job?"

Jaime considered his question. "If you're interested in being appointed guardian, the best thing you can do is hire your own lawyer to represent you at the hearing. And call your grandfather's court-appointed attorney. His name is Ron Martinez. Convince him that you can be trusted to take care of your grandfather, and he'll recommend you to the judge."

Karl was amazed and a little insulted that anyone would even question his intentions in that area. "Of course I can be trusted to take care of him! I would have been down here sooner if you'd bothered to call me."

Jaime leaned forward, keeping her voice level by sheer effort of will. "I didn't even know you existed. Your grandfather refused to answer my questions about his family or his finances. He wouldn't show me his checkbook or his address book. He wouldn't admit that there was any problem, and he wouldn't accept any help. If I had known that there was a suitable family member willing to take responsibility for him, Mr. Hallstrom, I probably wouldn't have had to file this petition in the first place."

Karl, too, leaned forward in his chair. "You know now, Ms. Mitchell. So all you have to do is cancel the hearing, I'll take my grandfather back to Seattle with me and we'll all live happily ever after."

Jaime hated to extinguish the glimmer of hope that she saw in his eyes, but she had no choice. "You can check with the court-appointed attorney, but I've never had a hearing canceled on those grounds."

Karl felt as if she'd purposely led him into the parlor and then jerked the rug out from under him. His resentment of her returned full force as he pushed to his feet and scooped up the hearing notice. "Then I guess we know where we stand. I'm going to fight you on this, Ms. Mitchell. As far as I'm concerned, you're the enemy."

"I'm sorry you feel that way," Jaime said sincerely.

Karl looked into her eyes and shook his head. "I think you're too hard and too cold to feel sorry about anything, Ms. Mitchell."

Jaime almost wished his accusation was true. Many years ago she'd learned to camouflage her vulnerability by projecting an image of self-sufficiency and cool control. At first it had been a constant struggle pretending to the world that she was strong and independent. Eventually it had become a habit—one that she was very good at. But her needs, her fears, her pain were all still there, behind the protective wall she'd built. At times it was still a battle to conceal them, but it was something she had to do in order to survive. But how could she make a man like Karl Hallstrom understand that? For some reason she felt compelled to try.

"If I let myself become emotionally involved with my clients, Mr. Hallstrom, I wouldn't be able to function in this job. I wouldn't be any good to any of them. I need to maintain a certain degree of distance to—"

"What you need is to get another job where you won't be able to use your clients' welfare as an excuse for your lack of caring."

"It's not an excuse, Mr. Hallstrom. It's a reason."

"Well, it's a lousy one!"

Biting back an angry retort, Jaime watched him walk away. As soon as she was alone in her office, she opened her desk drawer and pulled out a bottle of antacid and a box of paper cups. She poured and drank, then breathed a little more easily as the ache in her stomach faded to bearable proportions. She wouldn't let herself be upset. She didn't have time to waste thinking about Karl Hallstrom's accusations now. She had to get out to see the woman that Mr. Gonzalez had called about.

Jaime was standing up, stuffing papers into her briefcase when her phone rang again. With a groan she perched on a corner of her desk, her back to the doorway, and reluctantly lifted the receiver. It was a hospital social worker with another referral for the unit. Jaime listened to the voice drone on and jotted down the information she was given, her mind already on the field visit ahead. Finally she hung up the phone and reached for her purse.

"Listen, lady..."

Jaime felt a hand encircle her upper arm, and she whirled around with a gasp.

Karl found himself staring down into a pair of brown eyes that were wide with surprise and apprehension. He slowly became aware that she was trembling beneath his hand and that the trembling was just part of an incredible tension that flowed through her entire body. It pulsed against his fingertips, as strong and vibrant as an electric current.

He choked back his own exclamation of surprise. He'd been wrong. She wasn't hard and cold. She was soft, warm and unexpectedly fragile. And that cool control she was so proud of was stretched so far and so thin to cover her vulnerability that it was on the verge of snapping like an overextended rubber band.

Jaime looked up into Karl's blue eyes and felt the first wave of her fear recede as his expression slowly changed from annoyance to puzzled speculation. Initially his grip on her arm had been firm. But as he gazed down at her, she felt him relax his fingers until his touch was as light as a caress.

Suddenly she began to experience an attraction that frightened her more than the threat of physical violence ever could. She felt the unshakable inner strength of the man who stood so close to her, and she was drawn toward it like a thirsty woman to a shimmering fountain of water. Yet she knew she couldn't take even the smallest sip from those inviting waters, or she'd end up being engulfed by them.

It had taken her years of painstaking effort to build up her fragile facade of self-sufficiency and control. A man like Karl Hallstrom could sweep away that facade as if it had never existed.

Karl saw the fear in her eyes and felt a surge of protectiveness. He wanted to enfold this woman in his strength, to keep her safe, to shield her from whatever it was she feared. Then he flushed as he realized that he was the one who had brought that frightened expression into her eyes in the first place. Reluctantly he dropped her arm and stepped back.

Jaime took a deep breath and focused on her surroundings until they seemed to settle into their familiar lines. Only then did she trust herself to speak. "You came back to ask me something, Mr. Hallstrom?"

Karl's jaw tightened as he watched the expressionless mask slip back into place and hide the face of the enticing woman he'd glimpsed so briefly. He collected his thoughts with an effort. "Yeah. I forgot to get the phone number of my grandfather's court-appointed attorney, that Ron Martinez guy."

Grateful to have a concrete task to concentrate on, Jaime quickly looked up the requested information. She wrote it down on a scrap of paper and thrust it toward the man in her office. "Here you go, Mr. Hallstrom." She was anxious that he leave quickly before anything else happened to retrigger that strange attraction she'd felt surging between them.

She held her breath when she saw him hesitate as if he wanted to say something more to her. She was relieved when he finally just waved the paper at her and left with a muttered thank-you.

Those two words didn't make up for his previous comments, but they were certainly more than Jaime had expected. He'd seemed somehow preoccupied and disoriented. Could he have felt the same emotional pull that she had? Jaime dismissed the thought with a smile. Her over-reaction to his touch had probably been enough to scare him out of ten years' growth. No man would know what to say to a woman after the kind of show she'd put on. Well, what had happened, had happened. She couldn't do anything to change it now. Thank goodness she wouldn't have to see him again until the hearing. Whatever the outcome there, he'd be leaving town soon after. She really had nothing to worry about.

Gathering up her briefcase and her purse, she came out of her office and followed the hallway a short distance to a large open area. It was occupied by some file cabinets, the clerk's desk and the cubbyholes that served as mailboxes. Two of her co-workers, Maria Valdez and Sharon Ryan, had also emerged from their offices and were standing by the clerk's desk watching through the glass door as Karl Hallstrom negotiated the parking lot.

"That is one fine-looking man," Maria commented in a husky voice. She was in her twenties, single and darkly attractive. Her appreciation for Karl was obvious. She nudged Sharon. "Don't you think so?"

"You'd better believe it," Sharon agreed, causing Jaime to raise an eyebrow. In her mid-thirties and eight months pregnant with her first child, Sharon Ryan was a tall, sweet-tempered blonde who hadn't acknowledged the existence of any male other than her husband in the five years that Jaime had known her.

"Is he married?" Maria wanted to know.

"He said his grandfather was his only family," Jaime responded more sharply than she'd intended. She was surprised to realize that she found her friends' open admiration of Karl Hallstrom objectionable, and she was at a loss to explain why she should feel that way. Her lack of insight only made her resent the man more. "And, just for the record, his marital status does not interest me in the slightest."

Maria made a clicking sound with her tongue.

Sharon smiled. "Do I detect a little unprofessional hostility here?"

"Sharon, believe me, I tried very hard not to express that hostility to him. But you should have been trapped in that office with him the way I was. He's one of those men who just has to take charge and control the situation."

Maria laughed delightedly. "I think it's love!"

Jaime wasn't amused. "Don't even joke about that, Maria. I'm doing a competency on Ivar Hallstrom. Any personal involvement with his grandson—and potential guardian—would be a clear conflict of interest."

Maria's eyes sparkled. "I don't care. That man can conflict my interest anytime he wants to. He looks like some kind of Greek god."

Jaime made a face. "You two are acting like a couple of overage groupies. The only god that man reminds me of is Thor—the old Scandinavian god of war and thunder. His voice certainly thunders when he rants and raves. I can't say that I find that to be a particularly attractive quality, though."

The knowing look that Maria and Sharon exchanged was the final indignity as far as Jaime was concerned. "Okay, I give up! Think whatever you like. Just don't share your fantasies with me."

"She puts in an application for the supervisor's position, and she thinks she can give everyone orders," Maria teased.

"Just remember," Sharon chimed in, "I'm acting supervisor until the position's officially filled. So show a little respect."

A phone rang, and Jaime realized that the sound was coming from her office. With a fatalistic sigh, she used the clerk's phone to pick up the call. It was Ron Martinez, Ivar Hallstrom's court-appointed attorney. "Well, speak of the devil, Ron. Your name came up in conversation a few minutes ago. Listen, could I possibly call you back in the morning? I'm late for an appointment."

Ron's rapid-fire clipped words were an indication of his hard-driving personality. "Sure, babe, no big deal. You can give me the rundown on the Hallstrom case tomorrow. Just one quick question. Do you have any idea who Karl Hallstrom is?"

Jaime felt a chill of premonition. "He's the client's grandson, just come to town from Seattle for the hearing. I already gave him your name and number. He wants to be guardian. Where did you hear about him?"

"You know that five-thousand-dollar check Ivar Hallstrom wrote? I just found out from his bank that it was cashed in Seattle by Karl Hallstrom."

Jaime hung up the phone feeling angry and betrayed. Despite all denials to her friends, she had been attracted to Karl Hallstrom. Even when he'd been his most annoying, she'd found something likable about him. She'd been willing to excuse his behavior because she'd truly believed that he was only trying to protect his grandfather. And when he'd come back to the office and grabbed her arm, she'd imagined a subtle bond being forged between them, as if he'd somehow been able to sense her true motivations. She'd even thought that there had been an apologetic air about him, as if he'd been sorry for the way he'd acted toward her earlier. Now all she felt was foolish.

He'd probably been upset about the competency petition because he didn't want the truth discovered, the flow of cash cut off. Had she allowed sexual attraction—and that was definitely all it was—to distort her judgment?

Jaime pushed through the glass door and strode toward her car. She knew one thing for sure. If he was exploiting his grandfather, she'd make it her business to see that he didn't get away with it. Karl Hallstrom had spoken truer words than he knew when he'd said that she was the enemy.

Chapter Two

Jaime put her foot on the brake and turned the steering wheel of her old blue car. As she rounded the corner, the engine stalled out. Muttering under her breath, she coasted to a stop a few yards from her driveway.

It was almost six p.m., she was finally through for the day and now her car had to die under her. It was an appropriate ending to a trying day.

She was shifting into park when the glint of metal drew her attention to the driveway of a house diagonally across the street. Shading her eyes against the glare of the July sun, she saw a man, the top half of his body hidden by the open hood of a red four-door passenger truck. There was something tantalizingly familiar about the half of the man she could see—the half that was outlined in taut denim as he leaned over the truck's engine.

"Hi, Mom!"

The shout drew Jaime's gaze to a second, smaller figure standing by the truck. She smiled and waved. Then the man whose jeans she'd been admiring straightened up and emerged from behind the hood.

Jaime's mouth fell open in dismay. "Karl Hallstrom!"

Her son had already jogged across the street to her side, and his smile turned into a frown when he overheard her exclamation. Alex's green eyes revealed his puzzlement as he ran one hand through an unruly shock of wavy blond hair that no barber seemed capable of subduing.

Jaime fought back the urge to touch those golden locks herself, knowing from experience that a public display of affection would only embarrass him. Sometimes it was hard for her to remember that Alex was already fourteen, too old to be considered a little boy anymore.

"You know Karl, Mom?" Alex asked her as she got out of her car. "I was just going to introduce you. He's a really nice guy. He was outside checking out his truck when I got home from school. Boy, does he know a lot about engines! He was showing me..."

Jaime stopped listening to her son's words as the subject of the boy's admiring monologue came swaggering toward her. To her mind, there was just no other term fit to describe the pure male arrogance explicit in every stride the man took. But then maybe she was letting what she knew about his personality color her observation.

"Go into the house, Alex."

Her son stared at her as if he doubted her sanity. "But, Mom..."

Jaime watched Karl Hallstrom approaching closer and closer as Alex stood there arguing with her. She'd always dreaded the possibility of her professional life intruding into her private life, and now it had finally happened. Her carefully controlled temper was on the edge of snapping.

"Don't they give homework in summer school? You should be inside doing it, not outside talking to strangers."

Alex frowned, unable to comprehend his mother's anger. "Karl isn't a stranger! He's old Mr. Hallstrom's grandson from Seattle. He's come to visit for a couple of weeks."

"How do you know Ivar Hallstrom?" Jaime demanded, aware that the man's grandson was now standing a scant two feet away listening to every word.

"Mom, Ivar Hallstrom has lived across the street from us for five years! How could I *not* know him?"

"I've lived here the same five years, and I didn't know he existed until I got a referral on him."

"Mom, you could live someplace for a hundred years, and you'd stay inside the house and never meet anyone. I told you about Mr. H. He's a great old guy. He talks to me all the time about trees and Seattle and Sweden...." He paused as what she had finally penetrated. "What do you mean you 'got a referral' on him? For what?"

Jaime refused to cut the conversation short at that point and let the big man at her shoulder think she lacked the courage of her convictions. "He's been a little confused lately, Alex. I'm taking the case to court. The judge may have to appoint a guardian."

"What a lousy thing to do!"

Jaime felt the blood rushing to her cheeks. Out of the corner of her eye, she was sure she saw one side of Karl Hallstrom's mouth twitch with suppressed amusement. "Go into the house," she ordered her son in no uncertain terms. "We'll discuss this later, when I have time to explain it to you."

Alex stared into her eyes for a long moment as if debating the wisdom of arguing the point further. Finally he turned to Karl with an apologetic smile. "Well, it was nice meeting you anyway. Tell your granddad I said hi."

The big man's answering smile held such genuine warmth that Jaime hardly recognized him as the person who had stormed into her office. "See you around, buddy."

Jaime waited until she saw the door of her house close behind Alex before she turned to where Karl Hallstrom had been standing. She did a double take when all she saw was empty air. A clinking sound caused her to whirl around. He had opened the hood of her car and was leaning over the engine.

"Please leave my car alone. And I'll thank you to stay away from my son, too."

Karl straightened up, surprised by the open hostility in her tone. She'd been almost painfully polite to him before— even when he'd forgotten his own manners. He couldn't remember ever talking to any woman the way he'd talked to her earlier. He'd just been so upset about his grandfather, and she'd seemed so cool and uncaring.

But as soon as he'd realized that her ice-princess behavior was just a facade, his anger had evaporated very quickly to be replaced by the naturally protective feelings he had toward women in general. Jaime Mitchell, however, seemed to be holding a grudge. Or maybe her professional courtesy just didn't extend past five p.m.

Whatever the reason behind it, Karl found that her remark about keeping away from her son had annoyed him. He couldn't resist throwing her a little zinger of his own. "I had no idea Alex was your son. He certainly doesn't resemble you—physically or personality-wise. He's a nice kid."

Jaime's eyes narrowed. "Thank you...I think. Now if you'll excuse me."

She climbed back into the driver's seat and turned the key. After some initial hesitation, the car started up. Jaime revved the engine and watched in annoyance as Karl shut the hood. She drove the short distance to her driveway, an asphalt curve that came to within three feet of the small concrete slab that served as a front porch.

"That car needs a tune-up. And it could use a new set of tires, too."

Jaime glared up at him as she climbed out of the car, dragging her old, battered briefcase with her. "Tell me something I don't know."

He continued to dog her steps as she walked toward the rear of the car. "So why don't you have the work done?"

Jaime spun to face him, and he jumped backward just in time to avoid a painful crack in the knee as her briefcase swung with her. "If you must know, I'm putting it off because other expenses come first—like Alex's dental bills."

"Why doesn't Alex do the tune-up? He knows his way around an engine. He could easily install a set of plugs and points for you."

"Alex may have some mechanical aptitude, but he's only fourteen years old. He can't install his clothes in his closet half the time." There was a tiny, traitorous part of her—a part she chose to label weak and inadequate—that was actually grateful for this man's concern. Jaime knew that she couldn't allow herself to become dependent on that concern, but it was nice to think that he actually cared what condition her car was in.

"Your son is a lot more capable than you think," Karl was saying. "He told me that his father didn't live long enough to see him born. Given those circumstances, it seems like you could have let the kid assume a little more responsibility over the years." He shook his head as if deploring her parenting skills. "Well, if you won't trust Alex to do the job, what about your boyfriend? Can't he take care of it for you?"

Any gratitude Jaime may have been feeling was obliterated by Karl's words. She was so angered and offended by the implications of what he had said that she didn't know which question or statement to respond to first. And how dare Alex discuss his father with this man? But expressing her anger would only make her sound more defensive than she had already. She could only regain control of the situation by pretending a calm indifference.

"I appreciate your concern, Mr. Hallstrom, but I'm used to handling things on my own. I don't have a boyfriend who can take care of it for me, and I don't need one."

But the revelation that she didn't have a man to help her only made Karl feel more responsible and more determined to find a solution to her problem. "Then let me do the tune-up for you."

Jaime had almost reached the end of her patience. "No, thank you, Mr. Hallstrom," she said very quietly. She turned away in dismissal and inserted her key in the trunk.

Karl's expression clearly reflected his annoyance. "No one in their right mind would drive a car in that condition!"

Jaime's mouth dropped open, and she searched for words that would adequately express her contempt. "Do you always come right out and say everything you feel? Doesn't your brain edit anything out before you speak?"

"I'm honest enough to say what I really feel. I find I avoid a lot of frustration that way."

"Maybe that eliminates the frustration for you, but it certainly doesn't eliminate the frustration for the person who has to listen to you!"

"At least I'm not a member of the antacid-for-lunch bunch. I saw that bottle on your desk. If you're not careful, all those feelings you keep swallowing are going to eat a hole in your stomach a mile wide."

Jaime struggled for words to form a reply, but none came. He'd seen right through all her shields, and now she had nowhere left to hide. Fumbling blindly, she retrieved her purse, then slammed the trunk shut.

Karl watched her jerky, awkward movements and felt a rush of something that could only be described as tenderness. He looked down at her pale, tense face regretfully. "I guess you were right. Sometimes I could benefit from a little editing before I speak."

Jaime sighed, weary of sparring with him. "Maybe it's better if we drop this line of conversation."

"So tell me, why do you keep your purse in the trunk of your car?"

Jaime almost smiled. "Smooth change of topic there. Well, actually, the police have advised us to do it that way. I go into a lot of economically disadvantaged neighborhoods. If I don't carry a purse, no one can snatch it. I don't wear any jewelry, and I dress casually so I stand a better chance of blending in."

Karl let his gaze rove over her, appraising her. She did blend in. She was ordinary, unexceptional. So why did he find her so fascinating?

Their gazes met and held, and Jaime's heart rate accelerated. She had to force herself to look away. The man was so domineering, he bordered on being obnoxious. So why was she reacting to him this way?

"Excuse me," she murmured. "I have to be going."

She tried to walk around him, but he stepped into her path again. Unable to stop in time, she bumped into him and lost her grip on her briefcase. It hit the ground and popped open, papers spilling onto the driveway.

"You're a little klutzy, aren't you?" Karl observed as he bent to retrieve the papers.

Jaime bent at the same time and their heads collided.

"I guess that answers my question," Karl said as he massaged his forehead.

Jaime was getting more aggravated by the minute. "You're the one who wouldn't get out of my way! That body of yours is a lethal weapon."

Karl grinned at her suggestively. "So I've been told."

Jaime lowered her gaze, embarrassed by what he'd said and at a loss as to why she should feel that way. She'd been the object of some pretty direct come-ons in her lifetime, and she'd been able to laugh them off and forget them without any embarrassment or second thoughts. So why was this man able to make her feel like a seventeen-year-old schoolgirl with one mildly flirtatious remark?

"What is all this stuff, anyway?" Karl demanded, breaking into her thoughts.

"Case records, Mr. Hallstrom," she responded, absurdly grateful that they'd returned to a neutral topic. "Paperwork."

"You bring it home with you?"

The clear disapproval in his voice irritated Jaime beyond measure. "Obviously. It has to be done, and I don't have time during the day to do it."

"Are they paying you overtime for this?"

"No."

"And I thought that slavery had been abolished."

Jaime snatched the last case record out of his hand, shut her briefcase and stood up straight. "I don't recall asking for your advice, your permission or your approval. Good night, Mr. Hallstrom."

"Karl."

Jaime reluctantly turned back to face him, one hand on the doorknob. His blue eyes seemed to be mocking her, yet she felt it again—the tug, the attraction between them. "What did you say?"

"Call me Karl. When you say Mr. Hallstrom, I think you're talking about my grandfather."

Jaime considered his request. On the one hand, she didn't want to appear overly familiar with him. But in a way he was right. Two Mr. Hallstroms were a bit awkward and confusing. Besides, when other clients or their family members requested she call them by their first names, she complied with their wishes. And many of them knew her simply as Jaime. She wasn't going to treat this man any differently than she did anyone else. That would only be admitting he was somehow special to her, and that was the last thing she'd ever admit.

He was already smiling that lopsided, smug smile of his, as if he could read her thoughts—as if he thoroughly enjoyed watching her try to squirm out of the position he'd put her in.

Actually Karl was smiling over the fact that Jaime was taking so long to make such a simple decision. She was an unusual mixture of casual and reserved, and he hadn't even begun to figure her out yet. Again he wondered why he was so attracted to her. She certainly wasn't any raving beauty. More than anything, she reminded him of a thin, bedraggled little sparrow struggling to fly against the wind.

He kept picking up subliminal signals that plainly told him she wanted and needed his help and his caring. But every time he reached out to her, she slapped his hand. It was the most frustrating thing he'd ever experienced. Maybe it was just a matter for persistence and patience. Persistence he'd been born with, but patience wasn't one of his strong suits.

"Good night . . . Karl," Jaime finally said, as if bestowing some great favor. Then she turned and walked into the house.

"Good night . . . Jaime."

Karl watched the door close behind her, feeling inordinately pleased with himself. Only gradually did he become aware that he was standing alone in her driveway, grinning like an idiot. And all because a particularly aggravating woman had agreed to call him by his first name.

Perplexed and annoyed by his reaction, he crossed back to his own side of the street.

Suppressing an absurd urge to smile, Jaime dropped her purse and briefcase onto the living room couch. She bypassed the dining room table and turned into the adjacent kitchen. Opening the refrigerator, she poured herself a glass of ice water. Then she leaned back against the sink, sipping the liquid, lost in thought.

"Who told you that Mr. H is confused?"

Jaime looked up, startled to see Alex standing in the entranceway of the kitchen. For the past couple of months, his eyes had been on a level with hers, and she hadn't quite gotten used to this added height. Or to the fact that his voice was now at a lower pitch than hers—most of the time.

"Wilma has been helping Mr. Hallstrom with his bills and his chores for quite a while now, Alex. She's the one who noticed the change and asked me to evaluate him."

"No kidding? Wilma started all this? But she really likes the old guy!"

Jaime set her empty glass in the sink. "She was trying to protect him."

"From who?"

"From people who might be trying to take his money."

Alex's eyes narrowed. "You mean Karl, don't you? That's why you were so mad when you came home and found me talking to him. That's why you sent me inside.

Well, you're wrong! Karl would never steal money from his grandfather.''

"How can you be sure of that?'' Jaime demanded, surprised by the vehemence of his defense.

"Because I've seen them together, that's how. Karl loves his granddad!''

It was the same impression Jaime had gotten earlier in her office—before the court-appointed attorney's phone call. But she pushed that impression aside, not trusting herself to be objective when it came to Karl Hallstrom.

"Alex, I see seemingly concerned relatives, seemingly nice people, exploiting the elderly and the handicapped everyday. I can't just assume Karl is innocent because that's what I'd like to believe.''

"What did Karl say when you asked him about it?''

"I haven't. Yet.''

"Why not?'' Alex asked, genuinely puzzled. "Why are you so angry with him when you haven't even given him a chance to explain?''

Alex's words stung Jaime. She had to admit that there was some truth in them. After she'd gotten the phone call about the check, she'd worked herself into a real state of anger over something she knew from experience could have an innocent enough explanation. Had her anger just been a way of counteracting the attraction she felt for Karl, a good reason to hold him at arm's length?

She cut her thoughts off, disturbed by the direction they were taking. She shouldn't—she didn't—care about Karl Hallstrom one way or the other. She'd just do her job as if this were any other case.

"I need to try to talk to Ivar Hallstrom one more time before I talk to Karl,'' she told Alex. "He refused to tell me anything about the check before, but maybe he'll be a little less angry and a little more cooperative now.''

"Why do you want to talk to Mr. H before you talk to Karl?''

Jaime hesitated, knowing that her son wouldn't appreciate her answer. "Because Karl could tell me anything he wanted to and then persuade, or even force, his grandfather to back up the story. If I can get Mr. Hallstrom to talk to me first, I have a better chance of getting at the truth."

Alex looked disgusted. "You really think Karl is slime, don't you?"

"Alex, please try to understand. It's really not important what I think of Karl Hallstrom. He's not my client, his grandfather is. And his grandfather will be the one to suffer if Karl isn't as aboveboard as he seems."

"So why didn't you go across the street and talk to Mr. H as soon as you got home?"

"Because it was late, I was tired and I'd dealt with enough problems for one day. I'll talk to both of the Hallstroms tomorrow."

"And if you find out Karl's okay, then I can hang around with him?"

Jaime felt an acute flair of annoyance. How could she explain her feelings about Karl Hallstrom to her teenaged son when she didn't even understand them herself? "Whether Karl is exploiting his grandfather or not is irrelevant. Our having any type of personal relationship with the Hallstroms is out of the question. I'm supposed to give objective testimony at the hearing. I can't be objective if I start thinking of the Hallstroms as family friends, now can I?"

"*I* don't have to testify," Alex was quick to point out.

"Alex, if you're involved with these people, you're going to get me involved, too. Look what happened today with my car."

"Karl would have come over anyway when he saw you stall out and—"

Jaime had reached the end of her patience. "I don't want you over there anymore, Alex. Please help me out with this."

"I really like being around old Mr. Hallstrom," Alex said resentfully. "And Karl knows so much about engines. It's not fair to make me give all that up because of some dumb court order that shouldn't have been filed in the first place!"

"Sometimes life isn't fair, Alex. Sometimes it's hard to act grown-up and responsible."

"You want me to act grown-up and responsible about this, but when I want to do other things that are grown-up and responsible, you won't let me."

After the day Jaime had had, a conversation like this was the last thing she needed. "Are you bringing up the subject of the job again?"

Alex pushed ahead, all his eagerness and frustration pouring out at once. "Why won't you let me earn some money and help you? Mr. Monroe already offered me a part-time job at his garage. He said he'd train me to be a mechanic."

Memories from years past were triggered by the words "mechanic" and "garage"—painful memories that Jaime didn't want to deal with. She walked out of the kitchen and stood with her back to Alex, one hand resting on a dining room chair as if the furniture could lend her support.

"We've been over this before, Alex. What about your grades?"

Alex gave a long-suffering sigh. "Last reporting period, I got an A in math and a B in science. All the rest were Cs."

"Exactly. That's why you need to study harder. You don't need a job taking up any of your time. If you expect to get into a good college—"

"I told you, I don't want to go to college! I want to be a mechanic!"

"And I told you that when you grow up, you'll need to have a good job. And for that you have to go to college."

Alex felt helpless, fenced in. He was trying to use his mechanical aptitude to take on responsibility, to act like a man. But his mother wanted him to be a man her way. And her way meant he was supposed to be a straight A, paper-pushing preppie. For a long time, he'd believed that he could do that for her if he just tried hard enough. But finally he'd had to admit the truth—the grades he was getting now were the best he was ever going to get. He'd been trying to tell her that for a long time, but she just refused to hear it.

"Is going to college how you got *your* wonderful job?" he asked sharply.

Without another word, Jaime walked down the hallway and entered the bathroom, closing the door behind her. She wouldn't cry. Tears never helped anything. She wanted to give Alex all the best things in life, to make sure every opportunity was open to him. But all he wanted to do was goof off in school and go to work in some grubby garage. Well, he might be stubborn, but so was she. She wouldn't let him ruin his life the way his father had ruined his. For Alex's sake, she had to make him do the right thing, choose the right course.

Jaime stripped her clothes off and studied her reflection in the mirror on the back of the door. She looked so thin, so tired. Maybe before she went over to the Hallstroms' tomorrow, she'd put on some makeup. Maybe if she wore her hair down ...

Angrily Jaime jerked herself back to reality. She couldn't afford to have thoughts like those. Karl Hallstrom affected her too strongly. She made a solemn promise to herself. After she got the information about the check, she'd be very careful to avoid him until the day of the hearing. That was only two weeks from today. How difficult could it be to stay out of the man's way for that long?

That resolution brought her a little peace of mind. She stepped into the shower, determined to wash away the troubles of the day. She shampooed her hair vigorously, then toweled it dry. Dressing herself in the pajamas and robe she kept hanging on the back of the door, she threw her dirty clothes into the hamper and emerged from the bathroom.

The smell of frying hamburgers greeted her as she approached the kitchen. Alex looked up from the stove.

"I'm sorry for what I said, Mom."

Jaime closed the distance between them and took her son into her arms. "I'm sorry, too, Alex. I just want you to be happy. I know my job isn't the greatest, but at least I make my own decisions, I have some control. There's no boss standing over me every minute, telling me what to do." She pulled back to look at him. "I want that for you when you grow up, Alex. I want you to be someone I can be proud of—someone you can be proud of. Not like..."

Her words trailed off, but Alex could have finished the sentence for her: *Not like your father.* She never said the words aloud, but they were in her eyes along with the bitterness he always saw there whenever the subject of his father came up.

Jaime stepped back, uncomfortable under his probing gaze. "Not like other people who miss opportunities they should have taken and then regret it later." She touched his arm. "I know you want to get a job so you can be more independent and have more spending money. I couldn't even buy you those expensive sneakers you wanted."

Alex wondered why she never seemed to hear him no matter how many times he repeated the words. "Spending money and sneakers aren't that important to me, Mom. I really do want to help you."

"Do your best in school. That's all the help I need."

"I am doing my best, Mom. I swear it."

He turned away from her, frustrated by his inability to communicate with her. Every time the subject came up, they argued like they'd done tonight. His mother got upset, and he ended up feeling guilty and ungrateful.

He flipped the hamburgers over. "Sometimes, Mom," he said quietly, "I just feel like something inside me is getting ready to explode."

Jaime looked at him in surprise. "I guess everyone feels that way at times. There are never enough hours in the day, there's never enough money to do the things we really want to do." Suddenly she thought of an idea that might make him feel better. "What if we could afford to go on a real vacation this year? Maybe fly out and see California?"

Alex wanted to tell her that a vacation wouldn't solve the problem, but he just didn't have the heart. Someday he'd get her to understand. He just hoped it would be someday soon.

"Sure, Mom. Sounds like fun. But where are we going to get the money?"

"You let me worry about that. Okay?"

"Okay."

She kissed him on the cheek and smoothed his hair. He was a good boy. Everything was going to work out fine. It had to.

After they'd eaten dinner and finished the dishes, Jaime sponged off the tablecover and spread her paperwork out in front of her. Alex had already gone to his room to study and to watch TV.

She worked steadily, filling out computer forms and writing the narratives that she never seemed to have time to write during the day. When she finally paused to glance up at the clock, it was already eleven.

Gathering up the papers, she stuffed them back into her briefcase and set it on the couch by the front door so she wouldn't forget it in the morning.

She walked down the hall to Alex's room and peered inside. He was asleep, fully dressed, with the TV playing and his bedside lamp still burning. She skirted the assorted motor parts that were lying on newspapers on the tile floor in various stages of dissection. She had pleaded with him countless times to throw them out, but he only seemed to keep adding to his collection.

Prying his textbook out of his hands, she set it on the bedside table and covered her son with a sheet. When he was asleep, he looked so peaceful, as if he didn't have a care in the world. She bent to kiss his forehead, trying to remember a time when she had felt that way.

Switching off the light and the TV, she stood in the doorway and found herself wondering if Karl was in bed already. She'd bet anything that he slept the same way Alex did: soundly and straight through to morning. She tossed and turned and more often than not awoke feeling more tired than she had the night before.

She thought of the feelings she'd had in the office when Karl had first touched her. What would it be like to sleep in the same bed with a man like that? Would she feel comforted by all that strength and warmth? Would she, too, sleep soundly?

Then she remembered the sexy gleam in his eye when she'd referred to his body as a lethal weapon. She probably wouldn't get any sleep at all.

Annoyed with her thoughts, she walked into her own room, took off her robe and climbed into bed. It just wasn't fair! He had no right to invade her mind like this. Why was she so powerless to stop him?

Well, if that's the way it was going to be, she might as well let her imagination run wild and enjoy herself. But reality was another matter. Karl Hallstrom wasn't going to gain a foothold in her real life. She'd be extra careful and make sure of that.

Resignedly Jaime snuggled up to her pillow and gave in to her fantasies, drifting off to sleep wrapped in the arms of a red-bearded Swedish giant.

Chapter Three

Jaime sat bolt upright in bed, her heart thumping double time. The digital alarm said 9:25 a.m.

"Alex!" she yelled. Then she caught herself. What was she thinking of? Alex would have left at seven to catch his school bus. And she wasn't late for work. She was scheduled to do visits in the field today. But she'd told Mrs. Todd she'd be at her house by ten o'clock at the latest!

Leaping out of bed, Jaime ran to the bathroom, then back to the bedroom where she dressed in a blouse, jeans and an old pair of slip-on canvas deck shoes with thick rubber soles. She hurriedly brushed her hair as she drank a glass of milk.

Then she grabbed the package of heavy-duty garbage bags she'd bought for her afternoon visit and stuck them into her briefcase. Slinging her purse over her shoulder, she clipped her I.D. onto her blouse, shoved some money into her jeans pocket and picked up her keys.

She had just reached her car when the sound of voices raised in anger caused her to look across the street. Her neighbor, Wilma Woodruff, was coming out of the front door of the Hallstrom house.

Jaime had lived in the same house since she was a child. She'd seen old neighbors sell out and new neighbors move in, and she'd studiously avoided becoming involved with any of them. But Wilma was the original extrovert, pushy and persistent. She often dropped over unannounced, bringing a plate of homemade cookies and helping herself to a glass of Jaime's milk. She never seemed to notice the chilly reception she received.

Jaime told herself that she tolerated Wilma's visits because Alex adored the woman. She found it difficult to admit that she appreciated the motherly attention Wilma lavished on her and that she identified with the loneliness she sensed in the other woman.

"Why didn't you tell me you had a grandson, you stubborn old goat?" Jaime heard Wilma saying. "I would have called him instead of getting Jaime and HRS involved."

Ivar Hallstrom stood framed in the doorway, a very tall, impressive-looking man with a shock of white hair and vibrant blue eyes. Now his face was flushed, and his hair was disarranged. "I didn't tell you because it's not your place to be calling *anyone* about my business. I was doing just fine until you came along!"

Jaime started walking toward the scene of the argument. Even though she was already running late, she did need to talk to Mr. Hallstrom today. And Karl was nowhere in evidence. It was an opportunity she couldn't afford to pass up.

Wilma, obviously upset, was looking at the older man beseechingly. "We all get old, Ivar. We all need help eventually in one way or another. But you're afraid to admit anything's wrong. And if you refuse to even recognize the problem, how can anyone help you to do something about it?"

Ivar waved a hand as if dismissing what Wilma had said. "You've done more than enough already. Now go away, and take your social worker friend here with you!"

Fear, resistance, pride. They were all there in Ivar Hallstrom's face. Jaime hated stepping on this man's pride, but she had no other choice. "Mr. Hallstrom, listen to me. I know you sent that five-thousand-dollar check to your grandson, Karl. Can you please tell me why you did that?"

A slamming door was the only answer she received. Jaime sighed. She'd really handled that well. But would the result have been any different if her timing had been better?

Jaime looked toward Wilma and was surprised to see the older woman dabbing at her eyes with a tissue.

"What's wrong?" Jaime asked. She took in the familiar appearance of the dynamic senior citizen, with her lined face, flaming red hair and violet polyester pantsuit. And she braced herself for one more assault on the fortress she'd constructed to guard her feelings.

"Oh, Jaime, I don't think he'll ever forgive me for this. I wish I'd never gotten you involved. I didn't think it would go this far."

Before Jaime could respond, the front door of the Hallstrom house opened again, and Karl stepped outside. "What's going on?" he demanded. "I was taking a shower and suddenly all I could hear was people shouting at each other."

Jaime turned to confront him and realized with a shock that he was naked from the waist up. Against her will, her gaze was drawn to the rippling muscles of his wide chest and the auburn curls sprinkled across it. He was big and powerful-looking, but not with the massive brawn some weightlifters cultivated. His muscles looked natural, as if they were a result of good genetics and honest labor instead of any conscious effort to develop them.

As she watched, a bead of water trickled through the hollow in the center of his chest and down over his hard, flat abdomen. She had the absurd impulse to stop its progress with her lips, to taste the flavor of his skin with her tongue.

Karl watched in bemused fascination as the hostility in Jaime's eyes changed to a warmer emotion. He'd seen that look in enough women's eyes to know what it meant. He hadn't had a sensual thought in his head when he'd turned to face her, but the look she was giving him remedied that very quickly.

He let his gaze slide over her. Trim hips, slender waist, a glimpse of white lace at the neckline where she'd forgotten to fasten the top button of her blouse. Slightly parted lips just made to be kissed. And those hungry fawn-brown eyes that seemed to be eating him up alive.

Suddenly Jaime remembered herself and blushed furiously. She'd never had thoughts like this in her life before! What on earth was the matter with her? One minute she was angry, and the next she was wondering what it would be like to...

Desperately she tried to concentrate on what Wilma was saying. The older woman was addressing herself to Karl as if seeking absolution. "I swear, I didn't mean to hurt your grandfather."

When Karl spoke, Jaime could hear the barely controlled hostility in his voice. "What's done is done. Now we all have to live with it as best we can."

Shaking her head, Wilma turned and walked slowly back toward her own house. She looked older and more discouraged than Jaime had ever seen her.

"You didn't have to be so harsh," Jaime told Karl with a frown. "Wilma cares about your grandfather. He's very important to her."

Harsh? Had he sounded harsh? Karl had thought he'd succeeded in reining in his anger enough to be civil—even kind—to Wilma. "My grandfather's important to me too," he reminded Jaime. "I don't enjoy seeing him so upset."

"Neither do I. What's best isn't always what's easy."

The come-hither look had vanished as if it had never been. Karl wondered what she'd do if he stepped down from the porch and kissed her right now. Would the look come back, or would she slap his face?

As if she could read his intentions in his eyes, she quickly turned and began to walk away.

Driven by a compulsion he didn't even try to resist, Karl closed the front door and followed her. "You just can't make a statement like that and walk away, you know."

Jaime avoided his gaze, trying to sound more indifferent than she felt. "Obviously this is one topic we'll never agree on, so why bother discussing it?"

"Then why don't we talk about the mutual attraction we feel for each other?"

Jaime stopped beside her car and looked up at him. That was one subject she had no intention of discussing—ever. "I don't have time for this nonsense. I'm late for my field visits. And, just for the record, I do not find arrogant, overbearing men attractive."

Karl frowned darkly. "I'm not arrogant and overbearing."

"You were arrogant and overbearing in my office yesterday."

"Isn't anyone allowed to have an opinion that differs from yours? Am I supposed to apologize for that?"

"I think you *should* apologize for some of the things you said to me yesterday. And as for your glorified opinion, if you did my job for one day, that opinion would change in a hurry."

"Prove it," Karl challenged.

"Now how can I do that?" Jaime demanded. She threw her purse into the trunk, opened the door of her car and climbed inside.

Karl leaned down and gave her a smile that raised both her heart rate and her suspicions. "Take me with you on your field visits."

Jaime was already shaking her head. "No way!"

"What's the matter, not up to the challenge? You said one day would convince me. Are you trying to back out?"

"I—"

"Come on, Mitchell. You don't have one thing to lose except that superior attitude of yours."

"Superior attitude!" Jaime sputtered.

"If you convince me to change my opinion, I'll give you your apology—and anything else you care to name."

Jaime was about to repeat her refusal. She had no intention of spending all day in the field with an overgrown, ill-tempered, domineering Neanderthal. But then she stopped to consider. Maybe it wasn't such a bad idea after all. Karl was so angry about his grandfather, so quick to condemn. Let him go with her today and see what she did for a living. Maybe he *would* begin to understand her point of view. The fantasy of Karl groveling at her feet in apology was just too appealing to resist. "Okay, you're on."

"Great! I'll be right with you," Karl said with a grin as he walked away. His better instincts had been screaming at him to help her, while his baser instincts had been insisting that he make a move to get to know her better. Maybe he could find a way to do both if he spent the day with her. Of course he realized that it would only complicate matters if he got more deeply involved with the woman who had filed the competency petition on his grandfather. But he was a man who listened to his heart, not his head. Although that road was sometimes painful, it was never boring.

"Where are you going?" Jaime called after him.

"To get a shirt—unless you'd rather I went like this?"

Jaime groaned and leaned back against the seat. Somehow she'd forgotten about the physical aspect of being with Karl. Without exerting the slightest effort, he had the annoying ability to make her suddenly and achingly aware of the fact that he was a man and she was a woman. She'd never been ashamed of the sexual side of her nature. In fact she'd often wished that she could be more responsive. But why did her wish have to come true now, with a man who was so obviously wrong for her?

"Ready when you are."

Jaime's eyes snapped open as Karl climbed into the passenger seat and shut the door. She quickly looked away and refused to turn her head again, even when she sensed his gaze on her.

She shouldn't be thinking about this man's body. She ought to be asking him about the five-thousand-dollar check he'd cashed. Maybe the best time would be at the end of the day when—

Jaime was rudely jolted out of her reverie when Karl reached for the front of her blouse.

"You forgot to button the top button," he explained matter-of-factly as his big hands performed the task with speed and dexterity.

It was over before Jaime even had a chance to react. He hadn't touched her, only her shirt. Some men would have used buttoning her shirt as an excuse to put their hands where they didn't belong. With Karl it had been a nonsexual, caretaking gesture. His touch had kindness in it and...sensitivity.

Quickly, before he had a chance to notice her response, she turned on the ignition and revved up the protesting engine.

Karl smiled, full of good humor. "Senior citizens, beware! Jaime Mitchell rides again."

Jaime's jaw clenched, and her mouth became a thin, hard line. Kindness? Sensitivity? Where had she ever gotten the idea that those words could be applied to Karl Hallstrom?

"Hello, Miss Mitchell!" Mrs. Todd greeted Jaime at the door with a smile of welcome. "I was getting a little worried about you."

"I'm sorry I'm late," Jaime said. "I know that Emma has a doctor's appointment this morning." She turned to Karl who was standing beside her on the porch. "Emma is Mrs. Todd's aunt and one of my Home Care for the Elderly clients," she explained. "Mrs. Todd, this is Karl Hallstrom. He's...uh...interested in learning about social work, so he's doing visits with me today."

The middle-aged woman looked up at Karl and shook her head. "My, my, but you're a big one. Are you tame?"

Karl took the hand Mrs. Todd was offering him and grinned. "No, ma'am. But if you'll invite me in, I promise not to stay for lunch."

The older woman laughed as she escorted them into the living room of her home. It was neatly kept, but crowded with heavy, overstuffed furniture and brightly colored knick-knacks.

Jaime had been struck by Karl's genuine warmth, his gentleness as he'd carefully cradled Mrs. Todd's small hand in his. Those qualities hadn't been part of her first impression of him when he'd come barging into her office the day before. Perhaps his concern for his grandfather had overridden the innate sense of chivalry he seemed to exhibit in his dealings with women. For the moment at least, she was finding it very hard to fault his behavior.

"I wanted to talk to you about a problem I have, Miss Mitchell," Mrs. Todd said as her two visitors seated themselves on the plastic-covered sofa.

"A problem with Emma?" Jaime asked.

"No, it's not Emma. It's my daughter, Charlene. Her baby's due in a few months, Miss Mitchell, and she's been taking drugs. Cocaine, I think. I didn't find out until yesterday—about the baby or about the drugs."

Jaime hoped the shock she felt didn't show on her face. She dealt with a lot of disturbing issues in her line of work, but to be discussing a pregnant woman's cocaine habit in Mrs. Todd's quaint, plastic-covered living room seemed somehow inappropriate. At the least, it was totally unexpected.

Then Jaime realized that Mrs. Todd was speaking about her own daughter, and her heart went out to the other woman. "You say that you only found out about all this yesterday?"

"Charlene, she went to Los Angeles about a year back, saying that she was going to be a big-time movie actress. She always did dream big, that girl." Mrs. Todd smiled, her face shining with obvious pride. Then her smile faded.

"At first Charlene wrote me long letters saying how nice things were in California. She'd gotten a job as a cocktail waitress, and she was trying out for lots of film parts. Then she met this man named Jeremy Johnson. After that she hardly wrote at all."

"This man she met...is he the baby's father?" Jaime probed as gently as she could. "Did he come to Miami with her?"

Mrs. Todd's face twisted into a grimace. "He's here with her, all right. Dealing drugs just like he did in Los Angeles. He probably came to Florida because he was running from the California police."

"Do you think that your daughter will agree to go for counseling or consider treatment in a residential center?"

"Her boyfriend is dead set against it, and she does just what he says. I'm scared for her and the baby, Miss Mitchell. Real scared."

Jaime gave the woman's hand a squeeze, hoping to reassure her. "I don't really know a lot about this type of problem, but I think there's a law called the Mandan Act that might provide for involuntary commitment."

"You mean put her somewhere against her will?" Mrs. Todd shook her head. "I don't know for sure how bad her habit is. Besides, I want her to make up her own mind to get better."

"Sometimes people don't know their own minds when they're on drugs, Mrs. Todd. You think it over. I'll try to find out more information about other programs that might be available for Charlene."

After seeing Emma and chatting with the elderly, wheel-chair-bound woman for a few minutes, Jaime walked toward the front door with Mrs. Todd and Karl.

On the porch, the older woman laid a hand on Jaime's arm. "If Charlene drops by here one day, Miss Mitchell, and you're free, would you be willing to come talk to her? You might be able to persuade her to get help."

When Jaime hesitated, Mrs. Todd pressed on. "Please, Miss Mitchell. It would mean so much to me."

Jaime wondered what she had done to inspire such confidence. Mrs. Todd apparently had more faith in her ability than she did. "Sure. Give me a call the next time she shows up."

"Thank you. The Lord bless you, Miss Mitchell. And you, too, Mr. Hallstrom."

Karl seemed uncharacteristically subdued as they drove away. His mood lasted for about a mile before he turned to Jaime with a question. "You think you'll be able to help that lady's daughter?"

Jaime shrugged, trying to sound matter-of-fact. "I don't do a lot of work with substance abuse, but from what I hear, the odds are definitely against it."

Karl put his hand over hers where it rested on the seat. "Somehow, I don't think that will stop you from trying."

Jaime experienced a warm rush of feeling that had very little to do with sexual attraction. She was touched by his effort to encourage her.

Karl let the warmth of his large hand surround and enfold Jaime's cool fingers. He wanted to bring her hand to his lips and press a kiss in the center of her palm, but he knew she wouldn't understand his need to do so. He didn't understand it himself. He was astonished by the range of feelings this woman seemed capable of arousing in him.

When she had to lift her hand away from his to turn the steering wheel, Jaime was relieved. But, at the same time, she felt deprived and was annoyed with herself for feeling that way. She was glad when she saw Mrs. Levine's house on the street ahead.

Sarah Levine was one person Jaime always enjoyed visiting. She was ninety years old, but as alert and fresh-minded as a girl of sixteen. Jaime thought of her as ageless, despite her wrinkled face and shuffling gait.

From the beginning, Sarah had ignored Jaime's show of reserve and had treated her as she would her own granddaughter. Over the years, Jaime had gradually opened up and had come to tell the other woman more and more about herself. Now she considered Sarah more a friend than a client. To Jaime, Sarah's home was a safe harbor of order and acceptance in a world that was often chaotic and judgmental.

Mrs. Levine greeted Jaime with a kiss and a hug, and peered over her bifocals at Karl. "And who is this? A boyfriend finally?"

Jaime's smile was a little forced. "I'm afraid not, Sarah. This is Karl Hallstrom. He's just an acquaintance who's going on field visits with me today."

The older woman ignored Jaime and addressed herself to Karl. "If I've told her one time, I've told her a hundred times, Jaime, you're only young once. So live a little. But does she take my advice? No, of course not." She sighed and patted Jaime's hand in apparent tolerance. "Come, children. Come sit down at the kitchen table. I'll pour you some nice iced tea."

"The homemaker was just here to clean today," Mrs. Levine commented as she moved around in her kitchen. "And on Thursdays she shops for me. She's such a blessing."

"The State pays for Sarah's homemaker," Jaime explained to Karl. "And she gets delivered meals, too."

"It's true, I can't cook and clean like I used to," Mrs. Levine said as she set the cold, presweetened tea down on the table. "But I still make my own soup from scratch. Even the reverend from the church down the street sends hungry people to my home to eat my soup. I keep a pot simmering just in case someone should drop in."

Karl smiled. "I knew something smelled good."

But Jaime was too worried to offer any compliments. "Sarah, I thought we decided that it wasn't a good idea for you to let strangers into the house?"

"You mean *you* decided. Every human being is a stranger until you get to know him." She turned to Karl and patted his cheek with one plump, blue-veined hand. "Even this man, God bless him, was a stranger to me when he first came into my house. And look how nice he's sitting at my table now. I'll get you a bowl of soup, Mr. Karl Hallstrom, and you'll tell me all about yourself. Are you married, divorced, what?''

"Sarah," Jaime persisted. "This is serious! Don't try to change the subject."

The older woman waved her free hand as she ladled up the soup. "So what do I have that anyone would want to steal?"

"Even if they just *thought* you had something worth stealing, you could be in trouble."

Mrs. Levine set full bowls of the appetizing mixture in front of Karl and Jaime. "I'm an old woman. Should I expect to live forever? If I can't share what I have with other people, if I have to hide inside my house with the door locked and the windows closed . . . well, then I'm as good as dead already."

Jaime opened her mouth to pursue the subject further, but Sarah refused to allow it. "Eat your soup."

Jaime didn't even bother to protest that it was too hot outside to be eating soup, or that she wasn't hungry. She'd tried both arguments with Sarah before and neither had worked. Resignedly she picked up her spoon.

Karl reached for the salt shaker, and Sarah tapped his hand. "My soup doesn't need extra salt. But don't take my word for it. Taste it. You'll see for yourself."

Karl took a spoonful. "You're right, Mrs. Levine. As a matter of fact, this is the best soup I've ever eaten. You'll have to give me the recipe."

Sarah looked at Jaime. "Such a nice, handsome man, and he cooks, too. What more could any woman ask for?"

Karl smiled at Jaime's sour expression and examined the salt and pepper shakers more closely. "These look like silver."

"They are silver," Sarah told him. "My third husband, God rest his soul, gave them to me the first year we were married. Not a very romantic gift maybe, but he was romantic in other ways." Her eyes sparkled with memories. "I outlived all three of my husbands, and I loved them all. But the last one, he was like the other half of my soul." She wiped a tear from her eye. "Excuse me, children, but I have something to get from the other room."

Karl watched as the old woman shuffled out of the kitchen, a wistful smile on her face. He felt an emotion that was close to envy. Would he ever find the other half of *his* soul?

Jaime felt uncomfortable at the suggestion that there was another person somehow magically capable of completing her. At times she did feel that something was missing in her life, in herself. But she knew that it was up to her to grow, to improve, to fill that void. A woman couldn't depend on a man to do that for her. If she did, she was a fool.

"You really like her, don't you?" Karl asked, breaking in on Jaime's thoughts.

"It's hard not to like Sarah. She really believes that everything in the world can be made right with a little soup and a lot of kindness." Jaime smiled, unaware of the glow that suffused her face when she spoke of the other woman. "Besides, she's one of my success stories. She's a lady who's had the courage to admit her limitations. She accepts all the help we can give her. Because of the homemaker and the delivered meals, she's able to continue to live in her own home."

Karl looked at her, one eyebrow raised. "Are you trying to tell me that my grandfather should learn to accept his limitations?"

Jaime's smile faded. "I hope he does, for his sake."

Mrs. Levine came back into the kitchen, interrupting their conversation. She laid a beautifully crocheted black shawl on Jaime's lap. "I made it for you. It's a late birthday present."

"My birthday was six months ago, Sarah, and you know you already gave me a birthday present."

"So it's an early Christmas present instead. You won't be able to wear it until wintertime anyway."

"At least let me pay you for the yarn," Jaime pleaded.

"Don't be silly! What are two skeins of yarn? Nothing. Now forget the money and tell me about your Alex. How are his grades?"

Jaime and Karl spent the next half hour drinking tea, eating soup and talking to Sarah. Finally the elderly woman went to find pencil and paper to write out the soup recipe that she had promised to Karl.

While she was standing at the counter jotting it down, Jaime pulled a five-dollar bill out of her purse and stuck it in the bowl of plastic fruit at the center of the table.

Karl gave her a hard look, but said nothing.

Jaime was following Karl out of the front door when Mrs. Levine tugged at her arm and halted her progress. "Your Karl Hallstrom is a good man, Jaime."

"You just like him because he said your soup was the best he'd ever eaten."

Sarah shook her head. "Now *I'm* being serious. A man like that would take care of you, Jaime. And he would give you beautiful, healthy babies."

Jaime glanced toward where Karl was waiting on the porch. She prayed that he was out of earshot. "I can take care of myself, Sarah. And I've already had the only baby I ever intend to have."

The other woman only smiled and patted Jaime's cheek affectionately. "I've lived every minute of my life, Jaime. I've taken more than a few chances. And that's brought me my share of pain. But it's brought me my share of happiness, also. That's what life's all about. Don't miss out on it. Don't let it pass you by. Invest a little. You just might end up a winner this time."

Jaime and Karl were back in the car and on the road before he spoke to her again. "Why did you do it?"

"What?" Jaime asked, surprised by his question.

"The five dollars for the yarn."

Karl's tone was mildly curious rather than accusatory, but his question still made Jaime feel defensive. "She doesn't have much money. She can't afford to be wasting it on yarn to make presents for me.''

"Is that the real reason?"

Jaime flushed. She knew what he was implying. "I guess my independence *is* very important to me."

Karl chuckled. "So I've noticed. But you should look at it from the other side, too. Doing favors for others makes a person feel useful and—hopefully—appreciated."

Jaime looked at him skeptically. "You mean you offered to tune my car so you could feel good about yourself?"

"Basically, yes. And, if you want to know the whole truth, I think that any man who lets a woman drive around in a car in this condition when he can do something to fix it, just isn't much of a man. There, I said it. Is my chauvinism showing?"

Karl's attitude disturbed Jaime more than she wanted to admit. It would be so easy to let a man like this take charge of things. But she couldn't allow that to happen. She'd had to struggle for every bit of self-sufficiency she possessed, and she wasn't about to let anyone take it away from her.

"It does sound like you think a woman is incapable of managing her own life."

Karl was honestly puzzled. He'd never had a woman react with anything but gratitude when he offered to do repairs. They usually attempted to reimburse him. He declined; they thanked him, and that was that. Apparently Jaime was going to be a different story.

"I'm sorry if it sounded that way." He paused, searching for words that would express his point of view. "I have feelings where women are concerned. Protective feelings. They've been a part of me for as long as I can remember. They have nothing to do with what I know up here—" he tapped his head "—about women being capable, and equal, and all of that. And I'm not ashamed of those feelings. I even think that the world could use a few more men who feel the same way I do."

Jaime was growing more frustrated by the second. "Look, I don't mind a little old-fashioned gallantry. If a man wants to open a door for me, or help me on with my coat, or pull out my chair, I'm not going to spit in his eye. But when a man I hardly know *insists* I get my car fixed—''

"I was *offering*, Jaime, not *insisting*," Karl inserted, a little stiffly. "There *is* a difference, you know."

Jaime tried to see things from his perspective. "Maybe I am being too defensive. But I can't afford to be obligated to you. Especially under the circumstances."

Karl muttered a curse under his breath. "You thought I offered to fix your car so that you'd feel obligated to me?" He'd been hoping for a little appreciation, but the fact that she would actually feel obligated to him for something he'd freely chosen to do hadn't occurred to him.

"No," Jaime replied after a moment. "But that's how I'd feel. Can you understand that? If the situation were reversed, wouldn't you feel the same?"

Karl had to stretch to imagine that one. "Yeah, I guess I would. I just wish it didn't have to be that way."

Jaime had almost convinced herself that taking Karl along hadn't been such a bad idea after all, when he asked her to pull into the parking lot of B. J.'s Sandwich Shoppe.

"Why?"

"For lunch—if this place is okay with you."

Sarah's soup had been enough to fill Jaime up. She would rather have skipped lunch altogether, finished her field visits, then gone directly home. She shrugged noncommittally. "Fine."

Once inside, Karl ordered a dinner salad, a Reuben sandwich, chili, french fries and an ice cream soda.

Slightly nauseated by the thought of having to watch him eat all that food, Jaime just asked the waitress for her usual glass of milk.

"Have you seen a doctor about that stomach of yours?" Karl asked.

Jaime shook her head. "It's from stress—the job, money worries. I don't need a doctor to tell me that."

"So why don't you get a different job? One that pays better."

"I started working for HRS as a social work aide when I was nineteen and Alex was a year old. I got my B.A. tuition-free at a State university." Jaime paused and looked at the man across from her. "I guess what I'm trying to tell you is that I grew up with HRS. It's the only job I've ever had. And it's a secure job with good benefits. I'm going to graduate school now—again, tuition-free—to get my master's in social work. I'm only taking one course at a time, but someday..."

The waitress came with Jaime's milk and Karl's food. Jaime had expected a respite from conversation while he ate, but Karl took a bite of sandwich and went right on with his interrogation.

"Someday what? You'll be rich and famous?"

Jaime felt like laughing out loud. "If salaries are any indication of how important things are in our society, the welfare of people who can't help themselves must be at the bottom of the list."

"I never thought of it that way, but I guess you're right."

"I know I'm right." Jaime smiled a little apologetically. "I don't mean to sound preachy. It's just that I know what it's like to be poor and helpless. My father left Mom and me when I was twelve. Mom was almost fifty then, with very little education and no job skills. We existed on welfare and food stamps until I got a job with the state."

Jaime took a sip of milk and fiddled with the napkin on her lap. "I know what you're thinking. Mom could have gotten training, she could have found work. But after my father left, she just didn't care anymore. He was the strong one. He made all the decisions. When he left, she was lost without him. She just sat around waiting for him to come back."

"And you swore that would never happen to you," Karl said softly, comprehending the motivation behind her fierce independence.

"That's right. And it never will. I'll never be like my mother. She lived long enough to take care of Alex until he started school. When she passed away, she left me the house.

It's still mortgaged to the hilt, but it's mine. She gave me that much, but she never gave me any idea of how to be strong, how to achieve, how to survive. I had to figure that out for myself. You know how she died?''

Karl shook his head.

"She got a letter from some woman telling her that my long-lost father had died of cancer. That same day she was gone. The doctor said that it was her heart. But I knew better. She just had no reason to live anymore. Can you imagine being that dependent on another person?''

Karl swallowed the last bite of sandwich. "My father was killed in a boating accident when I was eight. A few months later my mother left to 'do her own thing.' I haven't seen her or heard from her since. I love my grandfather. But since the day my mother left, I haven't been dependent on anyone.''

Jaime sensed more pain beneath those words than Karl was willing to reveal. Had his mother's desertion affected him as profoundly as her father's leaving had affected her? She decided to probe a little further.

"I remember you told Sarah that you'd never been married. That surprised me. I'd have thought a man like you would want a traditional 'little woman' at home to cook his meals and darn his socks.''

Karl laughed at the picture she painted. "You have the wrong man. I enjoy cooking my own meals. And if a sock gets a hole in it, I just buy a new pair.''

"But when you do marry, your wife will be a woman who does things the way *you* want them done.''

It was a statement, not a question. The ice princess thought she had him all figured out. "I'll admit that I find sweet, agreeable women pleasant to be around. But over the years I've learned to appreciate the bittersweet ladies, too.''

Jaime was annoyed by his remarks. Maybe it was because he seemed to classify women like chocolate bars—as if they were different flavors to be selected and consumed according to his mood. Or maybe it was the gleam in his eye—the gleam that made it clear which category *she* belonged in.

"You talk as if you're quite a connoisseur, Karl. Have you just dated extensively, or do you keep your own harem?"

Karl just looked at her and smiled. "Harem" was one word people had used to describe his numerous and diverse female acquaintances—people who didn't know any better. "I guess I'm just too conservative to keep a harem." He was about to tell her in plain language that he hadn't slept with a woman in four months. On second thought, he couldn't resist throwing out a certain word just to see her reaction. "Actually I'm celibate."

Jaime almost choked on her milk. "Celibate?"

She couldn't have heard right! Did he really expect her to believe that? Why would a man with his obvious sex appeal choose not to take advantage of it? He'd only had to smile at the waitress, and the poor woman had been so disconcerted she'd nearly dropped his bowl of chili into his lap. He must be teasing her! Or maybe it was some kind of come-on. Was she supposed to feel challenged by his unattainability? Then she looked into those blue eyes and realized that Karl Hallstrom didn't need to use any gimmicks to seduce a woman.

"Are you...ill?" she asked tentatively, unable to resist pursuing the line of conversation.

Karl was amused by her delicately phrased inquiry. "No. I came out of a long-term relationship with a lady about four months ago, and I guess I just haven't felt the need to get...involved since then."

Of all people, Jaime could understand how being hurt in a relationship could cause someone to avoid involvement with the opposite sex. But Karl hadn't seemed particularly sad when he'd spoken about the broken relationship and his lost love. There was something else there. A sense of disappointment, of failed expectations, that touched Jaime's heart.

"But you didn't love her, did you?"

Karl shook his head. "I've always wanted to be in love, to have a wife and children. But I've never fallen in love."

His expression was self-derisive. "And no woman has ever fallen in love with me."

Jaime looked at him as if he'd just announced that the sky was green.

"It's true. After a few months of my company, the physical attraction starts to ebb, and they all seem to gravitate to other men. I stay friends with most of them. I fix their cars, loan them money, listen to their problems. And I get invited to their weddings."

"Maybe," Jaime said hesitantly, " . . . maybe you just don't need them enough."

"What do you mean?"

"You mentioned all the things you did for them and all the things you gave them. But maybe what you didn't give them was the feeling that you needed them."

Karl suddenly found himself on uncomfortable ground— ground he didn't want to examine too closely. "And what about you? Do you need anyone?"

Jaime found that the tables had been turned very neatly. She didn't like it one bit. "I have my son. And my friends."

"But surely there was a time when you wanted more?" Karl persisted. "After all, you married Alex's father. You must have been in love."

Jaime looked away, feeling a sudden chill. "At seventeen I didn't know the meaning of the word."

"How did he die?"

All at once Jaime was sure that she'd had enough of Karl's questions. She stood up abruptly. "I don't really care to discuss that right now. If you'll excuse me for a minute . . ."

Walking rapidly, she rounded a corner and entered another section of the restaurant. An intervening wall hid her from Karl's view, and she knew he wouldn't follow. He'd just assume that she'd gone to the ladies' room. If she hurried, there wouldn't be any problem.

After speaking to the cashier, Jaime sat down in a nearby booth and placed the form the woman had given her on top of the table. Only then did she realize that she was trembling.

She rested her elbows on the table and rubbed her forehead with both hands. She had to calm down; she was overreacting again. Karl didn't mean any harm. He was just trying to make conversation. She'd asked him personal questions, too, and he hadn't gotten upset. Still, the sooner he was out of her life, the safer she'd feel. Meanwhile she had more important things to concern her. Like that vacation she had promised Alex.

Determinedly Jaime sat up straight and began to fill out the job application in front of her. She'd seen the Help Wanted sign when she'd entered the restaurant, and the cashier had just told her that they could use a part-time waitress evenings and weekends. Now if she could only get her hands to stop shaking . . .

Karl looked up as Jaime came back to stand by their booth. She'd been gone a long time. In fact, he'd started to suspect that she'd walked out on him. He knew that his question about her dead husband had upset her. He hadn't anticipated that. After all, the man had passed away over fourteen years ago. Did she still care for him that much? The subject definitely touched her emotions in some way. Her shields had gone right up to maximum again.

"Are you okay?" Karl asked. "I'm sorry if I—"

"Forget it," Jaime told him brusquely. "Can we leave now? I have two more visits scheduled, and it's getting late."

Karl's eyes narrowed. They'd finally reached a point where they'd felt halfway comfortable with each other, and now they were back to square one again. And all because of one innocent question.

Resigned to the situation, Karl stood up. "I've just been waiting for you to make an appearance."

"Well, here I am. How much do I owe you for the milk?"

"I'll take care of it," Karl told her, the set of his jaw daring her to contradict him.

Jaime reached into her jeans pocket and threw two singles onto the table. "Fine. I'll leave the tip."

Karl stared after her as she walked away. Damn, he'd like to... The thought stopped there. He wasn't sure what it was he wanted to do to Jaime Mitchell. She was stubborn, exasperating—and the most intriguing woman he'd ever met.

He followed her to the register and frowned at her as he paid the check. And he made certain that he opened both the restaurant door and the car door for her.

"Are we even now?" Jaime asked archly as she climbed into the driver's seat.

"From the look on your face, I'd say so."

"Great. Now maybe we can get the rest of my visits over with."

"Why are you in such a hurry to do that?" Karl asked as she backed out of the parking space. "I kind of enjoyed the morning visits."

Jaime smiled smugly. "I saved the best for last."

"Well, it's about time! You told me that you'd be here yesterday."

Karl looked from Jaime to the middle-aged landlady who stood confronting them in the doorway of her apartment. The woman had the sourest expression on her face that he'd ever seen.

"As I told you over the phone, Mrs. Kent, I couldn't make it yesterday. I had an emergency."

The landlady grunted. "And I told you that I have to rent Mrs. Hunter's apartment. I'll put her things out on the street if you don't take them today! I guess it's not enough that I had to put up with that crazy old woman as a tenant all those months before you people finally got around to doing something about her. She set fires in the kitchen, she locked herself out every day, she went around begging the other tenants for food. And she never paid her rent—"

"I know all that, Mrs. Kent," Jaime said, feeling the strain on her patience. "That's why we had her declared incompetent and placed in an ACLF—an adult congregate living facility—where there's a staff to watch out for her."

"Well, I've been calling that lawyer who was appointed guardian every day since you took her away. He won't do anything. And there's no family to contact."

"Mrs. Hunter has no property and no income except for a small social security check. That means the lawyer we found to act as guardian isn't getting paid to do so. That also means there's no money to pay a moving man or anyone else for services. That's why I'm here. Now why don't you open her apartment for us, and we'll get started."

Mrs. Kent continued her grumbling as she led them up the two flights of stairs to Mrs. Hunter's apartment. "I hope you're taking the furniture."

"Only her clothes and whatever personal items we can find. I can't move her furniture, and there's no place for it at the ACLF anyway. Usually there's someone who will clean out places like this in exchange for the contents. Check with her guardian and see what he wants done."

Mrs. Kent shook her finger at Jaime as she unlocked the door. "That furniture is junk. I'll throw it out on the street, I tell you!"

"You do what you have to do, Mrs. Kent, and I'll do what I have to do."

Jaime walked into the dingy, musty-smelling apartment, and Karl followed. She breathed a sigh of relief when the landlady closed the door behind them and left them alone.

"Charming lady," Karl commented. "Now I see what you meant about leaving the best for last."

Jaime smiled, feeling a certain satisfaction. Only yesterday Karl had acted almost as unpleasantly as Mrs. Kent. Now he was coming around to her way of thinking. Maybe there was hope for him after all.

She spent the next hour packing papers, mementos and other personal effects into the garbage bags that she had brought along for that purpose. Mrs. Hunter's clothes fit into two battered suitcases that Jaime exhumed from the bedroom closet.

Karl made three trips down the stairs to the car until finally all that was left to take that Mrs. Hunter would have any use for was a small fan and a portable TV set. Jaime balanced the fan on her hip and pushed the lock in on the apartment door before following Karl and the TV down the stairs.

"What exactly is an ACLF, anyway?" Karl asked as they drove toward their destination.

"It's a licensed facility that provides clients with a room, housekeeping, laundry services, prepared meals, supervision of medication—even bathing, if necessary. The one we're headed for isn't the best, but it's all Mrs. Hunter can afford—even with the state supplementing her social security."

Karl saw what Jaime meant when they arrived at the large three-story complex. It was as dismal as Mrs. Hunter's apartment had been. "Don't they have minimum standards for these places?"

Jaime pulled the fan out of the trunk of the car. "Oh, it meets the minimum standards. And, in all fairness, the facility doesn't get enough money from the clients here to provide more than the minimum."

They met with Jeff Dunn, the administrator, who assigned a staff member to help them unload the car. Mrs. Hunter's room was on the third floor, but at least here there was an elevator.

Mrs. Hunter sat on one of the twin beds in her room and watched as they worked to get her belongings put away. She complained the whole time about her roommate, the food and the facility in general.

"I'll speak to the administrator about changing your roommate," Jaime promised. "But there's nothing that I can do about the rest of it, Mrs. Hunter. I'm sorry, but this is the only place I could find that would take you."

"How would you like someone to leave *you* in this place?"

Mrs. Hunter's parting comment was on Jaime's mind as they headed out on the way to their last visit. "I don't have a lot of options when it comes to placing a client like that one.''

Karl glanced over at her. "Then maybe it would have been better to leave her where she was."

"Mrs. Kent would have evicted her eventually. And Mrs. Hunter was at risk—in physical jeopardy. I had no alternative. I had to take measures to remedy that situation."

"And what about emotional jeopardy?" Karl asked. "What about how she feels?"

Jaime pressed her lips together and stared straight ahead. "If she doesn't survive physically, her emotional needs certainly aren't going to be met."

Karl thought about her statement. "Okay, I'll concede the logic of that point. But I don't think I'd want that choice made for me no matter how at risk I was. Don't you feel the same way?"

She still didn't look at him. "How I feel doesn't even enter into the picture."

Karl took in her grim expression and clenched hands and remembered the bottle of antacid on her desk. How long could she keep on the way she was going? Her stubbornness and determined independence suddenly reminded him of his grandfather. He smiled, wondering what she would say if she could read his thoughts.

But Jaime was too preoccupied with trying to locate the address of the next field visit to notice Karl's expression. Finally they came to a halt in front of a faded, rundown house.

"You can't go in here with me, Karl."

Karl paused in the act of opening his door and looked back toward her. "Why not?"

"Our unit handles the overflow of referrals for the abuse unit. This is an abuse referral, and by law, it's confidential."

Karl looked confused. "You mean child abuse?"

"I only deal with clients who are over eighteen. I mean adult abuse."

"Like beating up little old ladies?"

Jaime almost smiled at the oversimplification. "That could be one example of abuse. It could also mean confining an elderly or handicapped person against his will, depriving him of food, conning him out of his money..."

She trailed off as she saw the disgust clearly visible in Karl's expression. Was this a man who would exploit his own grandfather?

"I'm just here to investigate an allegation of abuse," she said, resuming her explanation and trying to concentrate on the task on hand. "A lot of times these referrals are false or exaggerated—especially the ones called in by anonymous informants."

Karl laid one hand on her arm as she moved to get out of the car. The warmth of his skin against hers was a distraction that she didn't need.

"Jaime, did it ever occur to you that someone capable of beating up an old lady just might do the same thing to you?"

"It's occurred to me," Jaime admitted. "Every time I go out on a referral like this, I have to swallow my fear—and sometimes my dislike for someone capable of hurting another defenseless human being the way I've seen people hurt."

Karl's fingers tightened on the soft skin of her arm, and she started when his other hand pressed against her stomach. "And what price do you pay for keeping all those feelings locked inside? Is it worth it?"

Jaime brushed his hands away, surprised as she realized how much of herself she had revealed to him today. She had never said those things to anyone else before. Why now? Why to this man?

She scrambled out of the car and slammed the door without giving him an answer. What right did he have to question her anyway? she wondered as she walked toward the house. When had he ever had to deal with people and their problems? He played around with wood for a living. She'd like to see him try to do this job!

Jaime paused in front of the gate and looked around the overgrown yard for any sign of life. She saw nothing unusual, but suddenly she had an ominous premonition of danger. She tried to throw off the impression, but it clung to her relentlessly. *Nerves,* she thought. *I have a case of the jitters from being confined in a small car with a big, obnoxious Swede.*

Jaime shook the gate without unlatching it, producing a loud clanging noise. She'd learned years ago that rattling a gate was a good way to flush out dogs that might be lurking in parts of the yard not visible from the street. This yard remained still and quiet.

She struggled to undo the latch. It was a tricky, complex mechanism, and she had difficulty opening it. At last she succeeded and stepped into the yard, closing the gate behind her.

Jaime was halfway to the front door of the house when a menacing shape rose up from behind a huge clump of weeds not ten feet in front of her. She froze, her heart thumping in terror. It was a full-grown pit bull terrier!

Jaime had never encountered that kind of dog face-to-face before, but she recognized it from pictures that she'd seen on TV and in the newspapers. The facts she remembered from those same sources weren't reassuring. The pit bull was a ferocious, mean-tempered animal traditionally bred to kill others of its kind in illegal dogfights. There were many cases in which the animals had also turned on people, often mauling and maiming them horribly.

She stared at the dog, and it issued a low warning growl. Desperately she deliberated her next move. If she turned and ran, the dog would almost certainly chase her. Even if she could make it back to the gate ahead of him, she'd never be able to get it open in time to escape. Could she climb over the fence? It had been years since she'd tried anything like that, and she wasn't very confident of her ability.

She risked looking away from the dog to examine the house. There was no sign of movement there. What about Karl? She felt a surge of hope. Maybe he'd notice her predicament and . . . But then she remembered that the car was parked facing the other way. Unless he actually turned around to look, he'd never see what was happening.

"How do you open this damned gate?"

A shudder of relief passed through Jaime as she heard Karl's voice behind her. She didn't dare turn her head to look at him. "How did you know?"

"I was watching to see that you got inside the house safely. Are you going to complain about that, too? Do you want me to go back to the car and let you handle Jaws there on your own?"

Jaime pressed her lips together, torn between fury and terror. "Since you're already here, why don't you shut up and do something about the situation?"

The volume of the growling increased as the dog, further agitated by the appearance of a second stranger, took a step toward Jaime. Involuntarily Jaime took a step backward. Teeth bared and ready, the dog charged.

Jaime dropped her papers and ran for her life. She saw Karl's white face and heard him cursing as he struggled with the stubborn gate latch. Her heart raced, pumping adrenaline throughout her system, and she ran faster than she'd ever run before. She was nearly at the gate. Only a few more steps.

Karl was leaning over the fence, reaching toward her. "Jump, Jaime! Jump, and grab onto me!"

Suddenly there was no time left to think. Jaime's hands grabbed for the material of Karl's shirtfront as her feet scrambled for purchase in the wire netting of the fence. Karl grasped her under the arms and lifted. She was almost home free!

Then a vise seemed to close around the thick rubber sole of her shoe, bringing her upward progress to an abrupt halt. "Karl! He's got my shoe!"

Karl grunted and heaved, and Jaime felt his muscles bunch under her hands. She heard the sound of canvas tearing, her shoe slipped off, and she was over the fence and in Karl's arms.

Jaime pressed against him, breathing heavily, shaking with reaction as he held her tightly. She stayed that way for a long time, eyes closed, absorbing all the comfort and security he offered. His warmth seemed to seep into her and become part of her. She felt his lips press against her hair, her cheek, her neck, and suddenly her trembling wasn't entirely due to fear.

Then a man in a passing car blew his horn and called out some very explicit encouragement. Jaime returned to reality with a jolt. All at once, she realized that she was on a public sidewalk with her arms and legs wrapped around Karl Hallstrom as if she planned to remain in that position for all eternity. He was supporting her bottom with both hands and, judging by the hardness of his body against hers, he was enjoying himself immensely.

She tried to pull away from him. "Karl!"

But Karl didn't hear her. He was totally lost in the scent, the feel, the taste of Jaime Mitchell. With a will of their own, his hands closed around her soft flesh, and his mouth moved to claim hers.

"Stop!" Her face scarlet, Jaime let her feet drop to the ground, pushing against Karl's arms until they finally gave. She hastily backed away from him, not sure what upset her more: the fact that Karl had put his hands on her, or the fact that she had enjoyed it.

Karl looked down at her, his face as red as hers. But whatever he'd been about to say was forestalled when a man appeared in the yard.

Clad in a pair of jeans and a dirty, torn T-shirt, he was broad and hulking with long, unkempt black hair and a beard that tumbled all the way to his chest. He looked like a bear whose hibernation had been prematurely disturbed. His height reminded Jaime of Karl. She noticed the similarity in personality the minute the man opened his mouth.

"What the hell were you doing trespassing in my yard, lady? You have no business provoking my dog that way!"

The expression on Karl's face gave new meaning to the word furious. "Provoking your dog? Why, you ignorant son of a—"

Jaime jumped into the conversation before Karl could finish his sentence. "I'm Jaime Mitchell, a social worker from HRS. Are you Clarence Damaris?"

The heavy set-man winced when she said his name. "Yeah, that's me. But everyone calls me C.T." He turned his attention to Karl. "And you better watch that big mouth of yours, mister, or I'm gonna shut it for you."

Jaime put both hands on Karl's chest, sure that she could halt his charge toward the other man. Instead she was carried forward by Karl's momentum and pinned between his body and the fence.

"It would take a better man than you to do that, *Clarence*!"

The volume of Karl's voice almost deafened Jaime, the dog was barking up a frenzy, and she could hardly breathe. Desperate, she grabbed Karl's beard with both hands. It was so closely trimmed that she had difficulty getting a grip, but she managed—barely.

"Hey, that hurts!" Karl protested.

"Being bulldozed into a fence by two hundred and twenty pounds of brawn with no brain isn't exactly my idea of paradise, either!" Jaime snapped, releasing her hold.

Karl immediately stepped back, his anger forgotten. "I'm sorry, I didn't realize. I didn't hurt you, did I?"

"I'm not made of glass, Karl. It was just uncomfortable, that's all."

She straightened her clothes and turned to C. T. Damaris with a forced smile. "If you'll excuse us, I'd just like to have a word with my friend here. I'll be right back."

She took Karl's arm and steered him toward her car. When they reached it, she opened the door. "Karl, I want you to get into the car and wait for me. I'll be out as soon as I can."

"Are you crazy? Are you going into the house with that—?"

"Shhh!" Jaime glanced in Damaris's direction and smiled again before turning back to Karl. "You've got to understand. It's my job to go in there. And I told you before, you can't go in with me. Just wait for me out here . . . please."

Karl didn't like the idea. His mind was telling him that it was her job and that she chose to do it. But his every instinct was screaming at him not to let her go into that house alone. "Don't you think you could use a little backup here?"

Jaime wanted to shake him. "I don't want to be protected from life, Karl, I want to live it. On my own terms. No pain, no gain."

"All right, I hear you. I just hope you don't get more pain than you bargained for."

"I knew you'd understand," Jaime told him sweetly.

"I understand. But I don't have to like it. You know where I am if you need me."

"Why don't you go get yourself a cold drink, then come back? I'll probably be a while."

Karl climbed into the car and slammed the door. "I'm staying right here."

"My guardian angel," Jaime muttered as she limped back toward the house.

When she reached the gate, she found Damaris holding her torn shoe in one big hand. "Sorry about that, lady. But Pumpkin here has been trained to protect the house. Isn't that right, girl?"

Pumpkin wagged her tail and licked her master's hand.

Jaime pulled on the remains of her shoe as she spoke. "I understand that your mother lives here with you, Mr. Damaris. I'd like to come inside and talk with her."

The man's expression turned suspicious. "She's taking her afternoon nap. Why do you want to talk to her?"

"An anonymous caller told us that you two aren't getting along with each other. I need to find out what the problem is and see if there's anything I can do to help."

"We don't need no help."

"Let me give you the facts, Mr. Damaris. The caller claims you're hurting your mother. I have to talk to her—alone—and see what she has to say about that."

Damaris was getting red in the face. "Anyone who says I hurt my mama is a damned liar!"

"Then you have nothing to hide. Just let me come in for a minute and talk to your mom."

"And what if I don't?"

"Then I'll have to come back with the police." Having made him aware of her authority, Jaime softened her tone. "Come on, Mr. Damaris. I don't want the police involved in this anymore than you do. And if what you say is true, I'll be in and out in a few minutes. Then you'll never have to see me again."

Damaris stared at her for a long moment before he gave her an answer. "Let me chain Pumpkin up first."

Half an hour later, Jaime climbed into the car with a smile on her face. It quickly vanished when Karl reached down and grabbed her foot. She tumbled back against the door as he lifted her leg and removed her torn shoe.

"What are you doing?" she demanded, embarrassed and confused by his actions.

His warm, probing fingers tickled the bottom of her foot, sending a jot of feeling all the way up her leg—and beyond. Suddenly all she could think about was how good his body had felt pressed against her own.

"Let go," she pleaded, her voice strained. She squirmed in her seat, trying to pull away from him.

Karl finished his examination and released her foot. "I saw you limping before. I thought maybe the dog had bitten you after all."

Jaime snatched her shoe out of his hand and tugged it back on. "I was limping because I was only wearing one shoe! If you had asked me instead of just grabbing me, I would have been glad to tell you that."

Karl watched as she started the engine with a roar and pulled the car out onto the road. "I'm not a man who takes advantage of frightened women, Jaime."

"Excuse me?"

"Look, I know you're upset about what happened after I pulled you over the fence. You barely escaped that dog. You were scared. You were looking to me for comfort, and you think I took advantage of the situation."

"In broad daylight. On a public sidewalk."

Karl's jaw clenched. "I just want you to know that I've never done anything like that before. For a while there I felt like I should be wearing a T-shirt with the word 'pervert' splashed across the front."

Jaime was finding it hard to hold on to her anger. In fact, the more Karl talked about the incident, the more vivid the memory of her own far-from innocent response became. "It's okay," she murmured, willing him to drop the topic.

But Karl hadn't finished his explanation. "While I was alone in the car, I had a chance to think about why I did it. I realized that it originated here." He tapped his chest above his heart. "Not lower down. It was just part of all the other emotions—the good emotions—I was feeling when I held you. When I realized that, I wasn't ashamed anymore. Do you understand, Jaime?"

Jaime didn't want to even consider the implications of that remark. She took refuge in sarcasm instead. "Oh, sure," she said lightly. "Stand back, world! Karl Hallstrom's expressing his feelings again."

Karl gave up trying to reach her. After a moment of tense silence, he changed the subject. "You never told me how it went in there. Are you going to take Damaris to court?"

Jaime shook her head. "I'm not really supposed to discuss it. But I can say that there's no reason for me to go back there."

In reality, if anyone was being abused in that house, it was C.T. Damaris. His mother was a tiny, spry little tyrant who snapped out orders like a Marine drill sergeant. After talking to them both, separately and then together, Jaime had found no reason to pursue the investigation any further. Mrs. Damaris had suggested that her son's ex-wife might have been the one who had called in the referral.

"She never did fit in around here," the older woman had asserted. "I think she was jealous of me."

Jaime certainly had no reason to doubt that.

Karl nodded, surprised but pleased. "Good. I'm glad you're through with those people." He paused, the words coming hard to him. "I have to say it, Jaime. That jerk, Damaris, deserved a punch in the nose. But I know I only made things harder for you when I started up with him."

Jaime was left groping for words herself. She couldn't believe that this was the man she had characterized as hopelessly arrogant a few hours before. An angry Karl Hallstrom had been attractive, but a contrite Karl Hallstrom was very nearly irresistible. "A-anyway," she stammered, "no one got hurt. And I know you meant well."

She was so involved with what had been said, that she almost missed her own driveway. Turning the car sharply, she pulled up in front of her house and turned off the engine. Her day with Karl was over. Now there was another issue confronting her. She couldn't delay any longer. She had to ask about the check his grandfather had sent to him. Yesterday she'd been reluctant to ask because she'd wanted to hold on to her anger. Now she wanted to go on believing that Karl was as good and decent as he seemed. She could only hope that his answer would show him to be innocent of any wrongdoing.

"Why did your grandfather send you that five-thousand-dollar check?"

She forced herself to look into his eyes, dreading what she'd see there. But she could detect no guilt, no evasiveness, only puzzlement.

"How did you find out about that?"

"Wilma knew he'd sent it out, but not who it was sent to. Your grandfather's bank gave that information to the court-appointed attorney. Yesterday, after you left my office, the attorney called and told me that you had cashed the check."

"Is that what started this whole thing? The check?"

"As I mentioned before, your grandfather's confusion has been a problem for some time. But I guess you could say that the check was the final incident, the reason that Wilma brought your grandfather to my attention."

"All this trouble and misunderstanding over a stupid mistake."

"A mistake?"

"My grandfather owns an old house in Seattle," Karl began. "He refuses to rent it or sell it even though he's lived in Miami for years. He claims he needs to keep it so he'll have his own place to stay when he comes to town to visit me. Of course, he always ends up staying with me instead."

Jaime couldn't help smiling, despite the seriousness of the situation. "It's probably a symbol of independence to him. He doesn't want to use it. He just wants to know that it's there—in case."

"It may be a symbol of independence to him, but it's a pain in the neck to me. It kept getting more and more run-down over the years, until finally I just couldn't let it go any longer. I had some work done on it, and I paid the bill. But the contractor misunderstood my instructions and sent the receipt to my grandfather by mistake. My grandfather insisted on reimbursing me even though I didn't want the money." He looked at her with an ironic smile. "So you see, all this was caused by one misdirected receipt. If it hadn't been for that, my grandfather would never have known about the repairs, he wouldn't have sent the check and you wouldn't have filed for an evaluation of competency. And we would probably never have met."

Jaime had to look away from the sudden warmth of his gaze. "When did your grandfather transfer ownership of the lumber company to you?"

"On my twenty-fifth birthday, over ten years ago. Why?"

Jaime stared straight ahead, as aware of Karl's growing anger as she was of her own tautly stretched nerves. "If the transfer had occurred recently, after your grandfather began to be confused—"

"You think I stole the company from him?"

"I didn't say that."

"But that's what you're implying."

Jaime risked a glance at him, then wished that she hadn't. "Let's just say that it would erase all doubt if you had proof of the date ownership was transferred and the receipt for the house repairs."

"My grandfather sent the receipt back to me with the check. It's in Seattle—along with all my company records. If you want proof, why don't you just ask my grandfather?"

"I did. Before I filed and just this morning. He wouldn't answer me."

Karl cursed softly. "I could try and persuade him to talk to you. He's upset, but maybe he'll listen to me."

Jaime struggled to find words that wouldn't sound insulting or accusatory. "Frankly, given your grandfather's questionable mental condition, a copy of the papers would be better."

Karl was both hurt and angered by her insinuations. After what they'd shared today, he felt he was entitled to a little trust. But he wasn't getting any. "You think I'm one of them, don't you, Jaime? Those lowlifes who go around exploiting old people. Well, I'm not! I wouldn't do something like that. Don't you know me well enough by now to realize that?"

Jaime clenched her fists in her lap. "That's just it. I'm not supposed to know you at all. I'm supposed to be making a judgment based on the facts."

"And what do the facts tell you? That I'm unfit to be my grandfather's guardian?"

Jaime answered slowly and deliberately, trying to hold her own temper in check. After all he'd seen today, didn't he understand that she was just trying to do her job? "The facts tell me that I have no conclusive evidence one way or the other. And the judge is the one who appoints a guardian. So you'd better make sure that your grandfather is willing to talk to *him*."

Karl leaned his head back against the seat and tried to let his anger and disappointment ease away. What had he expected after all? That the ice princess was going to open her heart to him, then melt in his arms? That a few hours together were going to change the way she felt about him? But those few hours had changed the way he perceived her. For a little while, he'd thought that the feeling had been mutual. It hurt to find out that he'd been wrong.

Jaime climbed out of the car and closed the door. She started to walk away, then realized that she couldn't. Not without saying what was on her mind. "Listen, Karl, thanks for helping me out today. Despite all our misunderstandings, you were there for me—whether I needed you or not. That's more than I can say for any other man I've known."

Karl sat up and leaned out the window, suddenly feeling a lot better. "You mean you only asked me those questions because you have to touch all the bases. You don't really believe I'd hurt my grandfather."

Jaime took a step backward. Just when had she lost control of this conversation? "That's not what I said."

"And if you weren't a social worker, if you were just another neighbor—would you say it then?"

"Don't ask me that, Karl. I *am* a social worker, and we shouldn't even be discussing this." She turned away. "I've got to go."

"What about our bet?"

Jaime paused, her curiosity getting the better of her. "What about it?"

Karl smiled a little sheepishly. "I guess this is my night for admitting my mistakes. I watched the way you dealt with your clients today. And I heard the things you were trying to tell me. I didn't always agree, but I understood. So this is your apology, Jaime. Some of the things I said in your office were way out of line."

Jaime was gratified by Karl's admission. He *had* come to understand her and her job a little better. He was reaching out to her, trying to meet her halfway. In return she owed him honesty. "In your grandfather's case, I was given a little time to consider some very limited options. I didn't have the luxury of choosing between what was right and what was wrong for him. The choice I had to make was between a greater wrong and a lesser wrong. I just tried to do the best job that I could.''

Karl got out of the car and came toward her. ''After today I know that.''

The corners of Jaime's mouth curved upward. ''In other words, you believe I'm misguided, but sincere.''

''That about sums it up.''

''Funny. That's just what I've been thinking about you. Goodnight, Karl.''

''Wait! What about the terms of our bet? What are you going to ask me for?''

''Oh, don't be silly! The apology was what I really wanted.''

''Nope. I insist. A Hallstrom never welshes on a bet.''

Jaime considered her options, then came up with a compromise she hoped would benefit all concerned. ''Then how about a tune-up for my car?''

Karl looked stunned. ''You're kidding! You'd actually allow me to do that?''

Jaime removed her car key from the ring and placed it in his hand.

''I wouldn't want you to feel useless and unappreciated.''

''But what about that independence you're so proud of?''

''It won't be in the least bit compromised. Alex is going to do the tune-up—under your close supervision—and I'm going to pay for the parts.''

Karl sighed. ''I know when I've been outmaneuvered. Okay, you've got a deal. But after the tune-up's finished, I'm taking us all out to dinner. You, me and Alex.''

''*I'd* like to take *you* out to dinner—to thank you for your help. But I have class in a couple of hours. It will have to be some other time.''

Karl winked at her. ''I'll be counting the minutes.''

Jaime began to back toward her front door. "Just so you understand. I enjoyed being with you today, Karl. But I just don't think—I *know* that things can't go any further with us."

Karl kept coming, closing the distance between them despite Jaime's retreat. "Why not?"

"The hearing. And after that you'll be going back to Seattle, and I'll be staying here. Even if that weren't the case, we're just such different people. It wouldn't work out."

Karl was getting too close for comfort. Jaime turned and hurried to the house.

"Jaime!"

"What?"

He followed her and stretched one arm across the open doorway, blocking her path. "Do you forgive me—for touching you today?"

Jaime's heart was pounding faster. But this time it wasn't from fear. "Yes. I forgive you. Now let me go inside."

His eyes searched hers. "What did you feel when I touched you?"

"Intense anger." *And intense excitement.*

"You didn't like it? Not even a little bit?"

"Not even a little bit."

"Liar," Karl whispered, turning an accusation into an endearment. "Stop pretending that you don't know what I'm talking about. You felt it, too—the attraction between us. It's driving me crazy, Jaime!"

He leaned toward her, but she ducked under his arm and into the house. "Good night," she told him firmly.

"I don't want to say good night and neither do you." Now his hand was pressed against the door, and there was no way that she could close it. She wasn't even sure that she wanted to close it.

He reached for her with his free hand, but she pulled away. "Please, Karl, don't! Okay, yes, I felt the attraction, too. I feel it now. But I can't begin to deal with someone like you in my life. Please, if you care even a little bit about what happens to me—if you want to help me—please, just leave me now, and give my car key to Alex when you are all finished with the tune-up.''

Karl hesitated. He'd never refused a woman who'd asked for his help. And he'd never disregarded a woman's emotional needs in order to satisfy his own desires. She was right. There was no time to build a relationship, no common ground to build one on. And anything less would be unfair to both of them. Despite that, he still wanted her. He didn't know whether it was his long abstinence, the companionship they'd shared today or some crazy physical chemistry. But he couldn't resist pushing his suit a little farther.

''Are you sure that's the way you want it?''

No, she wasn't sure! She hadn't been sure of anything since the moment she'd met him. ''That's the way it has to be.''

''Then good night, Jaime Mitchell.''

The sad look in Karl's blue eyes tugged at Jaime's heart as she shut the door. Unable to resist, she went straight to the living room window and lifted the edge of the curtain. She peeked out just as Karl was removing his shirt to examine the engine.

Why hadn't she let him kiss her? One kiss wouldn't have hurt. But in her heart she knew that it wouldn't have stopped with just one kiss. No, it was better that she had ended it now. Even so, she couldn't help appreciating the attractive picture Karl presented as he bent over the engine of her car.

''Hi, Mom.''

Jaime gasped and let the curtain fall closed. ''Alex! You scared me.''

''Yeah. I saw you jump. Who were you watching out there?''

Jaime swallowed hard. ''I...uh...Karl. He's getting ready to do a tune-up on my car. I, uh, I've never seen anyone do that before, so . . . I was watching.''

''Why didn't you just stay outside and watch?''

Yes, why not? "Well . . . I didn't want to make Karl nervous."

"Nervous? Karl? Go on out and watch. It won't bother him."

"No, no. I've got to . . . to get ready for class."

"Did you ask him about the check?"

Jaime clutched at the question like a life preserver. "Yes, I did. Everything seems to be in order, but—"

"Then I can go out and watch Karl do the tune-up?"

"Karl and I agreed that you could do the tune-up under his supervision. But I—"

She was interrupted by a wild whoop. "I'll get my tools!"

"Have you finished your homework?"

Alex nodded on his way out of the door.

She sank down onto the couch, holding her head in her hands. Her own son had caught her behaving like a Peeping Tom—or maybe in her case, it was a Peeping Tomasina. Thank goodness she'd been able to talk her way out of that situation! If Alex ever realized what had really been going through her mind . . .

"My mom was watching you from the window."

Karl peered across the engine at Alex. "What?"

"She was sneaking a peek from behind the curtain. I walked up and caught her and scared the heck out of her."

Just picturing the scene made Karl grin. "You shouldn't have done that."

Alex grinned back. "I know. But I really think she likes you, Karl. I've never seen her watch anyone else like that. I don't think she even noticed there was a window there until now."

Karl grunted. "With your mom, you never know. She was probably keeping an eye on me to make sure I didn't steal the hubcaps. I don't think that woman trusts me completely—yet."

"Nah," Alex responded. "She said that all that stuff with the check was cleared up."

"She told you that?" Karl asked, surprised and pleased.

"Uh-huh."

Alex watched Karl tinker with the engine for several minutes, gathering the courage to say what was on his mind. "Karl," he asked finally, trying to sound casual, "do you . . . do you think my mom is pretty? I mean, would you watch *her* out the window?"

Karl liked Alex, and he was amused and touched by the boy's heavy-handed attempt at matchmaking. He didn't have the heart to tell the kid that Jaime had already turned him down. So he thought about Alex's question, then answered it truthfully.

"Yeah, I'd watch her all right."

Alex hid a smile. This situation definitely had possibilities.

Chapter Four

"My feet hurt." Jaime leaned back in her chair and propped the offending appendages up on her desk. On Wednesday, the day after she'd filled out the job application, B. J.'s Sandwich Shoppe had called her. She'd worked there that night from six-thirty to ten-thirty and skipped class last night to do the same. Now it was Friday, and she had yet another night's work ahead of her.

Maria stirred her coffee. "I'm sorry to hear that your feet are sore, but who told you to go get a job as a waitress? Don't you have enough work to do around here?"

Sharon frowned and tapped Maria lightly on the arm. "Can't you be a little more supportive?"

Maria shrugged, apparently unaffected by the rebuke. "I'm trying to keep her from working herself to death. I consider that supportive."

Jaime sighed wearily and sipped her coffee. "It's only temporary. I'm trying to earn some vacation money. Remember?"

"What's the use of earning money for a vacation," Maria commented, "if you're too tired to enjoy it? Look at what you can have here and now, *niña*. One night with that big, handsome Karl would do you more good than two *months* in California."

Jaime felt the heat rising in her face at the thought. "Oh, stop teasing, Maria. If I thought you were serious, I'd feel insulted."

Sharon shook her head. "Maria, you really are outrageous."

"And both of you are so dumb! Jaime, you're working your fanny off so you can go on a vacation and relax. And, Sharon, your baby is due in three weeks, and you're still working—even though you have a husband on the police force who's getting paid all kinds of overtime."

Sharon threw her empty orange juice container into Jaime's wastebasket and folded her arms over her bulging stomach. "Don't start on me, Maria. I'm working because I don't want to sit at home listening to the clock tick while waiting for Junior to make his appearance. I'd go nuts! But don't worry, I'm going to begin my six-month maternity leave in another two weeks."

But Maria evidently read something more in Sharon's self-satisfied expression. "What else? Come on, what aren't you telling us?"

"After my maternity leave is over, I think I'm going to resign and stay at home with the baby. I—"

Jaime's feet came off her desk and hit the floor with a thud. "*You?* The workaholic! You're resigning?"

"Well, I'm not sure yet. I'll wait until it's time to come back to work, and then I'll decide. But I've waited a long time for this baby. Now I want to be there for his first step, his first word."

Jaime tried to adjust to the idea of doing her job without the benefit of Sharon's advice and support. It wouldn't be easy.

"And I thought that my announcement would be the shocker of the morning!" Maria said. "I went for a job interview with Catholic Services. I think I have a good chance of getting the position.''

"Oh, good," Jaime said with a notable lack of enthusiasm.

"Cheer up, I may not get it. And if I do, you can always become a full-time waitress. You said the tips are good.''

"Yes, but the benefits are lousy. Besides, I'm a klutz. I think I drop more food than I get to the tables.''

"Well, when you get the supervisor's position and the salary that goes with it," Sharon pointed out, "you won't need to worry about a second job.''

Jaime smiled a little sadly. "I know. But if you guys leave, I won't have a unit worth supervising.''

The phone rang, breaking the poignant silence.

"Jaime Mitchell's office.''

"You promised to call me back about the Hallstrom competency, Jaime Mitchell.''

Jaime's heart gave a guilty lurch. It was Ron Martinez, the court-appointed attorney. She'd put off calling him for days, but now the moment of truth had arrived. She balanced the receiver between her jaw and shoulder as she rummaged through her files with both hands, trying to find the case record.

"Sorry about that, Ron. It's been crazy around here—as usual. How's the baby?''

She listened to his pleasant chatter about his two-month-old son with half an ear while she continued her search. She'd dated Ron for two years. She could probably even have married him if she'd given him any encouragement in that area. But she'd felt only relief when he'd stopped seeing her in favor of the woman who'd eventually become his wife. Jaime was genuinely happy that Ron had managed to find what he'd been looking for.

Locating the Hallstrom file, she quickly gave him a summary of her initial assessment of the client and the current status of the case. She mentioned that Ivar was still refusing to talk about why he'd sent the check. And she related the explanation that Karl had given her. Then Ron asked the question that Jaime had been dreading.

"So what do you think of Karl Hallstrom? Are you going to recommend that he be appointed guardian?"

Jaime struggled to be objective, to separate what she knew from what she felt. When it came to Karl, that wasn't an easy task. "He seems to be honest and sincere and to care a great deal about his grandfather. But I wish we had proof of what he did with that five thousand dollars. And I'd also like to verify that the lumber company was transferred to Karl's name and when. If by some chance he is exploiting his grandfather, and he's appointed guardian—"

"You know as well as I do that if Karl Hallstrom is appointed guardian, he'll have to disclose all information about his grandfather's income and assets to the court. He'll have to account for every penny of his grandfather's money that he spends."

Jaime wrapped the phone cord around her hand and squeezed. "I know."

"Then what's the problem, babe? You've always been willing to leave the decision up to the judge before. What's different about this case?"

"Nothing really." Just Karl Hallstrom and her own desperate need to be sure of him, to have something concrete to back up her feelings.

"I have an appointment to see both Hallstroms at the grandfather's house tonight. I'll let you know what happens."

"Good luck," Jaime told him. "And say hi to Ginny and little Ronnie for me." She hesitated, and then decided to say what she felt. "I can hear the happiness in your voice every time you talk about them, Ron. I'm so glad for you."

There was a short silence, followed by a husky, "Thanks, babe." Then there was only the dial tone.

"See, that wasn't so bad," Maria told her as she hung up the phone. "I don't know what you've been so worried about."

"That, somehow, without my even realizing it, my . . . personal involvement with Karl is going to cloud my judgment."

"Jaime," Sharon inserted, "all he did was go with you on some field visits and help tune-up your car. Besides, if you believed that Karl was exploiting his grandfather, you'd never recommend him for guardian no matter how involved you were with him. You're one of the fairest, most objective people I know. You've got to learn to trust yourself more."

Jaime looked down at her coffee. "Maybe. But when it comes to Karl, I feel . . . I don't know . . . confused. The last time I talked to him, we sort of agreed to go out to eat one night. So I thought I might stop by his house after I leave the office today and offer to treat him to Sunday dinner. I think it would be a nice way to show him that I appreciate his help with my car. And I still have to reimburse him for the parts he bought." She smiled, anticipating Karl's reaction. "He probably thinks I've forgotten about that. But I haven't." Her smile wavered. "On the other hand, maybe I shouldn't be taking Karl out for any reason. With the hearing and all . . ."

Maria and Sharon exchanged a look that Jaime couldn't decipher.

"Dinner with Karl sounds like a great idea to me," Sharon responded.

"I was wondering when you were going to wake up," Maria said with a smirk.

Sharon nudged Maria with one elbow in the ribs before turning to Jaime with a wide smile. "It's very appropriate, and a very . . . uh . . . friendly gesture."

Pulling herself to her feet, Sharon began tugging at Maria. "Come on, let's go. We've got work to do!"

"Okay, okay, I'm coming! I don't know what you're so worried about. I'm not going to say another word. Not another word."

Maria walked out of Jaime's office, still grumbling, as Sharon paused in the doorway. "What about lunch later on?"

"No, I have to do some research on pregnancy and cocaine use—you know, for Mrs. Todd's daughter. There's a drug information center near here. I thought I'd drop by there on my lunch hour."

Sharon's hand went to her rounded stomach. "I can't even drink coffee anymore without feeling guilty. I'm glad you're the one dealing with this and not me." She tapped her lip with her index finger. "You might want to ask Linda in Children's Protective Services about this subject. I think she deals with some of the children whose mothers are habitual drug users."

"Thanks, I'll do that," Jaime told her. "So, have you decided on a name for the baby yet?" she asked, trying to shift Sharon's thoughts to a more cheerful subject.

"No, and I'm driving Ted crazy. Last night he told me I could name the baby Rumplestiltskin if I like as long as he doesn't have to see any of those baby name books ever again."

"Rumplestiltskin Ryan. It has a nice ring to it."

Sharon laughed. "I guess I've found the name then. But there are still a few minutes left on my break. I think I'll thumb through the name book one more time—just in case I have a girl."

Alone in her office, Jaime sat staring at the wall in front of her, lost in thought. Despite her friends' approval, she still had doubts about inviting Karl to dinner. But every morning when she left the house for work and saw Karl's truck in the driveway across the street, she couldn't help remembering the time they'd spent together. Through the day, she'd catch herself smiling at odd moments as she recalled a remark Karl had made or a look that had come over his face—or how she'd felt when he'd touched her.

It seemed as if they had shared so much during that day of field visits. Obviously, due to circumstances beyond her control, their relationship couldn't progress beyond its present stage. But she should pay him for the parts before the hearing. And buying him dinner seemed a nice, acceptable way to say thank-you for the time he'd put in on her car.

Of course, it was also a nice, acceptable way to spend some more time with Karl, to look into his eyes, to hear his voice again. He might make her feel threatened and angry and on the verge of losing control, but at least she was feeling again. And that was intoxicating. She knew he was bad for her, and she didn't intend to let things go any farther than they already had. But like a moth attracted by a flame, Jaime couldn't resist drawing just a little closer to Karl Hallstrom's enticing warmth.

Jaime gathered up her courage and knocked on the door. She'd rehearsed what she intended to say over and over again in her mind, but she was afraid she'd forget it all the minute she saw Karl's face. She was suddenly sure that this was the worst idea she'd ever had.

Then the door swung open, and Ivar Hallstrom glared out at her. "What do you want now?" he growled without preamble.

Jaime felt like retreating back across the street, but she refused to give the man the satisfaction. "I came to talk to Karl."

"Why? Does your car need more work?"

Jaime had to bite back a sharp reply. "My son did the actual work on my car, Mr. Hallstrom," she said evenly. "And that's not what I'm here to talk to Karl about now."

"Something to do with that damned fool hearing, I suppose. Three of those men from the court have been out here already asking me a bunch of questions. And another one's due to come tonight."

"Mr. Hallstrom, I know you're angry about all this. I wouldn't like it if it were happening to me. But you have to cooperate with these people—for your own sake."

"I don't *have* to do anything, young lady. I'll tell my story to the judge."

Jaime didn't think she'd be able to penetrate all the layers of denial, fear and resentment that the man had built up, but she made one more attempt. "I know you're a proud man, and I know you're used to taking care of things for yourself. But you have to realize that those men report to the judge, and he listens to what they say. You're only hurting yourself by not cooperating with them." She looked at him steadily. "Sometimes, Mr. Hallstrom, you have to bend, or you end up breaking."

"I don't need your advice. I've lived a lot longer than you, and I've managed fine so far. You should spend your time straightening out your own life, instead of messing up other people's. That boy of yours needs a father."

"Alex?" Jaime croaked, too startled by the unexpected turn the conversation had taken to even come up with a suitable reply.

"Yes, Alex. Who do you think I mean? That boy's worth ten of you. He's been coming across the street to me for years now, while you were busy chasing off to school and working yourself to a frazzle. He's helped me around the house and run errands for me and never once asked me for a penny." Ivar shook his finger at her. "What Alex needs is a father, someone to give him direction. You ought to be worrying about finding yourself a good husband, instead of worrying about what goes on with my bank account."

"Jaime?"

The sound of Karl's voice coming from inside the house signaled a welcome reprieve for Jaime. He appeared in the doorway wearing a chef's apron, a kitchen towel draped over one shoulder. "I thought I heard a social worker," he said, giving her a wink and a grin.

He seemed to be surrounded by a warm aura that reached out and engulfed Jaime, causing her to smile, too. Even Ivar dropped his aggressive posture.

For the first time, Jaime noticed just how strong Karl's resemblance to his grandfather actually was. Had Ivar been younger and bearded, she would have been hard put to tell them apart. And the expression in their eyes was the same when they looked at each other. At last she saw what Alex had meant. The love between these two men was plain to any observer. She felt a sharp twinge of regret and wished that fate hadn't brought Ivar Hallstrom's case to her attention. The competency had caused a tremendous amount of pain already, and Jaime knew that this was only the beginning.

"Don't stand out here, Jaime. Come on inside."

Karl took her arm and drew her into the house, and Jaime forgot all about regrets. She no longer felt sad and weary. All of a sudden she felt young and aware and very much alive.

Karl shut the door and stood in the living room staring into Jaime's eyes until Ivar's discontented grumbling broke the spell. "Well, Karl, you spent a good part of your childhood driving me to distraction by bringing home hurt creatures and trying to heal them. I guess I shouldn't be surprised by this turn of events."

Jaime was deeply shaken by the older man's statement. Were her scars so visible that even Mr. Hallstrom could detect them?

Karl turned to Ivar with a frown. "This may be your house, Granddad, but I won't stand here and listen to you insult Jaime."

"I wasn't insulting the girl. I was just stating a fact," Ivar said, his voice betraying his own hurt. "But now I see how things stand."

To Jaime it was like a scene out of a nightmare. The last thing she had wanted to do was cause more strife. She realized now just how wrongheaded an idea this visit had been. She had been right to have doubts about it, and she ought to have heeded them.

She moved to the door and began to open it. "Please, it's all right. I'm leaving now."

"Jaime—" Karl took a step toward her, but his reaction was cut short when he saw Wilma standing on the doorstep.

Ivar snorted in apparent disgust. "When these two leave, Karl, you can call me out to dinner. Until then, I'll be in my room."

He stomped off down the hall, and a few seconds later there was the sound of a slamming door.

Wilma passed by Jaime and Karl and followed in Ivar's footsteps, disappearing into the hallway. "How long do you intend to keep this up, Ivar?" Jaime heard the older woman demanding, her voice sounding tearful.

"Until Hades freezes over!" was the muffled reply from inside the bedroom.

Karl looked at Jaime. "She comes over here every day, and every day it's the same scene. You'd think she'd be discouraged by now."

A loud sizzling sound coming from the direction of the kitchen suddenly claimed his attention. "I think my sauce just boiled over! You wait for me right here," he said in a tone that left no room for argument. "Don't go away."

Before she could even respond, Karl had left the room.

Wilma reappeared, looking agitated and teary-eyed. "I don't know what to do, Jaime. I just don't know what to do."

Jaime put an arm around the other woman. "He'll calm down after the hearing. You two will be able to talk then."

Wilma shook her head. "You don't understand. If he's declared incompetent, he'll probably be going back to Seattle with Karl. And even if he isn't, things will never be the same between us again."

All at once Jaime understood. "You love him, don't you?"

Wilma hesitated, then nodded. "I suppose you think that's foolish at my age."

"No, of course not. I guess I just didn't expect it, that's all." She hugged Wilma in sympathy. "I'm so sorry. If there were a way to make it right for you, I would."

Wilma straightened her shoulders. "I'll find a way," she declared. "I got Ivar into this, and I'll think of a way to get him out."

The doorbell interrupted their conversation, and Jaime turned to open the door.

"Hello, Jaime! I didn't expect to see you here."

Karl came back from the kitchen just in time to see Jaime being swept into an embrace by a tall, dark stranger. The feelings that sight aroused in him came as a complete shock. He'd never been a jealous man, and he'd never been able to comprehend the reasoning behind that particular emotion when he'd seen others displaying it. Now he suddenly understood. It had nothing to do with reasoning. It simply existed. It sprang from some dark, primitive place deep inside, and he had no control over it whatsoever.

Jaime returned Ron's hug and smiled up at him as he kissed her on the cheek. "How's it going, counselor?" She fingered the lapel of his suit. "Hmmm. The suits are getting more expensive. I guess that means the clients are paying higher fees."

Ron chuckled. "The ones who pay me are."

Jaime took his arm and introduced him to Wilma. Then she noticed that Karl had come back into the room. He was glowering ominously, so she guessed he had burned his sauce after all—another disaster that she was at least partially responsible for. Well, she'd just introduce the two of them, then go home and get out of the way.

She walked toward Karl, tugging Ron's arm and wondering why the lawyer seemed to be holding back. "Karl, this is Ron Martinez, your grandfather's court-appointed attorney. Ron, this is Karl Hallstrom."

Karl was tempted to compress the other man's hand in a show of brute strength, but sanity intruded before it was too late. What was wrong with him? he wondered as he released the lawyer's hand and bared his teeth in a grim facsimile of a smile. He was only thirty-five. Was it possible that all this was part of some strange mid-life crisis?

"I guess I'll be going now," Jaime announced, heading for the door.

But Karl wasn't about to let her get away. "Excuse me for a minute, folks," he said as he followed Jaime out onto the porch. He shut the front door and found himself alone with her at last. "You're not going anywhere until you tell me why you came over here tonight," he informed her.

Jaime fidgeted under Karl's gaze, her mind suddenly blank. She'd already decided that issuing Karl a dinner invitation was a bad idea. But what other reason could she give for this visit? "Your sauce is going to be ruined," she said, a trifle desperately.

"It's already ruined, and you're not getting out of this conversation that easily. Why did you come over?"

The money for the parts! Now was the perfect time to give Karl the money she owed him. Then she should go home and not see him again until the hearing. That was what she ought to do. But she knew that it wasn't what she was going to do. "Remember when we agreed to go out to dinner together?" she heard herself saying.

"Dinner?" Karl echoed. It was the last answer he'd expected. Did this mean she'd changed her mind about their relationship? He tried to contain the grin that threatened to spread across his face at any moment.

"Yes, dinner," Jaime repeated. "I thought that we could go to a restaurant together."

"I've already cooked dinner for tonight. How about tomorrow?"

Jaime thought fast. She'd be working both tonight and tomorrow night, but she hesitated to tell Karl that. She didn't think his reaction would be positive, and there was no sense borrowing trouble.

"I'm busy tomorrow night, Karl. Actually, I was thinking of Sunday."

Karl's good humor seemed to evaporate. "You have a date with *him* tomorrow?"

Jaime frowned, wondering what he was talking about. "Him, who?"

"Him. The suit with the briefcase and the slicked-back hair."

"Ron?" Jaime asked in surprise. "I haven't been out with Ron in three years. He's married now."

Karl's mood took a sudden upswing. "Great! I mean, good for him." Then a new thought occurred to him. "You're not going out with anyone else, are you?"

"No. I just have a lot of running around to do tomorrow, and I know I'll be tired by tomorrow night."

That was true enough. She was scheduled to work in the restaurant tomorrow from six a.m. to six p.m. That was one heck of a lot of running around. But no matter how tired she was by Sunday night, she'd enjoy every bite of the dinner she was going to buy Karl.

"Sunday, then," he agreed with a smile.

"Seven-thirty?"

"Fine." Karl had no idea what had caused her to change her mind about going out with him, but he was thankful. He only wished it could be sooner than the day after tomorrow. There were only ten days left until the hearing, and he wanted to spend them all as close to Jaime Mitchell as possible.

Jaime saw the quickening of desire in Karl's eyes and was alarmed to find that her own pulse was racing crazily. "See you Sunday," she said. She'd meant to convey a cheery farewell. Instead the words came out sounding like a sultry promise.

She walked back across the street, feeling Karl's gaze on her every foot of the way. Even when she'd closed and locked her door, she didn't feel safe from the effect he had on her. If she was this disturbed by a simple conversation with the man, what would spending an entire evening with him do to her?

Jaime crossed to the dining room table wondering just what she'd gotten herself into. Then she glanced at the clock and realized that she didn't have time to worry. It was already six p.m. She had to be at the restaurant in half an hour. The feeling of elation she'd had while talking to Karl seeped out of her, and she felt bone-tired.

She went to the refrigerator for a cold drink and saw Alex's note taped to the door:

Rode bike to library. Back before dark.

Pouring her drink, she thought about how much she missed her son. She'd managed to fix him quick dinners on Wednesday and Thursday before going to the restaurant. But today she wouldn't get to see him at all. He'd been gone before she'd dragged herself out of bed this morning, and he'd be asleep when she got home tonight. And how much time would she be able to spend with him this weekend?

Fighting back a wave of guilt, she reminded herself that she was doing this for him. And her second job was only temporary. For some parents, moonlighting was a way of life.

She took her drink to the table and pulled the information she'd gotten from the drug center out of her purse. From talking with a counselor there, she'd already gathered that the problem of pregnant women and cocaine was more widespread than she'd ever imagined.

Now, as she sat reading through the material, her problems with Karl, Alex and her jobs faded into insignificance, and she forgot to watch the clock.

"What do you think?" Karl asked as he walked Ron Martinez to his car.

"Frankly? I feel your grandfather may be incompetent. But I also have to consider the fact that he isn't the most cooperative client I've ever talked to. It was hard for me to tell whether his refusal to answer certain questions was a cover-up for his not knowing the answers or just angry resistance to the whole procedure. Hopefully, the two psychiatrists—and the layperson—who've examined him will be able to clarify that for us."

Karl looked doubtful. "They each came out here, talked to my granddad alone and then left. None of them would discuss their findings with me. Even that layperson guy was closemouthed."

As he spoke to the lawyer, Karl noted that Jaime's car wasn't in front of her house. That made the third night in a row that she'd been out. He assumed she was at graduate school and wondered how she felt about leaving Alex alone so much.

Ron tossed his briefcase into his car and turned to face Karl. "If it turns out that your grandfather does need a guardian, I have no problem with your being appointed. Assuming, of course, that no evidence of exploitation comes to light between now and the day of the hearing."

"Exploitation?" Karl put his hands in his pockets and paced a few steps before turning back toward Ron. "Jaime keeps asking about that, too. My grandfather just backed up my story about the repair work and when the company was transferred but I guess that doesn't matter. In your opinion, he's too senile to know what happened."

Ron took a cigarette out of the pack in his jacket pocket and lighted up before responding. "I've been working on these cases long enough to believe that anything's possible. But your grandfather obviously trusts you and wants you to be guardian—if necessary. That carries a lot of weight with me. And, if you are appointed guardian, the lawyer you hired can serve as your representative here in Miami until you can arrange through the Seattle courts to transfer guardianship up there."

"Good enough." Karl shook the attorney's hand. "Thanks for coming out."

"It's part of the job." Ron looked into Karl's eyes for a long moment before he spoke again. "Are you involved with Jaime?" he asked finally.

Karl was surprised by the question. Once he'd ascertained that Ron was a part of Jaime's past and not her future, his feelings of jealousy had completely vanished. In fact he'd developed a grudging respect for the knowledgeable, straight-talking lawyer during the two hours Ron had been at the house. He saw no reason to be evasive with the other man.

"I'm not involved with her yet. But I'd like to be."

Ron smiled. "I thought you weren't too pleased when I kissed her."

Karl chuckled. "Did it show?"

"Slightly. I guess she told you that I'm happily married."

"She did. How'd you ever get her to go out with you anyway?" Karl asked, hoping to discover Jaime's motivation in his own situation.

"I met her doing a competency a lot like this one. I asked her out several times before she accepted. I think her friends finally nagged her into it. They were always after her about her nonexistent social life. We saw each other for about two years, on and off."

"Why'd you finally break up?"

"A lot of reasons. We got along well together. I enjoyed her company socially. The rest of our relationship..." He looked at Karl and shrugged. "Let's just say that it didn't do wonders for my ego. But it was the emotional chill that finally got to me. She just wouldn't let me touch her emotionally. I needed more than she was willing to give. Then I met the lady I'm married to now, and I realized how much was missing between me and Jaime. End of story."

He climbed into his car and started the engine. "I don't know why I'm telling you all this. Except you seem like a nice guy, and I don't want you to have to go through the pain I did." He paused and then continued. "I was in love with Jaime once, and I still care about her. But now I feel more sorry for her than anything else. And I feel sorry for any man who gets involved with her. Since her filing a competency on your grandfather hasn't stopped you—and Jaime herself hasn't managed to discourage you—I don't suppose what I've said will have much of an effect, either. So take care, friend. Take care."

Karl stood in the front yard and watched as Ron drove away. He had already suspected what the lawyer had told him about Jaime. But Karl was convinced that, in his case, things would be different. He'd seen the desire in Jaime's eyes when she'd looked at him, and he knew he'd see it there again on Sunday night. He'd backed off once because she'd asked him to. Now she'd sought him out again. The next time they came together, there'd be no turning back for either of them. He was going to defrost the ice princess once and for all.

Whistling in anticipation, Karl strode up the walk and into his grandfather's house.

Chapter Five

Karl set the grocery bags down on the counter and began to unload them.

Alex looked up from his seat at the kitchen table. "Are there any more? I could help you bring them in."

"This is it. But thanks for the offer."

Ivar paused after taking a bite of his sandwich to contribute to the conversation. "I told you Alex was a good boy. This morning we rewired a lamp together, we played some cards and then he fixed me lunch."

He reached across the table to ruffle the boy's hair, and Alex smiled.

Karl noticed the clear space on the table in front of Alex. "Why aren't you eating?"

"My mom left me a note this morning. She wants me to ride my bike over to the restaurant and have lunch there."

"The restaurant?"

"Yeah. Since she's been working that part-time job, I hardly get to see her anymore. Usually on Saturday we at least go to a movie or something together."

Karl turned to face Alex, the groceries forgotten. "You mean she's working a second job? When did this start?"

"Last Wednesday. She's working as a waitress at B. J.'s Sandwich Shoppe. She told me she put in an application when she had lunch there with you."

Karl began throwing the rest of the groceries into the cupboards none too gently. "She works hard enough as a social worker." Glancing over his shoulder, he saw the frustration he felt mirrored in Alex's expression.

"She thinks we need a vacation in California—as if that's gonna solve everything. What I need is to get a job and do my share. But no way. I'm supposed to sit home with dumb books all day and watch her..." Alex took a deep breath and blinked back the tears that threatened to spill out at any second. "I try to explain to her, but she just doesn't understand how that makes a guy feel. You know?"

Karl nodded. "Yeah. I know." He placed a roll of paper towels on top of the refrigerator, then moved to stand by Alex's chair. "Look, why don't I go to lunch with you and maybe we can talk to her about how you feel. Even if she doesn't agree, it'll all be out in the open instead of bottled up inside you."

A smile slowly spread over Alex's face. "You'd really do that for me?"

"I don't like to think of her working that hard, either, buddy." He looked at his grandfather. "Think you can spare me for an hour or two?"

Ivar pushed himself to his feet and carried his dishes to the sink. "If that's a polite way of asking if I'll be okay alone," he growled, "the answer is that I've taken care of myself for eighty-three years, and I can continue for another eighty-three if I have to."

Karl grinned, not at all intimidated. "I guess that's a yes."

Ivar gave his grandson a crooked smile and a solid whack on the shoulder. "Of course that's a yes. Now go on and get out of here. I'm just going to take my medicine, and then I'm going to watch a little television."

"But, Mr. Hallstrom," Alex inserted. "You just took your medicine a little while ago, before lunch. Remember?"

Karl was close enough to see the bewildered expression in his grandfather's eyes. He felt a small thrill of fear. He knew that his grandfather hadn't remembered at all.

Then the confused expression vanished as if it had never been, and Ivar was smiling again and patting Alex on the back. "Of course I remember. You two run along and have a good time now."

As Karl left the house with Alex, he wondered whether today's mistake with the medicine had just been an isolated incident, or if Jaime might not be right about his grandfather. That thought scared him more than he cared to admit.

He brooded about the occurrence all the way to B.J.'s. But once he'd pulled into the parking lot, all his thoughts turned to Jaime.

She was nowhere in sight as they entered the crowded restaurant, but Karl asked the hostess to seat them in Jaime's section.

Then, just as they were sliding into the booth, Karl caught sight of her. She was walking toward them, wearing tennis shoes and a ponytail. A bright pink apron with B. J.'s Sandwich Shoppe in red letters partially covered her T-shirt and jeans.

Was he imagining things, or was she thinner than before, the circles beneath her eyes darker? But he'd seen her only last night, and he hadn't noticed it then. Damn the woman! It seemed that he couldn't be sure of even the simplest fact when it came to her.

Jaime almost tripped over her own feet when she saw that Karl was with Alex. Darn! Why had he had to find out about this?

Feeling a little apprehensive, she approached the table. Karl was wearing a deep blue short-sleeved shirt that emphasized the color of his eyes, and even though the expression in those eyes left some doubt as to her welcome, she felt the familiar excitement at just being near him again.

Smiling, she set two glasses of ice water down on their table and handed them each a menu. "Welcome to B.J.'s, gentlemen."

Karl knew that he had no right to dictate what Jaime should and shouldn't do. But somehow that knowledge only frustrated him more, and he couldn't stop the words that seemed to come jumping out of him. "Do you think you can handle a job like the one you have and do this, too?"

Jaime planted her hands on her hips. She'd just been asking herself the same question, but she'd never admit it to him now. "Lots of people in this country work two jobs in order to support their families, and they're not whining about it."

"I don't care about anyone else. I'm talking about you."

"And I'm—" Jaime swung her hand to emphasize her words, and Karl's glass of ice water toppled into his lap.

Alex covered his mouth with one hand, trying his best to stifle a laugh.

Karl glared at Jaime, righting the glass and scooping a handful of ice back into it.

Still aggravated, Jaime grabbed several napkins from the table dispenser and tried to blot the water off the front of Karl's pants. "I'm sorry, I didn't mean to do that. But I hope it helped you to cool off."

Her innocent ministrations were having just the opposite effect, and Karl took hold of her wrists and pushed her hands away. "I'll do it," he told her very deliberately.

Suddenly Jaime understood, and her anger was replaced by acute embarrassment. Avoiding his gaze, she busied herself wiping the water from the booth and the table.

"What seems to be the problem here?"

Karl looked up at the balding man with the tie and the plastic tag that said Assistant Manager. From the expression on the man's face, Karl knew that Jaime was in imminent danger of losing her job.

Jaime was aware of the same fact. Mr. Fox hadn't liked her from the minute he'd seen her. And she *was* a klutz. He'd warned her about that once already. In fact, she would have loved to walk out on him right now and leave him with the lunch crowd, but she needed this lousy job.

She held her breath as Karl looked at the assistant manager and smiled.

"There's no problem here. I just spilled my water, and the lady is helping me clean it up."

Mr. Fox looked at Karl skeptically. Then, with a parting glare at Jaime that had "I'll get you next time," written all over it, he turned and stalked away.

Alex could no longer restrain his laughter, and even Jaime smiled. She should have known that Karl was a fair fighter. "Thanks, Karl."

"Anytime. But I still think you ought to quit."

Jaime sighed, too tired to continue the argument. "I may just do that if Mr. Fox doesn't get off my back. But it won't be because you said to. It'll be because I want to. Now hurry up and tell me what you want to order."

Karl blinked at her, then quickly glanced at the menu. "Two cheeseburgers medium-well, a double order of french fries and a vanilla milkshake."

"I'll have the same," Alex said. "Are you really gonna quit?"

"I haven't decided yet. You'll have to settle for one cheeseburger and one order of fries."

Alex made a face as Jaime took their menus and walked away. "I think she's still mad. I don't know what it is about you, Karl. But you're the only one I've ever seen get to her that way."

Karl took an inordinate amount of satisfaction from Alex's observation. Then he remembered the question that he'd wanted to ask the boy earlier.

"Alex, remember a little while ago when my granddad forgot he'd taken his medication? Has that ever happened before?"

Alex answered the question with obvious reluctance. "Well, yeah. Once in a while. I told him he ought to use this plastic gizmo that Mom told me about one time. It has a different compartment for each time you have to take the medicine. So when the compartment for that time is empty, you know for sure you already took the pill. But your granddad said he didn't need it."

Karl sat thinking about that until Jaime brought their food to the table. He watched her as she hurried away again. What was it she'd said at Sarah Levine's house? Something about having the courage to admit one's limitations and accept help. Maybe he'd talk to his grandfather when he got home.

"I know you've helped my granddad a lot, Alex. I appreciate that."

Alex peeled the wrapper off his straw. "You don't need to thank me. I like helping him. I never really had a grandpa. Mom's dad left her and Grandma a long time before I was born." A shadow seemed to cross his face. "Grandma used to take care of me while Mom worked, but she died when I was seven. She was real nice to me, but she was sad all the time. I don't ever remember her smiling. Not once."

"What about your dad's father?" Karl asked between mouthfuls of food.

Alex glanced in Jaime's direction. She was standing a few booths away writing down an order. "I never knew him, either."

Karl sensed he was close to learning more about the haunted look he often saw in Jaime's eyes. He pushed a little harder, not out of idle curiosity, but because he felt a real need to know. He wanted very much to understand what made Jaime Mitchell tick. "And your dad?"

Alex stirred his shake with his straw for a moment before he looked up and met Karl's eyes. "Mom gave me a picture of him, but I tore it up and threw it away a long time ago."

He waited for Karl's reaction. But when the man just sat regarding him with silent acceptance, he continued to talk, grateful that he finally had someone to tell the story to. "My mom and dad dated in high school. Mom said they loved each other, but that he died in a car accident before they could get married."

Karl puzzled over that information. Was that why Jaime had become so upset when he'd questioned her about her "husband"? Had she been reluctant to reveal the fact that she'd never been married—or was there more to it than that? Alex's skepticism had been apparent in the tone of his voice.

"You don't think that's the real story, do you Alex?"

The boy slowly shook his head. "I can see the hurt and the anger in Mom's face whenever she talks about him. I figure she loved him, but he didn't even care enough about her to marry her when she got pregnant. If he hadn't died, I bet I'd still never have seen him. I think Mom just told me that other story because he was my dad, and she didn't want me to feel bad about him."

Karl looked at the boy across from him, wondering if Jaime had any idea how perceptive this son of hers really was. But he was even more surprised by Alex's next words.

"My dad was nothing but a coward, Karl. He didn't amount to anything. In that picture I tore up, he looked a lot like me. I think my mom is afraid I'm like my father inside, too. She's afraid I won't amount to anything, either."

"Your mom loves you, buddy."

"She loves me, but she doesn't understand! She thinks I oughta be like her and get all As. But I can't, Karl. I have to work my butt off just to get those Cs. And I don't want to go to college. I want to be a mechanic!"

The frustration in the boy's voice touched a responsive chord in Karl. He'd felt the same way about school at Alex's age, and he certainly knew how hard it was to communicate with Jaime.

He polished off his first burger, giving Alex a chance to settle down before he spoke. "I wish I had gone to college when my grandfather wanted to send me."

"You didn't go to college?"

"Nope. I didn't like school that much, either. And I was in too big a rush. I wanted to start working in the company full-time. I wanted to be a man and do a man's job instead of wasting time in school like some little kid."

"So why are you sorry?" Alex asked as he reached for the ketchup.

"Because going to college is a lot more than learning English and math. It's going to football games—or maybe even playing in them. It's getting to socialize with people your own age and figuring out who you are, what you believe, where you fit in with the rest of the world. It's sort of a transition between being a teenager and being an adult." He looked at Alex's impassive face. "I guess I'm saying this all wrong."

"No, you're not," Alex assured him. "I understand what you mean. I just never thought of college that way before."

"Neither did I until I looked back and realized what I'd missed. And, eventually, I even started to regret not taking those English and history courses."

Alex wrinkled his nose in disgust. "Why?"

"Sometimes I'd be out with my friends—people who'd kept on going to school while I was busy working. Someone would mention a book I'd never read or some historical incident I'd never heard about, and I'd feel like a real dummy. I didn't like that feeling. I didn't like to think that my friends were moving on, learning and growing, while I was just standing still."

He paused, trying to gauge Alex's reaction. The boy was looking at him warily, as if he'd begun to suspect that his new ally was really on his mother's side of the college issue after all. "I started taking a course or two at night," Karl continued. "First I took a business course. Then I took an engineering class. I finally worked up enough nerve to register for a literature course."

"How bad was it?"

Karl smiled at Alex's sympathetic expression. "I survived. And I found out that I was smarter than I'd thought. I worked hard to get my Bs and Cs in high school. I didn't have a talent for memorizing and feeding back the teachers' ideas like some of those A students. I had to really understand the facts before I could do well on a test. But once I understood, I didn't forget the information the next day. It was mine for good.''

Karl could see that Alex was thinking over what he'd said, but then the boy seemed to reject it all with one sentence.

"I still don't think college is for me.''

"Maybe not. But just knowing you this past week, I'm willing to bet you'd make a damned fine mechanical engineer. And you have a while before you have to decide about college. Why close doors you haven't even come to yet?''

Alex seemed flattered by what Karl had said, but not flattered enough to agree with it. "Part of me wants to go to college so that Mom will be proud of me. But another part wants to grow up fast and get a job so I can pay my own way.'' He jabbed his straw into his drink and gave Karl a speculative look. "You don't think I'm like my dad, do you, Karl? I want to help Mom. I could get a part-time job now, but she won't let me. And I try as hard as I can in school.''

Karl was about to say something reassuring when Jaime came back to the table.

"Is our dinner date still on for tomorrow?'' she asked Karl a little uncertainly.

He gave her a look that sent a shiver all the way down to her toes. "It takes more than a little ice water to discourage me.''

Jaime couldn't help feeling a warm glow of anticipation that had nothing to do with paying off debts. "Good. Alex and I will be ready at seven-thirty.''

"Mom, did you forget? I'm supposed to...uh...have dinner at Tony's house tomorrow. I'm sleeping over. Remember?''

Jaime frowned, and Karl turned his head to hide a smile. He didn't know whether Alex's excuse was legitimate or another juvenile attempt at matchmaking. But the possibilities it opened up were definitely intriguing.

"Alex, I don't remember you mentioning any sleep-over. And you have school the following morning."

"Aw, Mom! Tony only lives a couple of blocks away. I'll be home in time for breakfast. I won't be late for school, I promise."

"I don't think so."

"Aw, Mom! Mrs. Angelo's been cooking all week, making pizza and lasagna and stuff just 'cause I said I was coming over. And Tony and I are going to study late for a test we have Monday. Tony's real smart. He helps me a lot. I bet I'll get at least a B on that test."

Jaime was lost the minute Alex brought higher grades into the argument. "I guess it will be okay. But this is the last time on a school night. And you have to swear to me that you're going to study. Do I have your word?"

"I promise, Mom," Alex said, meaning it. He'd study all night long if it meant a chance to get Karl Hallstrom for his stepdad.

Of course, long shots like that only worked out on TV, but what did he have to lose by trying? He'd have to call Tony real quick and set things up with him. What if Mrs. Angelo didn't agree? Alex didn't even want to think about that. He was feeling bad enough already about all those lies he'd told. But they were sort of white lies. He'd told them for a good reason. Now if everything would just work out between Karl and Mom!

"I'd better get back to work now," Jaime said.

She tore the check off her pad and placed it on the table, then counted five one-dollar bills out of the tips in her apron pocket. "This is for Alex's lunch. See you tonight, sweetheart."

She leaned forward to kiss her son, and he shifted in his seat in embarrassment.

Karl watched her walk away and smiled as he pulled out his wallet.

"She's not going to like that," Alex warned him.

"The customer's always right," Karl told him with a wink. "And listen, buddy, I didn't forget. Tomorrow when

I go to dinner with your mom, I'll mention how you feel about school and about getting a job. It might be easier for her to talk about how she feels if you're not there."

"Maybe. Thanks, Karl."

"Sure thing."

"You won't mention what I said about my father, will you?"

"Not if you don't want me to. But I think *you* should discuss it with her."

Alex shook his head, unable to put his feelings into words. "She's just . . . she's not ready to hear that."

"What you're telling me is she's still treating you like a little kid, and you're playing along with it. If you want her to start treating you like an adult, you've got to let her know how close you are to becoming one. If she had a chance to hear what you told me today, I think she'd realize that you're not a little boy anymore."

"Maybe you're right," Alex said as he stood up to leave. "I just don't want to hurt her, that's all."

Karl put his arm around the boy's shoulders as they walked to the cash register together. "I know how you feel. But sometimes that's the only way a relationship can grow."

Jaime watched them as they left the restaurant and idly wondered what they were discussing. As she made her way back to their booth, she half expected to see her five dollars still lying on the table. Instead she found the crisp new twenty that Karl had left for her tip.

Jaime smiled as she pocketed the money and started clearing away the dirty dishes. Karl might have won this round, but tomorrow night it would be her turn. And she was going to enjoy every minute of it.

Chapter Six

Jaime looked into the mirror and wrinkled her nose at her reflection. She had only fifteen minutes until seven-thirty when she was supposed to meet Karl, and she was not thrilled with the results of her efforts. She'd showered, blow-dried her hair and applied her seldom-used makeup. Her red silk dress had a ruffle at the chest area that made her small breasts appear larger. Its short, full skirt concealed her narrow hips while emphasizing her tiny waist and long legs. What more could she do?

Jaime hadn't been on anything approximating a date in the last year, and she hadn't had time to even take notice of that fact until tonight. She supposed that long dry spell must be why she was so nervous. After all, this wasn't a real date. She had only asked Karl out to dinner to repay him for his kindness.

Her hands shook so as she applied her perfume that she almost dropped the bottle. She met the gaze of the woman in the mirror and was forced to admit the truth at last. She wanted Karl Hallstrom. But it was one thing to recognize her fantasies and another thing entirely to play them out. And Jaime Mitchell had no intention of leaving reality behind tonight.

With a final glance at the mirror, she turned away, picked up her purse and eased her aching feet into a pair of red high heels. Whatever else happened, at least her career as a waitress was officially over. She'd actually enjoyed the flabbergasted expression on Mr. Fox's face when she'd told him what he could do with her job. She hoped the rest of the evening would go as well.

Leaving the bedroom light burning, she walked to the kitchen and reread the note that Alex had left for her:

Gone to Tony's house. Back tomorrow for breakfast.
                                                    Love, Alex

She frowned in annoyance. Alex knew that any time he went out, he was supposed to write down an address and phone number where he could be reached. She had wanted to call Mrs. Angelo and check on him before she left. Now there was no way she could do that.

Her gaze traveled to the kitchen clock. It was already seven-thirty. There was nothing she could do about Alex now. She'd try looking through the telephone book for the Angelos' number when she came home.

As Jaime switched on the outside light and stepped onto the porch, she reminded herself that she was a grown woman. Fluttery feelings and sweaty palms were for teenagers. But she couldn't ignore the thrill of excitement that ran through her when she saw Karl standing in the driveway across the street.

He was faced away from her, rubbing the gleaming hood of his truck with a cloth. She was surprised to find that he looked as good in a suit as he did in a work shirt and jeans. She'd imagined he'd appear out-of-place and ill-at-ease in a jacket and tie. But the cut of the dark blue material only served to delineate and enhance the powerful lines of his body.

As a matter of fact, the closer Jaime drew to Karl, the better he looked. When a hot, slow-moving breeze carried the musky scent of his cologne to her, she closed her eyes for a second and savored the fragrance.

Karl turned at the sound of Jaime's approaching foot-steps and hoped that his surprise didn't show. She'd en-hanced her features with subtle makeup and fixed her hair in an attractive style. And that was a pretty dress she had on. A pretty, *short* dress. With a sense of deep appreciation, Karl noticed that Jaime Mitchell had been hiding the long-est, most attractive pair of legs he'd ever seen. He would dearly love to start at her toes and kiss his way up those legs, inch by beautiful inch. And then... And then he'd show her just how good a man could make a woman feel.

Karl felt himself growing more enthusiastic by the sec-ond and desperately tried to concentrate on some other subject before his enthusiasm became embarrassingly ob-vious. He'd definitely been abstinent for too long! He couldn't remember the last time he'd reacted to a woman so strongly with so little provocation.

With some effort, he raised his gaze to Jaime's face. She looked younger somehow. Maybe it was the expression she was wearing. A kind of shy anticipation. Seeing it there didn't do much to dampen his troublesome enthusiasm.

"You look beautiful, Jaime," he said, and meant it.

"I'm glad you think so," she murmured. Her cheeks grew pink, and the expression in her eyes was warm and welcom-ing.

Karl stood there fascinated, unable to look away. He felt a little drunk, but he hadn't even had one beer. What the heck was wrong with him?

Finally he forced himself to turn and walk to the other side of the truck. He opened the door for her, and she brushed past him to climb inside, her skirt riding up to mid-thigh as she sat down.

Karl slammed the door a little harder than necessary, the sultry scent of her perfume only adding to his torment as he slid behind the wheel. He didn't dare look at her. Straightening his tie, he tried to focus on the idea of dinner. But for once, he wasn't interested in food. He wanted to devour Jaime instead.

But now that she'd finally accepted the invitation he'd issued after field visits last Wednesday, he intended to savor their time together. He was determined to make the entire evening a night to remember.

"I made reservations at a great seafood place," he said as he backed the truck out of the driveway. "I ate lunch there a few days ago, and I'd like to try it for dinner—if that's all right with you."

Jaime was a little taken aback. She had made reservations at a nearby steak house. After all, she was the one who'd asked him out to dinner, not the other way around. Then she decided that it wasn't worth fighting over. The dinner was for Karl, and she was willing to take him to any restaurant he preferred.

"That's fine with me," she said, her smile only a little forced. Mentally she totaled up the money she had in her purse and crossed her fingers.

As the hostess seated them, Karl congratulated himself on his choice of restaurants. He'd selected this particular place with Jaime in mind. He knew her well enough by now to realize that his spending an exorbitant amount on dinner would only make her feel uncomfortable. This place was nice, but not elegant, affordable rather than expensive.

Jaime examined the menu and began to relax a little. She could handle these prices.

"How about some champagne?"

Jaime moved her menu aside to look at him and almost knocked her butter dish off the table. She had no idea what brand Karl was considering or how much it would cost.

"I...uh...don't drink alcohol very often. But, please, go ahead if you'd like."

Karl put the wine list down. So much for that idea. "Maybe I'll just have a glass of white wine instead. What are you ordering for dinner? Their lobster is delicious."

"I'm going to have steak."

"You're ordering steak in a seafood restaurant?" Karl asked, doubting that she was serious.

"I don't like fish," Jaime confessed.

"You don't like— Well, why didn't you say so? We could have gone somewhere else."

"No, this is your night, Karl. And I'm fine, really. These places always have steak or chicken as alternate selections."

The waitress came to take their order, and Karl frowned in perplexity. This is your night? What did that mean? He'd never figure this woman out! One minute she was as assertive as all get out, the next she wouldn't even challenge his choice of a restaurant. Maybe all the time he'd been planning the evening to please her, she'd been planning it to please him. Did that mean she had other plans for him later on? He certainly hoped so. Maybe this *was* his night, after all.

He smiled and raised his glass. "To us."

"To us," Jaime echoed as she clinked her soda glass with his wineglass.

She thought that she'd be content to stare into those beautiful blue eyes for all eternity. Then she smiled as she realized how silly she was being.

"What are you smiling at?" Karl wanted to know.

"This was my last day at B. J.'s," Jaime improvised. "I'm a one-job woman again—at least temporarily."

"You know, before Alex told me that you were working, I noticed your car was gone, but I thought you were at night school."

"I only go two nights a week," Jaime told him. She wasn't used to sharing her hopes and dreams, but Karl's quiet interest seemed to encourage it. "I hope my graduate credits will help me get the supervisor's position that I've applied for. It's more pay and a lot less client contact." She patted her midriff. "Maybe even less stomach trouble."

Karl somehow couldn't picture Jaime sitting behind a desk doing paperwork all day. "But you're so good with people, Jaime. That's the kind of work you were meant to do."

Jaime took a sip of soda and shook her head in denial. "I like my clients. I like to help them. But what do I really accomplish? All I have time to do is put bandages on problems that require major surgery. And sometimes I think I hurt more than I help."

"Well, I think you're wrong. You try your best, and you do a damned good job. I went on field visits with you, remember? I saw you with Sarah, Mrs. Todd—even good old Clarence. I know what I'm talking about."

"Well, at least one of us thinks I'm a smashing success." She smiled self-consciously, suddenly realizing that they'd been talking about nothing but her all evening. She'd never had that experience with a man before. Most of them seemed perfectly content to talk about themselves nonstop, but they weren't very good listeners. Karl was different.

"Tell me about what *you* do for a living," Jaime coaxed.

She listened, enthralled, as Karl described how his great-grandfather had come to Seattle from Sweden over eighty years before and built the sawmill that was still part of Karl's company today. He went on to tell her anecdotes about some of Seattle's founders that were as funny as they were unbelievable.

"Seattle's history is stranger than fiction," Karl said as he polished off the last of his wine. "It's a fascinating place to live even now, a city with something for everyone." He looked at her speculatively. "You and Alex ought to pay me a visit someday. I'd be glad to give you a tour."

"Maybe I will," Jaime said impulsively, surprised at how much the idea appealed to her. "Tell me, did the men of Seattle really import a boatload of brides from New England?"

"More than one. If they hadn't, I probably wouldn't have red hair."

"What do you mean?"

"One of my non-Swedish ancestors, my mother's great-grandmother, came to Seattle with Mercer's second expedition. She was an Irish maid from Boston named Katherine Flynn.''

"Aha!" Jaime exclaimed. "So that's where you got that temper."

Karl grinned. "My red hair can probably be blamed on Katherine, but my temper I inherited from Granddad. The two of us used to scandalize Grandma. She was very quiet and reserved—a proper Swedish lady."

The waitress arrived with their dinners, and Jaime became aware of the pensive expression that had come over Karl's face. "What's wrong?" she asked, wondering at his sudden change of mood.

Karl smiled wanly, surprised that she had noticed. "I was just thinking about my grandfather." He hesitated, debating the wisdom of sharing his thoughts with her. But the concern in her eyes was too genuine to resist. "That first day in your office, Jaime, you tried to tell me that Granddad was having problems with his medication. But I wouldn't listen. The other day, I saw it for myself. I tried to discuss the situation with him, but he denies the whole thing."

Karl paused to cut himself a bite of swordfish, his frustration evident. "So I've been watching him closely and reminding him when necessary. But even if he goes back to Seattle with me, I can't stay with him all day. What am I going to do?"

Jaime was pleased that Karl finally recognized Ivar's problem, but seeing his uncertainty and pain brought her little satisfaction. "You could try enrolling him in an adult day-care center. They have activities—like arts and crafts—and they can monitor his medication."

Karl chuckled. "Can't you just see my granddad weaving baskets?"

Jaime smiled as she buttered a roll. "You're right. He'd never agree to a day-care center. You still might be able to hire someone to live with him and help him out."

"Another idea he's sure to love."

"Well, there's always placement," Jaime suggested reluctantly.

Karl sat back in his chair and pushed his plate away. "He wouldn't consent to that. And I can't—I won't—force him. Because I won't, having him declared incompetent isn't going to help me deal with his problems. It will only kill what's left of his pride."

Jaime reached out and touched his hand. "I know. It's not going to be easy for either of you—any way you look at it."

"He's always been so strong, able to deal with anything that came his way. It scares the hell out of me to see him not able to face up to this."

"Give him time, Karl," Jaime urged. "He may have a deeper strength than even you know."

Karl saw the warmth in her gaze and felt a surge of optimism. "Maybe you're right."

When the waitress came by to inquire about dessert, Jaime passed. Karl, his appetite and good mood restored, ordered coffee and Boston cream pie.

"This is good, but I make it better," Karl declared after the first bite.

Jaime had no reason to doubt him. "When we had lunch together the other day, you did mention that you enjoyed cooking. Who taught you?"

"My grandfather took over all the cooking after my grandmother passed away. I guess I just picked it up from him." He smiled at her over his coffee cup. "I enjoy it, but for someone who loves to eat as much as I do, it's a pretty necessary skill."

His smile was contagious. Jaime's lips curved upward in response to his gentle humor. "Necessary or not, I'm really impressed with anyone who can follow a recipe. I think even Alex is a better cook than I am."

At the mention of Alex's name, Karl remembered his promise. He hated to bring up a touchy subject when things were going so well with Jaime, but he felt an obligation to the boy.

"Alex has been talking to me, Jaime," he said, knowing full well that he was rushing in where angels feared to tread.

"About what?" Jaime asked, inferring from Karl's tone that she probably wouldn't like the answer.

"His feelings about school and getting a job."

"His job right now is to do his homework and prepare for college," Jaime said coolly.

"He's giving that his best shot, and he's probably doing as well in school now as he's ever going to do," Karl told her. "It really upsets him that you don't believe that."

Jaime felt her temper rising and tried to curb it. The last thing she wanted to do at this point was to get into another argument with Karl. "You've known him a week. I've known him fourteen years. I think I'm better able to judge what's best for him."

Karl drained his cup, wishing the coffee were something stronger. He tried to figure out what the hell to say next. He was sorely tempted to repeat what Alex had said about his father and use that to illustrate how little Jaime really knew about her son. But he had told Alex he wouldn't mention that. And he had no desire to see Jaime hurt, either.

"I think I understand Alex better than you do because he's a lot like I used to be—and because we're both males."

Jaime carefully folded her napkin and placed it on the table. "I do not believe that people have to have the same sexual equipment in order to communicate with each other. But the longer we talk, the more I disprove my own point. So let's just move on to something else."

Karl leaned forward, his voice intense. "I just have one more thing to say, and it has nothing to do with sex. I understand why you want Alex to go to college, Jaime. I agree that he'll do fine there—if he makes up his mind that he wants to go. But you're defeating your own purpose by pushing him to make As in subjects where he's only average. Accept him as he is and ease up. Compromise a little. Let him get a part-time job doing what he loves. I guarantee he'll compromise with you in return. Otherwise he's going to start pushing back, and then you're both going to be sorry."

He sat back in his chair and gave her time to absorb what he'd said before he spoke again. "That's all. End of lecture. How mad are you?"

Jaime thought about it. "I suppose you have the right to express your opinion," she told him grudgingly. "And I seem to have a problem staying angry with you because— even though you're wrong—I know you mean well. I know you're trying to help Alex."

She paused, steeling herself for an assault of her own. "You just told me something I didn't want to hear. Now it's my turn."

Karl looked apprehensive. "What?"

"Here's the money I owe you for the car parts. Alex said this was the amount."

Karl stared at the bills she was extending across the table. It was the last thing in the world he had expected and the last thing he wanted to accept. He would have blown three times that much on flowers or perfume for a lady and never thought twice about it.

He raised his gaze to her face. What was he supposed to say? Keep your money, sweetheart. It's small change to me. No, he couldn't hurt her like that. He'd stepped on her pride before, and he wouldn't make that mistake again.

He took a deep breath and swallowed his own pride. It was a mouthful, and it hurt like hell going down, but he managed it.

He reached out and took the money. "Thank you, Jaime."

Jaime gave him a wide smile. Just for a second there, she'd thought he was going to refuse. But in the end he'd taken it. He'd finally accepted her as an equal. He finally understood.

At that moment, the waitress brought their check. Karl counted out the bills Jaime had given him, then reached for his wallet to add the balance.

"Oh, no," Jaime exclaimed. "I'm paying!"

The look Karl gave her could have been lethal to someone with a weak heart. In that instant he forgot all about

Jaime's pride, her sweet smile and her long, sexy legs. He could have cheerfully strangled her where she sat.

He turned his attention to the hovering waitress, his voice ominously quiet. "Give us a few more minutes."

"Sure thing," the woman quavered, beating a hasty retreat.

Karl's cool gaze swung back to Jaime. "What do you mean, you're paying?"

Jaime looked at him, a little bewildered. "Karl, I told you the other night—before you started on the tune-up—that I was going to take you out to dinner to thank you for your help with the car."

Karl's anger receded as he recalled that conversation. "Now that you mention it, that does sound kind of familiar. I guess I just didn't—"

"—take me seriously? Well, I was very serious. I'm paying for dinner tonight."

Karl stared at her across the table. What could he do to stop her from paying? Make her arm-wrestle for the check? Then he smiled, despite himself. "Damn, lady! I don't think my ego can survive a woman like you."

Jaime smiled back at him. "Oh, with your ego, I don't think you have a thing to worry about."

"Thanks for the vote of confidence."

Karl watched her add her own money to the bills on the table.

"Aren't you going to take some of the money back?" Jaime asked.

"I'll leave it for the tip," Karl told her, a challenge in his eyes.

"You do have a reputation as a big tipper," Jaime commented drolly.

Karl followed her out of the restaurant, wondering why he wasn't angry. Had he actually come to understand the way the woman's mind worked? It was a frightening thought.

Jaime stood back and allowed Karl to open the door of the truck for her, and they rode all the way home in a silence filled with unspoken thoughts. Then Karl pulled his truck into her driveway and switched off the headlights and engine.

Jaime watched him apprehensively as he let out a slow breath and turned toward her.

"Why do I put up with you?" he asked lightly.

Jaime looked at the dark outline of his face and barely restrained herself from touching it. "For the same reason I put up with you, I guess. I . . . like you. But—"

She broke off abruptly as Karl leaned closer. "Like? You mean the way you like the right wallpaper pattern or a cute puppy?"

Jaime pulled on the door handle and practically tumbled out of the truck in her haste to put distance between them. She heard his door slam as he got out to follow her, and her heart pounded in a strange mixture of dread and anticipation.

When she reached the porch, she turned to confront him. "I like you as . . . as a friend."

Karl walked to within a few steps of her, his gaze level and unwavering. "We're more than friends, Jaime."

"We can't be, Karl! For heaven's sake, we have nothing in common. I don't understand what keeps pulling us together."

"Don't you think I've been asking myself that question ever since I touched you for the first time? On the surface you seem so cold, so remote and self-sufficient. All the things my mother was. All the things I learned to hate."

"I—" Jaime began, but he laid a finger across her lips, startling her into silence.

"Hush and let me finish because I may never be in the mood to say this again."

Jaime did as she was told, her mouth tingling where his finger had pressed seconds before.

"I didn't understand what it was about an independent little iceberg like you that seemed to draw me like iron to a magnet. Then I realized that every time I was with you, I was picking up signals. Signals that contradicted the things you were saying to me."

"What are you talking about?" Jaime asked, genuinely puzzled.

"You want me, Jaime Mitchell—and not as a friend. Maybe you even *need* me."

Jaime took a step backward, feeling as if all her clothes had suddenly been stripped away and she were standing naked in front of him.

"That's not true!" she asserted, knowing all the while that he told the truth. She was just shocked and humiliated to discover that he'd been able to see through her camouflage.

Karl followed her, refusing to allow her to escape. "What you mean is that you didn't know it showed. Well, I'm sorry if that fact embarrasses you. You're vulnerable, just like everyone else in this world, and it's about time you admitted it."

"No!" Jaime cried, her icy facade cracking at long last. Anger, hurt and humiliation threatened to overwhelm her, but she made one last desperate attempt to regain control. "I have nothing more to say to you until the hearing," she informed him, her voice cool and level. "I'm going inside now. I refuse to stand here and put on a display for my neighbors."

But Karl wasn't about to be put off again after he'd come this far. He was like a bloodhound that scented the imminent capture of his quarry. The real Jaime Mitchell wasn't going to escape him his time. He was going to find her and bring her out into the open no matter what the consequences.

"Just what are you afraid of, Jaime?" he persisted. "What deep, dark secret are the neighbors going to find out?"

Jaime stumbled in her haste to reach the front door, to get inside her house, to lock herself away from this man and his disturbing words. Hands shaking, she turned the key and pushed the door open. Then she glanced back at Karl and hesitated in confusion when she saw that, far from pursuing her, he was backing away from her. She watched in horror as he cupped a hand on either side of his mouth, faced the street and yelled as loudly as he could.

"Hey, everybody! Guess what? Jaime Mitchell is human!"

"Damn you! You . . . you Swedish meatball!"

Throwing her purse onto the couch by the door, Jaime stepped back outside and advanced on the annoying hulk dominating her front yard. The fact that he was taller by a head and outweighed her by at least a hundred pounds didn't alter her determination to throw him off her property.

She came to a halt a foot in front of him. Shaking her fist in his face, she proceeded to call him every name, decent and indecent, that she could think of. Then she went on to invent a few more.

When she reluctantly paused for breath, she became aware of the fact that Karl was staring at her with a peculiar expression on his face that had nothing to do with anger or smugness. She stared back, unable to resist voicing the question on her mind.

"Just what do you think you're looking at?"

"The real Jaime Mitchell. The one who's capable of feeling anger and passion and who's capable of expressing those emotions. I always knew she was there somewhere deep inside you, shouting to be let out. I've been waiting to meet her. Waiting and wanting . . ."

Mesmerized by Karl's softly spoken words and the strangely compelling expression in his eyes, Jaime watched his mouth draw closer and closer to her own. Her anger had drained away as swiftly and as inexplicably as her fear had the first day he'd stormed into her office. That same acutely sexual awareness pervaded all her senses as his big calloused hands gently cupped her face. Then his lips took possession of hers with the same firm determination he showed in everything else he did.

Jaime made one halfhearted attempt to free her face from the large frame of his hands. Then his tongue slid inside her mouth, and she lost all will to resist.

She felt a dull sense of wonder at the intensity of her arousal. Before this night, she'd never truly desired a man, never believed herself capable of real passion. But Karl held her and kissed her until her heart beat in rhythm with his, until the blood flowed through her veins like sweet mulled wine to carry the heat of desire throughout her body.

Making an inarticulate sound in her throat, Jaime shifted her mouth to take the strokes of his tongue even deeper.

Karl drew in his breath sharply, dizzy with sensation. The enticing scent of her perfume, the softness of her skin, the wet warmth of her mouth, had aroused him. But her unexpected response to his kiss caused a primal exultation to course through him. His lips still pressed to hers, he tightened his arms around her waist and lifted her feet off the ground.

Jaime felt as if she were floating on air. She was vaguely aware that she was being borne into the house. She heard the front door shut behind them and the click as Karl reached back and threw the dead bolt. Then she was being lifted completely into his arms and carried down the hallway toward her lighted bedroom.

Driven by the urgency of his desire, Karl pressed her back against the bed. Without conscious thought, he brought his hand up and cupped one small, silk-covered breast.

Jaime tore her mouth away from his in a last attempt to hold on to her sanity. "We have to stop this," she whispered. "It's... it's a conflict of interest."

Karl smiled down into her flushed face, punctuating his words with kisses. "I know what...I'm interested in...and it's pretty obvious...you're interested in...the same thing.... I don't think there's...any conflict at all."

Jaime felt herself succumbing to the warm, moist persuasion of his lips and tongue. Her hands crept up beneath his jacket to caress the muscles of his back and shoulders, and she made no protest as his fingers fumbled open the buttons of her dress and released the clasp of her bra. His mouth left hers, and she felt abandoned until she realized his intent. Then the fire building in the depths of her abdomen threatened to rage out of control.

Jaime's skin had felt so cool to Karl when he'd first touched it. Now it was flushed and burning hot beneath his lips and tongue as he nibbled and licked his way down her soft neck to the twin mounds that beckoned him. He felt her quiver as his warm breath fanned across her nipple, already a hard, aching peak rising from the center of her breast. Then he took her inside his mouth.

Jaime felt his tongue moving against her flesh, and the sensation seemed to pierce through the center of her being. Aching with the need to join her body to his, she arched her pelvis against him in a silent plea.

Karl was lost to all rational thought. He knew only that he wanted to bury himself to the hilt inside the woman who was surging beneath him. And if that didn't happen soon, he was going to explode. Determinedly he pushed the skirt of her dress up and tugged at the waistband of her panties.

Jaime surfaced long enough for reason to intrude. "Karl, no. We can't. I'm not ready for this. I have to—"

Karl didn't even pause in his efforts. "Trust me, sweetheart," he breathed against her neck. "I'll take care of it. Just trust me."

Jaime froze beneath him, a vision of a similar night fifteen years before replaying itself in her mind. It wasn't Karl's desire-flushed face above hers, but that of Alex's father. "Trust me, baby," he'd told her. "I'll protect you. Trust me." That night had changed her life forever.

Gradually Jaime's head cleared, and her sense of reality returned with a jolt. She was lying half-naked beneath a man she hardly knew—a man who was strong enough to take what he wanted whether she agreed or not.

She pushed against his shoulders as hard as she could. But his mouth continued to seek hers, and his hands pulled her panties down over her hips.

Real fear began to course through Jaime as she realized just how helpless she was. It rose to her throat in a panicked scream.

"Let me go!"

Karl looked down at her in dazed bewilderment, as shocked as if she'd hauled off and slapped him. He'd been too absorbed in his own arousal to notice that she was no longer responding to him. But now he felt her coolness, the rigidity of her body under his. What had gone wrong? Had he only imagined her passion?

He pushed back and sat up on the bed, watching as Jaime straightened her clothing to conceal herself from his gaze. But it was really her feelings, her emotions that she was trying to hide. She'd withdrawn into herself again. The ice princess reigned supreme.

"What's wrong, Jaime? Tell me."

Jaime turned her back to him and buried her face in a pillow. "Go away," she told him in a cold, lifeless voice. "Please just go away and leave me alone."

"I'm not going to go away," Karl said softly, resting one hand on her hip. "I'm going to get this misunderstanding cleared up—even if I have to stay here all night."

But his gentle persistence evoked no positive response in Jaime, only fear and a cold anger. Who was he kidding? He didn't care about her! He was just determined to carry on with his seduction until she gave him what he wanted.

She had thought that she wanted it, too. She'd been fighting her desire for him ever since the first time she'd seen him. She'd practically invited him into her bedroom tonight. She'd enjoyed his touch.

But then she'd remembered the price of unguarded feeling, the cost of misplaced trust. Pain. Pain that she couldn't afford.

Jaime moved away from Karl's touch and huddled at the edge of the bed. "I don't want to talk. I don't want to make love. I just want to be left alone. Go away!"

Karl stood up, anger coursing through him as passion had only moments before. He had been so close to knowing her, to touching the real Jaime. She'd been warm, open, willing to share herself with him. Then, in the blink of an eye, she'd turned cold, hard, unyielding. And she wouldn't even tell him why. She wouldn't even let him close enough for that. Instead she was dismissing him from her life, cutting off all the feelings of tenderness and caring between them before they had a chance to grow.

The unfairness of it, the hopelessness of his position, hurt Karl beyond bearing, and he lashed out at the woman who was the cause of his pain.

"Fine. I'll go. I'll leave you alone. You have a great life, Jaime. Keep right on the way you're going. Don't let anyone get close to you. Hide from any real feelings. Just crawl back into your isolated, *frigid* little shell. I don't know why I even bothered trying to thaw you out in the first place!"

Jaime listened to his retreating footsteps, the resounding slam of the front door making her jump like the impact of a physical blow.

Karl was gone, but the words he'd spoken still lingered in the room. Jaime ached with the pain those words had caused her. She wanted to cry, but somehow she couldn't. Instead the unshed tears seemed to gather together inside her chest and form yet another layer of protective ice around her heart.

Chapter Seven

"You're late, Alex. Hurry or you're going to miss your school bus!"

Jaime rubbed a hand over her blurry eyes and tried to concentrate on getting the milk into the cereal bowl. Given her state of mind and the sleepless night she'd spent, that wasn't a simple task.

She'd lain awake from the time Karl had left until she'd heard Alex come in at ten to seven. Then she'd stumbled out of bed still wearing her smudged makeup and the hopelessly wrinkled red silk dress.

But Alex didn't seem to notice her strange appearance. He sat at the dining room table in brooding silence, picking listlessly at the cereal she served him.

"Why didn't you leave Mrs. Angelo's address and phone number in your note?" Jaime demanded, suddenly remembering that she'd intended to ask Alex that question as soon as she saw him. She hadn't given him a thought since her argument with Karl, and that lapse made her feel even worse.

"Sorry," Alex muttered, his mind still on what had happened to him the night before.

The sleep-over had been a bad idea from the beginning. When he'd left the restaurant Saturday, he'd suddenly remembered that Tony Angelo was spending the week with a friend in Fort Lauderdale. And his other friend, Eric, was out of town on vacation.

As a last resort, he had called Mike Walker, a guy who sat next to him in history class. It had seemed like everything was going to work out when Mike had said he could come over. But he had arrived to find that Mike had agreed to dinner and the sleep-over without his mother's consent.

Mike had just shrugged it all off. "Take it from me, Alex. If I'd've asked her ahead of time, she would have said no for sure."

Alex soon realized how true that statement was. Mrs. Walker had handed him a piece of the frozen pizza she'd made for dinner as if she were giving him a piece of gold. And she'd spent the whole meal smoking and staring at him like he was some display in a museum.

First she'd wanted to know his mother's name. Then she'd asked what his father's name was. His answer hadn't seemed to surprise her at all. But what she'd had to say after that had sure surprised him. He hadn't been able to sleep for five minutes the whole night.

"I asked you why you didn't leave the number and the address."

Alex looked up at his mother, too tired and upset to avoid the issue any longer. "I didn't want you to check up on me. I stayed at another guy's house because Tony was in Fort Lauderdale. I arranged the sleep-over *after* you told me about your date. I wanted you and Karl to be alone."

Jaime was shocked speechless. Then her face turned a mottled shade of pink. "Karl and I had no reason to want to be alone."

"Can't you see what a great guy he is?" Alex persisted, despite his mother's reaction.

But Jaime was shaking her head. "I want you to stay away from that man. I don't want to ever catch you speaking to him again. Is that clear?"

All Alex's remaining hope that Karl and his mom would get together evaporated abruptly. Anger and defiance took its place. "Why can't I be friends with Karl? Because he talked to you about how I feel about school and getting a job? Didn't you like what he had to say?"

Jaime was in no mood to debate the subject. "Don't argue with me, Alex. Not this morning. Just do what I tell you. The man's a bad influence. He has a terrible temper. For all I know, he could be lying about his grandfather's money."

Alex had heard more than he could stand to hear. His own pain suddenly overcame his reluctance to hurt his mother. He couldn't suffer in silence any longer.

"Oh, so Karl's a liar. And you won't tolerate lies, will you, Mom? Except when they're your lies about my father!"

The glass Jaime had been holding in her hand dropped to the floor and shattered against the tile.

"Mrs. Walker talked to me last night. She said she used to go to school with you and my dad. She said he didn't die in any car accident. He was a mechanic who was part of a stolen-car ring. He was shot by the police during a raid."

Jaime sank onto a chair, her legs refusing to support her.

"Is it true?" Alex demanded.

Jaime looked at him, her eyes glistening with unshed tears. "Yes," she whispered. "It's true."

"And he was never going to marry you, was he? That was a lie, too."

Jaime wanted to cover her ears, to block out what Alex was saying. But she'd run away from the truth for too long. "I didn't mean to lie to you, Alex. But I just couldn't bring myself to tell you about your father. I just wanted to protect you."

She was pleading for understanding, but she received none from her son.

"Don't you think I knew you hated him? I could tell by the look in your eyes every time you talked about him. I just wasn't sure why. But I found that out last night."

He stood and picked his book bag and lunch money up off the table. "And I found out why you push me so hard about school. My old man was a high school dropout. He was a quitter, a loser and a thief. Well, you tried Mom, but I guess there's too much of him in me."

"No! You're my son, not his!"

Alex was out the door before she had time to say anything more. She ran out after him and followed him down the street, calling his name. For once, she was oblivious to the fact that she might be attracting unwanted attention from the neighbors.

Ignoring her, he jogged around the corner and disappeared from view.

Panting, Jaime got to the end of the block in time to see her son boarding his school bus. She watched helplessly as the doors closed behind him and the bus carried him out of reach. Feeling numb, she walked slowly back to the house.

Standing in her sunlit kitchen, she swallowed a large dose of antacid. Then she squatted down and cleaned up the pieces of the glass she had broken. She refused to waste any more time worrying over what had happened last night with Karl. And Alex . . . She'd talk to him tonight after he'd had a chance to calm down. She had to get to work now. She had to maintain control.

"Everything will be all right," she told her reflection as she dressed in clothes suitable for the office. But the thin, pale woman in the bedroom mirror didn't look convinced.

At two o'clock, Jaime was gathering her papers together to go out on field visits. She was functioning on automatic pilot, barely paying attention to what she was doing. When the phone rang, she jumped. It as the administrator of the ACLF where she'd placed Mrs. Hunter.

The more
you love romance . . .
the more
you'll love this offer

FREE!

Mail this heart today! (See inside)

Join us on a Silhouette® Honeymoon
and we'll give you
4 free books
A free Victorian picture frame
And a free mystery gift

IT'S A
SILHOUETTE HONEYMOON—
A SWEETHEART OF A FREE OFFER!
HERE'S WHAT YOU GET:

1. Four New Silhouette Special Edition® Novels— FREE!

Take a Silhouette Honeymoon with your four exciting romances—yours FREE from Silhouette Reader Service™. Each of these hot-off-the-press novels brings you the passion and tenderness of today's greatest love stories . . . your free passports to bright new worlds of love and foreign adventure.

2. Lovely Victorian Picture Frame— FREE!

This lovely Victorian pewter-finish miniature is perfect for displaying a treasured photograph. And it's yours FREE as added thanks for giving our Reader Service a try!

3. An Exciting Mystery Bonus—FREE!

You'll be thrilled with this surprise gift. It is useful as well as practical.

4. Free Home Delivery!

Join the Silhouette Reader Service™ and enjoy the convenience of pre-viewing 6 new books every month delivered right to your home. Each book is yours for only $2.74* each—a saving of 21¢ off the cover price. And there is no extra charge for postage and handling. It's a sweetheart of a deal for you! If you're not completely satisfied, you may cancel at anytime, for any reason, simply by sending us a note or shipping statement marked "cancel" or by returning any shipment to us at our cost.

5. Free Insiders' Newsletter!

You'll get our monthly newsletter, packed with news about your favorite writers, upcoming books, even recipes from your favorite authors.

6. More Surprise Gifts!

Because our home subscribers are our most valued readers, when you join the Silhouette Reader Service™, we'll be sending you additional free gifts from time to time—as a token of our appreciation.

START YOUR SILHOUETTE HONEYMOON TODAY—JUST COM-PLETE, DETACH AND MAIL YOUR FREE-OFFER CARD

*Terms and prices subject to change without notice. Sales tax applicable in NY.

Get your fabulous gifts ABSOLUTELY FREE!

MAIL THIS CARD TODAY.

GIVE YOUR HEART TO SILHOUETTE

Yes! Please send me my four Silhouette Special Edition® novels FREE, along with my free Victorian picture frame and free mystery gift. I wish to receive all the benefits of the Silhouette Reader Service™ as explained on the opposite page.

PLACE
HEART STICKER
HERE

NAME _____
(PLEASE PRINT)

ADDRESS _____ APT. ____

CITY _____ STATE ____

ZIP CODE _____

235 CIS ACEV
(U-SIL-SE-01/91)

SILHOUETTE READER SERVICE™ "NO-RISK" GUARANTEE

—There's no obligation to buy—and the free gifts remain yours to keep.
—You pay the low subscribers'-only price and receive books before they appear in stores.
—You may end your subscription anytime by sending us a note or shipping statement marked "cancel" or by returning any shipment to us at our cost.

OFFER LIMITED TO ONE PER HOUSEHOLD AND NOT VALID TO CURRENT SILHOUETTE SPECIAL EDITION® SUBSCRIBERS.

© 1991 HARLEQUIN ENTERPRISES LIMITED

If offer card below is missing write to:
Silhouette Reader Service, 3010 Walden Ave.,
P.O. Box 1867, Buffalo, NY 14269-1867.

DETACH AND MAIL TODAY!

BUSINESS REPLY MAIL

FIRST CLASS MAIL   PERMIT NO. 717   BUFFALO, NY

POSTAGE WILL BE PAID BY ADDRESSEE

SILHOUETTE READER SERVICE
3010 WALDEN AVE
PO BOX 1867
BUFFALO NY 14240-9952

NO POSTAGE
NECESSARY
IF MAILED
IN THE
UNITED STATES

"Hi, Jerry," she said with forced cheerfulness. "I've been meaning to call you about Mrs. Hunter. Has she been any happier since we brought the things from her apartment?"

"That's what I'm calling *you* about. Mrs. Hunter disappeared from the facility last night. I notified the police, and they're looking for her. But there's no sign of her so far. Jaime? Jaime, are you there?"

"Yes, I'm here, Jerry," Jaime responded, her voice as calm and steady as she could make it. "I have to fill out an Unusual Incident Report. What time did you discover she was missing?"

After ten minutes of questions and answers, she laid down her pen and hung up the phone. All she could hear was Mrs. Hunter's accusing voice: "How would you like someone to leave *you* in this place?" Now the woman was out wandering the streets, confused and in danger because of an inadequate placement that Jaime had made.

She sat in her chair, staring at the wall in front of her, her thoughts going around in circles. Disembodied voices echoed inside her head.

"How would you like someone to leave *you* in this place?"

"You won't tolerate lies, will you, Mom?"

"Just crawl back into your isolated, *frigid* little shell. I don't know why I even bothered trying to thaw you out in the first place!"

"Jaime?"

She blinked, and Karl's features came into focus.

"Are you all right?"

"What are you doing here?" Jaime pushed her chair away from her desk and swung her legs to the side.

She intended to get up, to leave the office. But Karl wouldn't allow it. Before she could even stand, he had placed a hand on either arm-rest, effectively imprisoning her in her chair.

Knowing that she couldn't force her way free, Jaime turned her face away, determined to ignore him.

Karl bent over her, leaning so close that she could feel his breath against her cheek. "You don't have to talk to me, Jaime. Just listen, please. I came to apologize. I'm sorry for what I said to you. I was angry because I came so close to getting you to trust me, so close to touching the real you that I could taste it. Then you put that damned wall up between us again, and it was more than I could stand."

What Karl's passion and anger had failed to do last night, his tenderness threatened to do today. The ice surrounding Jaime's heart began to melt. She was still afraid of the attraction she felt for him. But that attraction was still there, stronger than ever before.

She wanted to turn her face toward him. She wanted it so badly that she ached inside. Instead she sat very still, her nails digging into her palms.

Karl mistook her stiff posture for anger, and he leaned even closer to her. "I know I don't deserve it, but give me one more chance, Jaime. Last night I saw that you were frightened. But when you wouldn't even tell me what was wrong, I got mad and said some things guaranteed to make the situation worse. I've always been real proud of the fact that I don't hide my feelings, that I say what I mean. I called it honesty. Last night I realized that's just another word for self-indulgence. I was so busy worrying about my own feelings that I hurt yours in a way that's almost past forgiving. But—"

"Stop it!"

Jaime turned to face him, unable to bear his self-condemning monologue a second longer. The time had come to make her own confession.

"What you said last night is true. With a partner, I've never been able to..." She let her words fade away on a soft, low note of misery.

Fighting to maintain her rapidly dwindling control, she closed her eyes. But Karl refused to let her retreat into herself again. Putting a hand under her chin, he lifted it marginally.

"Look at me," he entreated. "Please don't shut me out."

Slowly, reluctantly, Jaime opened her eyes and met Karl's intent gaze.

"There are very few truly frigid women, Jaime. But there are a lot of stupid, clumsy, impatient men who use that word to cover up their own inadequacy. I never knew I was one of them until last night."

Karl sank to his knees in front of her chair. "Give me another chance. And I'll give you my solemn promise that I'll control my temper—I'll never speak to you again the way I did last night."

Jaime felt an overwhelming rush of tenderness and a yearning that she didn't want to resist. As if of their own accord, her fingers rose and buried themselves in Karl's thick, soft hair. She felt him hesitate in surprise before he pressed her back against the chair and covered her lips with his.

Then Jaime was lost in a maze of desire that had no beginning and no end as Karl deepened the kiss, making her feel more than any man had ever before. The clean, sharp odor of pine filled her senses as his hands covered her rib cage, his thumbs brushing the soft undersides of her breasts.

She turned her face aside, breaking their kiss with a low moan, and he trailed a line of kisses along her jawline to her earlobe. She gasped as he nipped the sensitive skin gently. Then he rolled the nodule of flesh between his lips and suckled it as he flicked it with his tongue.

His voice was a slow, hot whisper in her ear. "I want to do this to you here...." His fingertips barely brushed her nipples, but she shivered violently. "And here." His thumbs lightly traced the crevice between her thighs before his hands returned to her face. "I'll make you feel so much that you won't be able to turn away, so much that you won't be able to deny it ever again."

He drew back, and Jaime became aware that they were both shaking. "Say you want me, Jaime."

She shook her head, stubbornly clinging to the last vestige of control.

"If you had a door on this office," Karl growled, "I'd lay you down right now and prove to you how much you want me."

Reminded of where she was, Jaime pushed him away and stood up. "How could I have let you... Anyone could have walked by!"

Karl got to his feet. He dusted off the knees of his jeans, willing his pulse to slow, his heart to stop racing. "No one walked by. I was keeping one eye on the doorway."

Jaime couldn't believe that she'd actually forgotten herself enough to carry on with Karl right at her own desk. But, somehow, the idea of him being alert enough to keep watch while she'd been practically swooning with passion upset her even more.

"You're insufferable!" she exclaimed.

Karl grinned, having recovered himself enough to be able to see the humor in the situation. "Sure I am, but I'm kind of cute, too. Don't you think so?"

Standing there with both hands in his pockets and an innocent expression on his face, he reminded her of a mischievous little boy who'd been caught pulling a prank—a little boy who was confident that his charm would save him from punishment.

Jaime wavered between exasperation and amusement. "Nothing as big as you are could ever be called cute," she told him finally, with a smile she couldn't quite hide.

He moved toward her again, but she dodged out of his way. "Karl! We need to talk."

"What would you like to talk about?"

"Us...our relationship...our chemistry...whatever you'd like to call this thing between us. It just can't go any further than it already has."

The playful light faded from Karl's eyes. "I thought . . . I was hoping that we could put last night behind us and start fresh."

Jaime avoided his gaze. "I don't blame you for what happened last night. It's just . . . well, it's the whole situation. You know I have to testify at the hearing."

"And after the hearing?" Karl persisted.

"After the hearing, you'll be going back to Seattle, so there's really nothing else to discuss."

"There's this."

Before she could even protest, Karl pulled her into his arms, and his mouth found hers. He held her gently but firmly, refusing to permit her to escape his embrace or the warm caress of his lips.

But, as always, it wasn't his strength that conquered her resistance. She succumbed to the sheer pleasure of his kiss as they had both known she would from the first moment he'd touched her.

When he finally drew back to look down into her face, the longing in his eyes almost overcame all of Jaime's resolutions. Almost.

"This doesn't change anything."

"Why not? And I'm sick of hearing about the conflict of interest and the time factor. So tell me the real reason. Is it that you don't trust me? That you don't believe I'm strong enough for you to lean on?"

Jaime backed away from him, crossing her arms over her chest. Her answer was a choked whisper that he had to strain to hear. "I don't know if the strength I see in you is the truth or an illusion—and I don't know which possibility terrifies me more!"

Karl reached one hand toward her. "I'm for real, Jaime. You can bank on it. What terrifies you about that? Tell me what you're afraid of."

The phone rang, and Karl cursed vividly. "I ought to pull that damned thing out of the wall!"

"I thought you were going to control your temper," Jaime said pointedly. Feeling as though she'd been granted a reprieve, she picked up the receiver and watched apprehensively as Karl paced to the other end of the tiny room. "This is Jaime Mitchell. May I help you?"

"Miss Mitchell, I'm so glad I found you in! Charlene is here at my house now. Can you come talk to her?"

It took Jaime a moment to place the voice. Then she realized that her caller was Mrs. Todd, the Home Care for the Elderly caretaker with the pregnant daughter on drugs.

Jaime hesitated. She could hardly hold her own life together at the moment, let alone give advice to someone else. It might help if she could ease the ache in her stomach, but she didn't dare reach for the antacid with Karl watching her every move. The pain had begun this morning during her argument with Alex. Then she'd heard the news about Mrs. Hunter. Last, but not least, Karl had shown up at her office to confront her. She just didn't need to try and counsel a drug user on top of all that. Yet, she couldn't justify a refusal to herself.

"Does Charlene know you're calling, Mrs. Todd? Has she agreed to talk with me? And what about her boyfriend?"

"I wouldn't let that man in my house, so I'm glad she came alone. As for Charlene, I told her all about you, and she said she was willing to hear what you had to say. She's sitting here right now, calm as you please, waiting for you."

She's probably a lot calmer than I am, Jaime thought. "All right, Mrs. Todd. I'll be there in about fifteen minutes."

"I'm going with you," Karl said as soon as she'd hung up the phone.

Jaime thought about his offer. This visit wasn't one she wanted to make alone. But Sharon had called in sick, and the other workers were out on their own visits. Maria and the clerk were the only ones in the unit at the moment, so Jaime really couldn't justify taking Maria away from the office to accompany her.

Mrs. Todd already knew Karl. He wouldn't really be intruding. And Jaime had read enough in the newspapers and seen enough on the six o'clock news about drug users and drug dealers to be more than a little nervous. She could use the support Karl's presence would lend her. But the price she would ultimately have to pay for that support was just too great.

"I'm sorry, but I have to do this alone."

She picked up her purse and started to leave, but he grabbed her arm. "How can I just stand by and let you walk into a dangerous situation alone?"

Jaime pulled free and looked up at him, determined to make him understand. "I have to deal with a lot of potentially dangerous situations in my job, Karl. I have to face them on my own or pretty soon I won't have enough strength left to face them at all."

"That's a crock! You'd take another worker with you and never think twice about it. Why am I different?"

"Because another worker is just there as a silent partner. It's still my referral. I call the shots. If anything went wrong while you were out on a case with me, you'd try to take over. You have a quick temper and you're too outspoken. Remember the Damaris abuse referral? Instead of defusing a situation like that one you'd tend to make it worse. That's bad enough under any circumstances, but when it comes to my work, it's totally inappropriate."

Karl took a step closer to her, refusing to concede the point. "I told you before that I was wrong to interfere with Damaris. Give me a chance to prove myself, Jaime. I swear, no matter what happens, I won't say anything, I won't do anything, unless you ask me to. I give you my word."

Jaime looked into his eyes, trying to gauge the depth of his sincerity. She was aware of the seconds ticking by. Charlene wouldn't wait for her forever. And even if she said no to Karl, she wouldn't put it past him to follow her to Mrs. Todd's house anyway. It was probably better to have him where she could keep an eye on him.

"Come on," Jaime said finally, coming to a decision she hoped she'd have no cause to regret.

Alex stood in the convenience store, leafing through an auto mechanics magazine. He tried to concentrate on the page in front of him. But instead he kept hearing the things he'd said to his mother that morning and seeing the wounded expression she'd had on her face as his bus pulled away.

When he'd arrived at school, things had gone from bad to worse. Mike Walker hadn't been able to resist spreading the word about Alex's criminal father. By the time the story got back around to Alex, it was even worse than what had really happened. At lunch, he overheard one girl tell another girl that his dad had been executed in prison for killing a cop. Even the few kids he'd called his friends had started looking at him funny and avoiding him in the hallway.

Then after school, two boys he hardly knew came up to talk to him. They weren't scared off by the story about his father. In fact, they seemed to think his dad was some kind of hero. All the time one part of Alex was laughing with them and embroidering the story even more, another part was feeling pretty disgusted. But he'd agreed to walk over to the corner store with them. Anything was better than going home and seeing the hurt look in his mother's eyes.

He was sorry he'd said those things to her at breakfast. He thought that a real man, like Karl, would have been strong and kept it all to himself. But Karl was the one who had urged him to talk to his mother, to let her know how he felt. Then this morning his mother had forbidden him to speak to Karl again because he was probably a liar and definitely a bad influence—Karl, the man who had tried to convince him that he needed to go to college.

More confused than ever, Alex put the magazine back on the rack and wandered down the aisle. His eyes scanned the rows of brightly labeled canned goods without really seeing them. One thing he was sure of, his knowing about his dad wasn't going to make any difference in his mother's attitude toward him. Except maybe she'd clamp down even harder. The anger surged again, drowning out the regret. It wasn't fair the way she treated him! It wasn't his fault that his old man had been a dropout and a criminal.

He passed a display of candy bars and on impulse decided to buy one. His mother kept harping about cavities and dental bills, but he didn't care about bills anymore. Let her work herself sick if she wanted to. She wouldn't let him help. She wouldn't listen.

Still brooding, Alex walked up behind Ray, one of the kids he'd come to the store with. He was surprised to see the boy slide a package of batteries inside the front of his shirt.

"What are you doing?" Alex whispered.

"What does it look like I'm doing? Joe is up front talking to the guy behind the counter and distracting him, and I'm stealing stuff."

"But what if you get caught?"

"Are you sure your old man killed a cop?" the boy said scornfully. "You sure sound like a wimp to me."

The remark stung. Now even these kids thought he was a jerk. "I'm not a wimp."

Ray looked at him assessingly. Before Alex knew what was happening, the other boy had pulled the candy bar out of his hand and slipped it up under Alex's shirt. "There. Now you're not a wimp," he said with a smirk.

Alex just stood there and watched the other boy walk away. The candy wrapper felt cold and scratchy against his stomach, his pulse was racing like he'd just run the hundred-yard dash and he felt a little sick. Had his dad felt like this when he was breaking the law? Maybe he was meant to be bad like his father. Maybe that was part of his genes, like green eyes and blond hair. If he could inherit a love of cars and a hatred of school, then maybe he could inherit being no good, too. His mother already thought he was just like his father, so what did he have to lose by acting like him?

Suddenly Alex became aware that the other two boys were heading toward the door. He was going to be left alone with the guy who worked in the store. The man seemed to be watching him. Or was that just his own guilty conscience?

Alex's throat went dry, and he felt cold all over. He had only one thought left in his head: to get out of the store as fast as he could.

He followed the other boys, his footsteps seeming drawn out, delayed. Every sight, every sound seemed to be magnified. It was like being stuck in some crazy movie where he could only move in slow motion and the soundtrack was the pounding of his own heart.

He had almost reached the door when the feeling of unreality vanished and his brain seemed to start functioning again. What did he care what anyone else thought about him—his so-called friends, those two little creeps, even his own mother? It was what he thought about himself that mattered. And he thought he was about to do something terminally stupid.

He pushed the door open and stepped over the threshold, slipping one hand up inside his shirt. He'd take the candy bar out now, where the guy couldn't see him. Then he'd just step back inside and tell the man he'd forgotten to pay. It didn't matter if the guy believed him or not. He'd just put his money on the counter, and that would be the end of that.

Then he'd go and find Karl and talk to him. His mother might not like that, but there just had to be a way to work things out between Karl and his mom—between himself and his mom. There had to be a way, but he sure wasn't going to find it stealing a candy bar from a convenience store.

With his money in one hand and the candy bar in the other, Alex turned to go back inside.

Chapter Eight

The door swung open, and Mrs. Todd looked up at them. "Hello, Miss Mitchell. Oh, and you brought that nice Mr. Hallstrom with you!"

Karl just smiled. Jaime gave him a quelling look as soon as Mrs. Todd's back was turned.

They followed the older woman into the living room where another woman waited. Once she'd probably been beautiful. But now she was thin enough to make even Jaime appear pleasantly plump—all except for the swollen abdomen that attested to her pregnancy.

She raised her eyes as the newcomers entered the room, and Jaime was startled by their clear amber color—and by their blatantly hostile expression.

From what Jaime could tell, the woman didn't appear to be on drugs at the moment. But she did appear tense. She sat poised on the edge of the couch as if she might leap up and flee given the slightest provocation.

If Jaime had doubted her ability to deal with the situation before, she was sure she was out of her depth now. She wasn't naive enough or egotistical enough to believe that what she had to say could actually help this woman. But for Mrs. Todd's sake, she was willing to try.

"This is my daughter, Charlene. Charlene, this is Miss Mitchell and Mr. Hallstrom."

The sullen amber eyes didn't even blink.

Karl took a chair in the corner, trying to make himself as unobtrusive as possible. Mrs. Todd sat on the sofa next to Charlene, and Jaime sank into a nearby chair.

"When is your baby due, Charlene?" Jaime began.

She counted every tick of the living room clock during the silence that followed. Mrs. Todd opened her mouth to speak, but Jaime shook her head and tried again.

"Are you hoping for a boy or a girl?"

There was no answer to that question, either. Charlene obviously wanted to be here less than she did.

"Your mother asked me to come talk to you about how a pregnant woman's use of cocaine can affect her unborn child. All right?"

There was still no response. Jaime felt as if she were speaking into a vacuum. She plunged ahead, intent on getting the ordeal over with as quickly as possible. "When you use cocaine, you cut down on the supply of oxygen that reaches your baby. That may lead to things like premature birth, developmental delays—even mental retardation."

Charlene was staring straight ahead, apparently unhearing as well as uncaring. Doggedly, Jaime continued speaking. "Many cocaine-exposed babies seem to be constantly irritable. They can cry continuously. They can be impossible to soothe. It would be hard for a mother who's not on drugs to cope with a baby like that. A mother who's on drugs—"

"Oh, so now we're talking child abuse, right?"

Jaime sat back in her chair. If a silent Charlene had been intimidating, a vocal Charlene was even more so. But deep inside, she felt a small thrill of triumph. At least she was getting some reaction. She looked from Charlene's angry gaze to Mrs. Todd's tear-filled eyes and searched for words that would communicate rather than condemn.

"Okay, Charlene. Forget about abuse, and birth defects, and all the rest of it. The only reason I'm here is because your mother asked me to come. She loves you a lot, Charlene. So I know you have to love the baby you're carrying, that you want a good life for it. How can you give it that kind of life if you're high all the time?"

There was silence for so long that Jaime almost gave up hope of hearing an answer. Then there was a terse whisper. "It's hard. It's hard not to get high when the stuff's all around you."

Jaime couldn't believe it. Charlene was actually admitting that there was a problem. "What if you moved back in with your mom?" she suggested, looking at Mrs. Todd for approval.

"I already asked her to come live with me, but she won't leave her precious boyfriend. All he is, is a no-good drug pusher. He turned my baby into an addict, and now she's making her baby into one!"

Jaime touched Mrs. Todd's arm to stop her tirade, but Charlene had retreated into resentful silence again.

"Charlene," Jaime said softly. "No man is worth what you're doing to yourself and to your baby."

"What do you know about needing a man, *Miss* Mitchell? You can't know how I feel!"

Jaime searched her heart before she answered. "Everyone carries their own special brand of pain inside, Charlene. Maybe mine's not the same as yours, but to me it's just as real."

"Oh, sure! What pain do you have? Don't you have enough money to go on a vacation to Europe this year? That really breaks my heart!"

"Charlene!" Mrs. Todd said angrily. "Miss Mitchell came here to help you!"

"I didn't ask for her help. She doesn't understand, and neither do you!"

Instinctively Jaime knew that her only hope of reaching Charlene was to talk to her woman-to-woman, to share a part of her own past. But she had spent so many years hiding her pain away. How could she reveal it now—and to a stranger? How could she rip through all the protective layers of scar tissue that she'd built up so carefully?

She wanted to get up and just leave. She'd given Charlene the information she'd brought with her. What the woman did with it was up to her. Then Jaime looked into Mrs. Todd's face and knew that she couldn't live with herself if she left like this. Maybe she could just tell about part of her pain—a part that might relate to the decision Charlene had to make.

Aware of Karl's gaze on her, Jaime began to speak before she had a chance to change her mind. "When I was in high school, I wasn't sure who I was or what I wanted. Sometimes I felt if I disappeared from the face of the earth, no one would care or even notice."

She glanced at Charlene. The woman was sitting with her lips pressed together, looking at the floor. Jaime had no idea whether she was listening or not.

"One day a boy noticed me—really noticed me. When he asked me out, I felt alive for the first time in my life. He had blond hair and green eyes. He also had a bad reputation that included a couple of minor brushes with the law. But all I saw was someone daring, attractive, confident—someone who was all the things I wasn't. I thought that he was beautiful. I thought I loved him."

Even Mrs. Todd had looked away by now. The only one in the room who would meet Jaime's gaze was Karl. And his gaze was so intense that Jaime nearly lost her train of thought.

"Before long, I found out that my new boyfriend expected a little more than adoration from me. He kept pressuring me to...go all the way. I kept holding back. I guess deep inside I knew that he was wrong for me."

Jaime stared down at the hands she had clasped in her lap, gathering the courage to continue her story. "One night he got tired of waiting for me to give in. He pinned me underneath him in the back seat of his car, and he...he..." Words failed her at that point. After a long pause, she began a new sentence. "He said he loved me. He said that I could trust him. But he didn't call me again. Two months later, when I went to him and told him I was pregnant, he said that that was my problem."

Karl cursed under his breath, longing to punish the man who had hurt her, longing to take her pain away, and knowing that neither thing was possible.

Jaime, oblivious to Karl's thoughts, looked up to find Charlene's face turned toward hers. She continued speaking, determined to say it all. "My mother was too ashamed to go with me to the hospital, and there was no money for a private doctor. I had my baby on my own in a charity ward a week after my eighteenth birthday. All the labor rooms were full that day, so I lay on a stretcher in the corridor for hours, hurting worse than I'd known anyone could hurt. Strangers walked by, and they all ignored me as if I didn't exist. I felt more alone than I'd ever felt in my life before."

With great effort, Jaime pulled back from the horrible memories and returned to the present and the woman who faced her now. "I grew up that day, Charlene. I learned that life wasn't fair. But I swore that I'd live it the best way I knew how—for my child and for myself. I learned that, in the final analysis, the only one I could depend on was myself."

"Well, I'm not you, Miss Mitchell. I have a man who's willing to take care of me."

"Do you really think he's done such a good job so far, Charlene? Or do you just stay with him because you're afraid you can't make it on your own?"

"You don't know anything about my baby's father!" Charlene responded defiantly.

But Jaime could hear the doubt in the other woman's voice. She leaned forward to press her point home. "No, I don't know your baby's father, but given what I do know about the situation, I'm willing to bet that if there are any consequences to your using drugs, he'll leave you to face them by yourself. If you have a handicapped child, he'll take no responsibility in caring for it. And if he won't, Charlene, you're going to have to. Start now. Go to a rehabilitation center. Get counseling. Do it for your child's sake—and for your own.''

Charlene looked away again, and Jaime knew that she'd done all she could. It was up to Charlene now. She stood to leave, feeling a little awkward about the revelations she'd made. But somehow she felt freer, too, as if by sharing them, she'd finally been able to let go of some of the pain that she'd been carrying around for so long.

''Charlene, here's the number of a woman at the detoxification center if you decide you want—''

The sound of the front door being thrown open interrupted Jaime in mid-sentence.

''I told you to stay out of my house, Jeremy Johnson!'' Mrs. Todd informed the young man who entered the room.

''And I told Charlene to stay away from you, old woman, but she don't listen so good.''

He was handsome and expensively dressed. But he seemed agitated, strung out, filled with more nervous energy than he could possibly expend. And when he looked at her, Jaime saw that his pupils were dilated.

She tried to quell the fear that was attempting to take her over. The man had no reason to harm anyone in the room—unless he felt threatened. She glanced at Karl, sending him a silent reminder of his promise.

''What's going on here, anyway?'' Johnson demanded. He eyed Karl with apparent suspicion, then his gaze shifted back to Jaime.

''I'm a social worker. I came to talk to Charlene about getting counseling.''

''She's doing just fine the way she is. She don't need no social worker running her life for her. Ain't that so, Charlene?''

Charlene hesitated, then nodded her head.

Suddenly Jaime's concern overcame her fear. If only she could make Charlene see what was obvious to her. ''If you care about the baby, why do you give Charlene drugs?''

Johnson laughed and stepped closer to Jaime. ''That baby is Charlene's business, missy. I don't make her take anything. I just make it available. Want a free sample? I bet I could turn you on real good."

Out of the corner of her eye, Jaime saw Karl tense in his chair as if he wanted to jump up and grab the other man by the throat. It would only take one word from her to unleash him. Would she be strong enough not to say it?

"I think I'll pass, Mr. Johnson," she said quietly. "I have better things to do with the rest of my life. Can't we talk about the baby?"

"Like I said, what Charlene does about the baby is her business. And I have better things to do with *my* life than stand here and listen to some preachy, uptight do-gooder who don't know nothin' about nothin'."

Mrs. Todd stood up, her voice strident with outrage. "You get out of my house, you trash!"

Johnson turned toward her, but Charlene was already off the sofa and pulling on his arm. "Come on, Jeremy. Let's go!"

Johnson smiled down at her. "Baby, I got no reason to stay!"

When the front door closed behind the couple, Jaime was torn between relief and a feeling of opportunity lost. If only she had . . . Then she wondered where she'd gotten the idea that anything she had to say could have possibly made a difference. She must be living in a dream world!

"I'm sorry that had to happen," Mrs. Todd said as she escorted Jaime and Karl to the door.

"I just hope it wasn't all for nothing," Jaime responded.

"At least Charlene had a chance to hear what you had to say, Miss Mitchell. I take some comfort from that."

When they were alone on the porch, Jaime turned to Karl. "Thank you for keeping your word, for not interfering."

Karl grinned at her, his admiration obvious. "I didn't have any reason to, did I? Is there anything you can't handle?"

Jaime smiled shakily. "I think I've about had my limit for today."

Karl gave her a sideways glance as they walked down the steps together. "So, do you trust me now?"

Jaime couldn't bring herself to lie, no matter how much she would have liked to. "I wish that I could give you an unqualified yes. I can't. Trust doesn't come easy to me—especially where men are concerned. But today was...a beginning."

They had reached her car. Karl opened the door for her to climb inside, then shut it behind her. He leaned down and looked into her face. "Jaime, all those years ago, when Alex's father... Why didn't you call the police?"

Jaime hadn't considered that question in years, and she wasn't pleased that it had been dredged up again. "I encouraged him. I led him on. It was as much my fault as it was his. He just lost control...."

"Who sold you that idea?" Karl asked angrily. "Him?"

The startled look in Jaime's eyes told Karl that he was right on target. "You led me on last night. As you keep reminding me, I'm not the most controlled person in the world. Did I go ahead and take you against your will?"

"No," Jaime said in a choked whisper.

"No. I ranted and raved and acted like a damned fool. But I didn't force myself on you. He could've stopped, too. Don't you dare carry that guilt around inside you for one minute longer, Jaime Mitchell, because you didn't do anything wrong. Do you hear me?"

For the first time, Jaime let herself think objectively about what had happened, as a thirty-two-year-old woman and not as a seventeen-year-old girl. She gave Karl a tremulous smile. "Yes, I hear you. And you know what? For a Swedish meatball, you're pretty smart."

Karl felt himself getting lost in her eyes. As if it had a will of its own, his mouth was moving closer to hers. Then a car horn blared nearby. He looked up to locate the source, and the spell was broken.

Maria brought her car to a stop behind Jaime's and climbed out. "Jaime, thank goodness you're still here! The police called you at the office. Alex was caught shoplifting!''

Jaime pulled up in front of the convenience store, her knuckles white against the dark steering wheel. She'd insisted on taking her own car, not knowing where she'd be required to go next. Karl had given in grudgingly and followed her in his truck.

She ran into the store, the fear caged inside her making the emotion she'd felt at Mrs. Todd's house seem a dim shadow in comparison.

She saw Alex first. He was pale, unsmiling, his eyes downcast. Nearby, a uniformed policeman was filling out a form, asking questions of a middle-aged man behind the counter. The man's face looked like an angry mask. Then she saw Sharon's husband, also in uniform, standing a little to one side.

Ted came forward and took her arm, steering her back toward the door. She glanced at Alex, but he refused to meet her gaze. Her son. The one part of her life she'd been able to keep separate from all the ugliness and pain. This couldn't really be happening.

Ted's voice was calm and reassuring. ''Sharon's been home on sick leave all day. Maria called her from the office, and then Sharon called me at the station. I was just going off duty anyway, so I came on over to see what I could do.''

''Thank you,'' Jaime said. She hoped she didn't look as helpless as she felt. She heard Karl move up to stand behind her, and she would have given anything to be able to lean back and let his strength support her. But Alex was her son. In order to help him, she had to find her own strength within herself.

''What happened?'' she asked Ted.

''According to the owner, Alex came in with a couple of other kids. The owner thought that he saw Alex take something and collared him when he was on the way out. There was a candy bar in Alex's hand that was never paid for.''

"A candy bar?" Jaime repeated in disbelief. "But he had enough money to buy a candy bar if he wanted one!"

"Kids shoplift for a lot of reasons, Jaime," Ted told her. "To be one of the crowd, for kicks, to get even with their parents."

Jaime thought back to the argument she and Alex had had only that morning, and remembered the things that Karl had said to her in the restaurant. Suddenly she understood.

Ted continued, apparently unaware of the affect his words had had. "Alex claims he was turning around, coming back in to pay for the candy when the owner grabbed him. But he also admits to stealing it in the first place."

"Let me talk to him," Karl said.

Jaime shook her head. "No, Karl. This has got to be between me and him."

She crossed the room to where her son was standing, slouched against the ice cream cooler. He didn't even look up when she said his name.

"Alex? Alex, why did you do it? Because you were angry with me?"

Alex turned his face even farther away from her. He was afraid and ashamed and more sorry than he could have put into words. And he was sure that if he took even one look at his mother's face, he'd break down right in front of everybody and start bawling like a baby.

When he finally trusted himself to speak, his voice was harsh and raspy with repressed emotion. "I did it, Mom, okay? It was the stupidest thing I ever did, and I'll never do it again! Is that what you want to hear?"

Jaime squeezed her eyes shut and pushed the pain down deep inside. She willed herself to remain calm. "All right, Alex. We're both upset. Maybe now isn't the best time for us to talk."

There was no response, only a visible tightening of his throat muscles as he swallowed. Automatically she reached out to touch his hair. But at the last second, she remembered how he hated it and drew her hand back. She forced herself to leave his side and return to where Ted and Karl stood waiting.

"What happens now?" she asked.

"Well, as I was explaining to Karl, you have two choices. You can let things take their course here, and Alex will be released into your custody pending a court hearing. I'm almost certain the judge will decide to put him on probation since this is his first offense."

"And what's my second choice?"

"Well, the guy here is pretty mad. This store isn't part of a chain. He owns it himself so he takes this personally. And he's had a lot of trouble with kids ripping him off. I don't know if it would work, but I can try and talk him out of pressing charges. He owes the other cop here a favor."

Jaime's every instinct urged her to make the second choice. But would that really be the best choice for Alex?

"If the charges are dropped, Ted, if he gets away with it this time, do you think that it will encourage him to try it again?"

Ted looked thoughtful. "It might. But I think Alex is worth the benefit of a doubt, Jaime. And if we're wrong—well, next time I won't be calling in any favors."

Unable to prevent herself, Jaime looked to Karl.

"Let Ted try, Jaime. Alex is a good kid. He deserves a second chance."

Jaime nodded, more reassured than she would have felt comfortable admitting. "Okay, Ted. See what you can do."

After fifteen minutes of discussion, the owner reluctantly agreed to drop the charges. Jaime apologized and tried to thank him.

"If you want to thank me, lady, you just keep that lousy kid of yours out of my store! I don't ever want to see his face around here again! You understand me?"

A wave of humiliation washed over Jaime, and she hardly noticed that Karl had brushed past her and was leaning over the counter. "You have a right to be angry, mister, but you have no right to shout at this lady. *You* understand *me*?"

The subdued owner hastily nodded as Jaime pulled on Karl's arm, urging him toward the door. "Karl, please! You promised me you wouldn't interfere unless I asked you to."

As the door of the store closed behind them, Karl lifted a hand to touch her face. "It was a personal situation, not a professional one."

Jaime forced herself to pull away from the comfort of his touch. "I can fight my own battles, Karl—personally and professionally."

"If I haven't learned anything else about you, Jaime, I guess I've learned that. You didn't need me to step in, but it was something *I* needed to do. You weren't a social worker in that store, you were just my woman. And I couldn't stand by and not speak up for you."

Somewhere deep inside, Jaime felt a thrill of pride when Karl called her his woman. But it was drowned out by a stronger emotion. Fear. She shook her head in denial. "I'm not anyone's woman but my own."

She experienced a flash of remorse when she saw the hurt in Karl's eyes, but they were interrupted by Ted before she could say anything else.

"I've got Alex in my car," Ted told her. "I'd like your permission to take him to Youth Hall for a little guided tour."

After what had just happened, Jaime wanted to take Alex directly home. She didn't want him going to Youth Hall with Ted or anyone else. "I don't know...."

"I'll be with him every minute, Jaime. I promise you he'll be safe with me. And afterward I'll take him out for hamburgers, and we can talk. It's not even four yet. I'll have him back to you by eight at the latest."

Jaime nodded. It wasn't what she wanted, but maybe it was what Alex needed. "If you think it will help, Ted. Will Sharon be okay by herself?"

"I already called her to let her know what's going on. She wants me to take the time for Alex."

"Thank you so much, Ted. And thank Sharon for me, too."

She watched Ted's car until it disappeared in traffic. "Why wouldn't Alex look at me?" she whispered.

"Give him time, Jaime," Karl advised. "He's just as upset and confused as you are right now. It'll be different when you can talk to him alone."

"I hope so."

Karl stepped close and hugged her. "It will be."

Jaime desperately wanted to lay her head against his broad shoulder and let him soothe away all her hurts. But if she did that, she knew she wouldn't be able to let him go until she'd taken all he had to give. Tensely, she waited for him to release her.

Finally, discouraged by her lack of response, Karl stepped back. "I've got to put some gas in the truck. I'll meet you at home."

Jaime nodded and hurried back to her own car, glad to be out of the way of temptation. She pulled out into traffic with every intention of going home. But soon she was replaying the events of the day in her mind, not really paying attention to direction.

She could have handled it all: Karl, her job, her past, the drug dealer. But Alex had sent her into a tailspin that she just couldn't seem to pull out of. The loneliness, the suffering, the hard work had all been worth it to her because there was Alex. And now she'd suddenly been rudely confronted with the fact that all she'd done hadn't been enough. She'd failed at the most important thing of all, the only thing that mattered to her: being there for Alex.

And Karl? Karl was just waiting to hold her, to comfort her, to make all her decisions for her. A minute ago she'd even looked to him to help her make up her mind about Alex! When he got through with her, she'd be unsure of herself and her ability, a weak little fool—just as she'd been in high school. Then when he returned to Seattle, how would she be able to get herself back together, to pick up the pieces of her life?

Turning into the driveway, Jaime shut off the ignition. Then she realized that she hadn't driven home after all. She was at Sarah Levine's house!

She climbed out of her car, her mood already lifting. Maybe that's just what she needed to clear her head. A nice long talk with Sarah.

She rapped on the door, noticing the unfamiliar car that was parked beside hers in the driveway. Wondering if it belonged to Sarah's homemaker, she waited expectantly for the cheery "Hello, Jaime!" that never failed to brighten the gloomiest day.

When the door finally opened, she was surprised to see a much younger woman than Sarah, a woman who was a stranger to her. "I'm Jaime Mitchell, Sarah Levine's social worker. Is Sarah home?"

All the light seemed to go out of the other woman's face, and suddenly Jaime knew. But knowing was more than she could bear. Maybe she was wrong. She *had* to be wrong.

The woman had Sarah's sweet smile, but hers was touched with sadness. "I'm Sarah's granddaughter, Rachel Morris. She used to write to me about you. Please come in."

Not knowing what else to do, Jaime followed the other woman inside and sat down in her usual chair. She couldn't help but notice the half-filled cardboard boxes, the disarray where order had been before. Sarah was packing up some old things to give to charity. That was all. Sarah was in the bedroom, and in a second she'd come out and make them all tea and—

"I . . . I'm afraid my grandmother is dead, Miss Mitchell."

Jaime couldn't pretend any longer. The words had made it real. All the warmth seemed to seep out of her body to be replaced by an insidious, numbing cold. "How?" she whispered.

Tears welled up in the other woman's eyes. "They caught the man who did it. He was a young man who came to the door saying that he was hungry. She invited him in and gave him lunch. Apparently he saw the silver salt and pepper shakers on the table and tried to steal them. My grandmother noticed and struggled with him. He pushed her down and fled."

The tears were now running freely down Rachel's cheeks. "He said he didn't mean to hurt her. But she was so elderly, so frail. Oh, God! Why did she fight with him? Were those old silver shakers more important to her than her own life?"

But Jaime was beyond responding to any question, especially when the answer involved a wise woman's foolishness and missing halves of souls.

Without a word of farewell, she got slowly to her feet and walked out the front door.

Chapter Nine

Jaime couldn't remember how she'd managed to get home. But, for some reason, that fact didn't concern her very much. She felt detached, insulated, as if she were sleepwalking through a dream. Slowly she pulled the keys from the ignition, walked up to the house and unlocked the front door.

Moving through the living room and down the hallway, she entered her bedroom. She switched on the wall-unit air conditioner and pulled off her sandals. Her dress and brassiere soon followed.

Listlessly pushing the clothes in the closet back and forth, she searched for an empty hanger. Then she saw it. The black shawl that Sarah had made for her.

Jaime reached for the garment, her fingers shaking as she drew it off the hanger. She wrapped herself in the shawl, then crossed her arms to hug its folds against her chest. Without warning, the strange insulation surrounding her cracked, then shattered.

A low, animallike moan seemed to begin in her stomach and push its way up through her chest to her throat. It grew louder and louder until her whole body vibrated with the sound of it.

"Noooooooooo!"

Sobs shook her, dry, heaving sobs that made it difficult for her to stand. Her back against the wall, she slid to the floor and drew her knees up under her chin.

Tears began to trickle and then to stream. She cried for all the lost ones like Mrs. Hunter who were doomed to live out their final years confused, alone, unloved; she cried for Mrs. Todd's grandchild who would be born into a world defined by drug abuse and pain; she cried for her beloved Sarah who had given only love and kindness and who had been repaid with senseless violence. And she cried for Alex, the son she loved but didn't understand. Most of all she cried for herself, to release all the tears and all the pain she'd kept locked inside for so many long years.

"Jaime?"

Suddenly she wasn't alone anymore. She was being lifted onto the bed to lie cradled in the strongest, gentlest embrace she'd ever known.

"Jaime, what's wrong?"

She grabbed at the material of Karl's shirt with both hands, as if he were her only hope of salvation, and choked out the words. "Sarah . . . a man killed Sarah."

Karl couldn't believe it. "God, no!"

"Karl . . ."

He stroked her hair, trying his best to soothe her. He had wanted to break through the barrier surrounding her feelings; he had wanted to see her true emotions. But not like this, never like this.

She cried for longer than he would have thought it possible for anyone to cry, while he held her shuddering body against his, feeling more helpless than he'd ever felt in his life. He rocked her, he murmured to her, he tried to comfort her, until finally she seemed drained of tears. She lay quiet in his embrace, still clutching his shirt.

"Why?" she asked in a hoarse, hollow voice. "Why did she have to let a stranger in? And why didn't she just let him have those damned salt and pepper shakers?"

Karl squeezed his eyes shut, feeling close to tears himself. So that was the way it had happened. "It was her choice," he said finally. "You heard what she said the other day—she wasn't about to shut herself away from life. And those shakers meant more to her than any monetary value they may have had. She said that the husband who gave them to her was like the other half of her soul."

Jaime's hold on his shirt threatened to tear the material. "There's no such thing as the other half of someone's soul! How could she give up her life for that nonsense?"

"It wasn't nonsense to her," Karl asserted softly. "And who knows? Maybe she's with him now."

"Do you really believe that?" Jaime asked, searching his face.

"I believe it's possible."

"I don't think I believe in anything anymore." She buried her face against his chest. "It hurts so bad, Karl. It all just hurts so bad! Sarah, and Charlene's baby, and Alex..." She looked up at him earnestly. "I love Alex, Karl."

Karl pushed the stray strands of hair away from her tear-streaked face, longing to lift the burden of sorrow from her. "I know you do, Jaime. He loves you, too."

"No, not anymore. Today he found out that I lied to him. He found out that his father was killed by the police when they raided a stolen-car ring. He'll never forgive me for not telling him the truth."

Karl's arms tightened around her protectively. That bastard seemed to keep reaching out of the past and hurting both Jaime and Alex, and there was nothing he could do about it. He remembered the words that Alex had spoken only two days before: "You don't think I'm like my father, do you, Karl?" If only he'd taken the time to reassure the boy...

Jaime continued talking, oblivious to the direction Karl's thoughts had taken. "All these years I've been working so hard, trying my best to make ends meet. But I didn't spend enough time with Alex, Karl. I never really tried to understand him. I just expected him to grow up the way I wanted him to, to go to college, get a job I approved of.''

Karl tried to find words that would encourage her without glossing over the problem. ''Jaime, there may be some truth in what you say, but you're not to blame for what happened in that store. The boy's fourteen years old. He decided to shoplift, not you. And I believe he tried to do what was right in the end—just like I believe he'll forgive you for lying. He's old enough to understand that you only did it to protect him.''

But Karl's words failed to ease the guilt Jaime felt. She kept talking, the thoughts flowing from a deep reservoir of pain inside her. ''My mother wanted me to give Alex up for adoption. I just couldn't. Alex was a part of me. I loved him even before he was born. But maybe my mother was right. What have I been able to give Alex? If he'd had two parents—''

''Stop it, Jaime!'' Karl said fiercely. ''Don't do this to yourself. You gave Alex life, you gave him love, you offered him everything you had to give. He'll come through this. There's nothing wrong with your relationship that can't be fixed if you just sit down and talk to each other.''

''You really think so?''

Karl reached for the box of tissues on the bedside table and gently patted her face dry. Then he kissed first one swollen eyelid, then the other. ''I know so.''

Jaime looked up into his face and saw all the strength and warmth that had drawn her since the first time she'd touched him. From that first day, she'd fought her longing. But now her need was too great, her defenses too low. Placing a hand on each bearded cheek, she touched his mouth with hers. The soft caress of Jaime's lips threatened to obliterate all of Karl's good intentions and the last remnant of his self-control. He wanted nothing more than to pull her toward him and make her his at last. But he just couldn't take advantage of her weakened defenses.

Taking a deep breath, he pulled away from her. "No."

Jaime shivered, chilled by his sudden withdrawal. "Don't you want me?"

"I want you, but not like this. Not when you're . . . when you—"

"Not when I need you so much?" Jaime whispered.

Karl's heart soared. At last Jaime was admitting that she needed him! But she was upset, exhausted, in no condition to make a decision like this. "It wouldn't be right," he told her reluctantly. "You'd only be sorry in the morning. Just let me hold you, Jaime. What you really need is sleep."

But for once Jaime didn't want to think about tomorrow. Now was all she cared about. And now she couldn't bear the loneliness, the emptiness, for even a second longer. She wanted to hold Karl close, to feel him touch her, to have that basic affirmation that she was alive. She was alive, and she mattered to another human being.

"I don't want to sleep, Karl," she said, reaching up to drape her arms around his neck. "I want you."

Her mouth pressed against his in a sensual caress that threatened to take his breath away. He raised his hands to her shoulders, intending to push her away. "Jaime—"

But before he could complete his protest, her tongue was insinuating itself between his lips. Karl lost track of the words he'd been about to say. Unable to resist any longer, he pulled her into his arms and answered her warm invasion with sinuous thrusts of his own.

When she slid down on the bed, he followed her, his mouth still joined to hers. Vaguely she was aware of her legs shifting under his, parting to cradle his hips.

"Hold me, Karl," she whispered. "I'm so cold. Hold me and make me warm again."

His head reeling, Karl braced himself on his arms and looked down at the woman beneath him. Her lips were curved in a half smile and slightly swollen from his kisses. He wanted her more than he'd ever wanted any woman before, but he knew that for her sake he must somehow find the strength not to take her.

Then her hands moved up, and she drew the folds of the shawl apart until the bare flesh beneath was revealed to his gaze. Unable to look away, Karl watched as her soft, pink nipples reacted to the cool air of the room. He nearly groaned aloud.

Burying her fingers in his hair, Jaime pulled his head toward her. "Love me," she begged.

Karl had no resistance left in him. His heart pounding in anticipation, he allowed his mouth to be drawn slowly, inexorably, toward the rosy center of one pale breast.

He traced the hard nipple with his tongue, smiling as he felt Jaime arch under him. Then he drew the entire aureola into his mouth.

Jaime had yearned to be held, to be comforted. In return she meant to give Karl the physical release he needed. It seemed a fair bargain. But as his mouth tugged at her breast, a shaft of pleasure coursed through her that was so intense she had to bite her lip to keep from crying out.

Yet she was afraid to surrender to the sensation, afraid that if she relinquished control of her body her heart would pay the price. Closing her eyes, she tried to ignore his caresses, tried even now to make herself immune to the strange power this man had over her.

Oblivious to the turmoil raging within Jaime, Karl continued to take his fill of her. Murmuring his appreciation, he kissed and licked his way back up to her mouth. He delved his tongue inside before moving on to suckle her earlobes. Then he returned to her breasts again, his tongue flicking one peak while his fingers toyed with the other.

Jaime had closed her eyes against the sight of his lovemaking, but she couldn't shut out the exquisite sensations that threatened to shatter her stubborn resistance. Then, just when she thought she couldn't withstand the sensual assault a second longer, he moved away from her.

Her eyes still tightly shut, Jaime felt him slide her panties off. But she didn't realize that he'd removed his own clothing until his body covered hers. The burning heat of his skin was a physical shock, and she shivered involuntarily.

"You're so cold, Jaime. So cold," he murmured. He drew her more closely against him, enfolding her in his warmth until she gave a small sigh of contentment.

She could have stayed like that forever, fulfilling a desire more basic than sex, a need stronger than passion. But eventually, inevitably, just holding her wasn't enough for Karl. His fingers slipped between her thighs.

Against her will, Jaime moved into Karl's caress. It was wildly pleasurable. At the same time, she found it wildly frightening. She had to block the feeling out, to protect herself from its intensity. But when one gently probing finger began to press its way inside her, her body responded to ease its passage.

Karl kissed her forehead, her cheeks, her mouth. "Your body's ready to be loved, Jaime. Are you ready?"

Jaime's eyelids fluttered open, and she looked up into the bluest, kindest eyes she'd ever seen. "Yes," she answered. And for the first time in her life, it was very nearly true.

She wanted to feel Karl surging in her arms, to watch his face as he was overcome by passion. For that instant, he would be hers alone. And suddenly Jaime wanted to know that instant as she had wanted few things in life.

Positioning himself, Karl pressed forward and found her warm, wet and ready to receive him. He groaned as he pushed into her yielding warmth, and she gasped as he stretched her and filled her more completely than ever before. He seemed to be touching every nerve, every cell, every fiber of her body.

Then Karl began to move, rocking against Jaime slowly, marveling at his own control. He wanted more than just the pleasure her body could give to his. He needed to arouse this woman. He needed to fulfill her—emotionally as well as physically. He had to make her open herself to him until no secrets were left unshared.

Jaime lay motionless beneath him, fighting against the tide of feeling, still trying to hold this man at a safe emotional distance. But he just kept moving inside her with a steady, relentless rhythm, every sensation building on those that had gone before until she thought she would shatter into a million quivering pieces. And part of her longed for that to happen, longed for Karl to be the one to make it happen.

Unable to help herself, she opened her eyes and looked up at the handsome, tense face so close above her own.

"Let go," Karl whispered, his voice begging, cajoling. "I won't hurt you, Jaime. Trust me. Please trust me."

Shaking with the effort, Jaime clung desperately to her last shred of control. She knew that she could never trust any man enough to give herself completely. Yet this man almost restored her faith in life—in him.

Karl moved his hand downward between their bodies, seeking and finding the small, hidden center of her pleasure. He massaged it gently, determined to take her with him as he drew closer and closer to the point of no return. "Come with me, Jaime," he pleaded hoarsely. "I want you with me."

Struggling to resist the thrust of his body and the caress of his fingers, Jaime watched Karl bend his head and slowly draw one taut nipple into his mouth.

A single cry escaped her lips as the last barrier fell. Clutching Karl's shoulders, she arched upward to meet him. Spasms started deep inside her and traveled outward until they shook her entire body.

Still moving against her, Karl raised his head to watch the passion play over her features, to see the flush spread over her face and neck. Being a witness to her fulfillment gave him as much satisfaction emotionally as the tight warmth of her body was giving him physically. He felt a rush of raw, primitive triumph.

"You're mine now, Jaime," Karl said fiercely. "Now and always."

A warning bell went off in Jaime's mind, but its sound was drowned out by the beating of her own heart. "Yours..." she echoed breathlessly, "...always."

The feeling evoked by Jaime's words and the intimate caress of her soft inner flesh spread through Karl's nervous system like fire blazing across dry tinder. Unable to hold back any longer, he put both palms flat against the mattress and drove to a shuddering climax.

Jaime whimpered with pleasure, holding him tightly, straining to absorb all he had to offer.

Quivering, whispering her name, Karl rolled them both onto their sides and kissed her deeply. He ran his hands over her warm, damp skin until, gradually, she relaxed against him.

Jaime pressed her cheek to his chest and sighed, a weary vagabond who had finally found a home. Physically Karl had introduced her to sensations that were beyond anything that she'd ever felt or even dreamed of feeling. Emotionally she felt an unfamiliar sense of fulfillment.

Secure in the circle of Karl's arms, her body still joined to his, Jaime drifted into the sweetest sleep that she had ever known.

Chapter Ten

Morning sunlight streamed into the small, blue-walled room, throwing a pattern of light and shadow across the rumpled bed and its sole occupant. But Jaime didn't appreciate the beauty of the pattern. She was huddled against the headboard bathed in a cold sweat of gut-wrenching, mind-numbing panic.

How could I have been so stupid? she asked herself. *How could I have been so irresponsible?*

It was easy, an inner voice answered. *And it felt so good.*

Jaime blushed hotly even though she was alone in the room. *I've just betrayed every one of my personal and professional standards!*

In Karl's case you were already doing that mentally and emotionally. Last night you just added "physically" to the list.

I let him touch me in a way no man has ever touched me. I gave him a part of myself I've never given before.

It was beautiful and right.

It was a stupid, dangerous thing to do—like stepping off the curb into the path of a speeding car. And the words I said to him! "Yours... always."

That's how you really feel, isn't it?

"No!" Jaime wailed out loud.

Tossing her bedcovers aside, she sprang out of bed and began pacing the floor, trying to get control of her thoughts. She had her life all arranged. Everything was going just fine. No man was going to walk in at this late date and mess things up—especially not a man like Karl Hallstrom. He'd been dominating and demanding before. What could she expect now after... after...

Jaime finally sat down on the bed, her hands pressed together in her lap. Maybe she was overreacting to what had happened. After all, Karl wasn't exactly inexperienced. Maybe last night had meant nothing more to him than sensual pleasure, a natural release of the sexual tension that had been crackling between them since they'd first met. But, for some reason, that possibility didn't comfort Jaime at all.

She glanced at the alarm clock. Six-thirty a.m. She'd awakened fifteen minutes before, alone in her bedroom, the door shut. But she'd still been able to hear the clanging, scraping noises that meant breakfast was being prepared. And there were other, muffled sounds, two distinct voices that she managed to identify as Karl's and Alex's even though she couldn't quite make out the words.

She wished that she could hear what they were saying. Did Alex know that Karl had spent the night? What would her son's reaction to that be? He'd seemed so distant, so unreachable yesterday. That had hurt her more than anything he'd done. Had Ted's efforts helped the situation, or was this just the beginning of a lifetime of antisocial behavior for Alex? No, she wouldn't believe that! He wasn't like his father. He was her son, and she loved him enough to work at helping him. They'd talk. They'd go to counseling if they had to. They'd make it somehow, together.

It was easier to think about the possibilities than it was to actually go out and face Karl and Alex. But she couldn't very well hide in her room forever. She had to leave for work soon.

Resolutely she gathered up underwear, a pair of slacks and a shirt. She shrugged into her robe and quietly slipped into the bathroom for a shower.

When Jaime walked into the kitchen a few minutes later, she found Karl in front of the stove scrambling eggs and frying bacon while Alex hovered in the background, admiring his technique.

The enticing aroma made her mouth water, and the sight of Karl dressed in jeans and a shirt, his hair freshly combed, only heightened the effect.

"Where did all this food come from?" she asked, voicing the first question that popped into her head.

Karl turned to look at her, and the expression on his face told her that he liked what he saw. Jaime felt a traitorous surge of pleasure, but she willed herself not to return Karl's smile. She had to get a hold on her emotions!

Karl was puzzled by Jaime's lack of response. On waking that morning, he'd felt a little uncomfortable himself as he'd recalled the words he'd said to her the night before. But as soon as he'd seen her standing in the morning light, questioning his invasion of her kitchen, he'd been able to remember only the pleasure that they'd shared.

Didn't she feel the same way? He hadn't imagined that look in her eyes last night. Maybe she was withdrawing because she felt threatened by their intimacy. With Jaime, that would be a predictable reaction. After all, she'd shared more of herself with him than she'd shared with any other man. He had to give her time to get used to the idea of being that close to another human being. He had to move slowly.

Deliberately he returned his attention to the food. "I brought some stuff over from my house this morning," he said casually. "Having breakfast together just seemed like a nice idea."

He looked at Jaime for confirmation, but she quickly turned away. "I don't have time to eat. I've got to get to the office."

There was a moment of strained silence during which Jaime heard only the sound of sizzling bacon and the pounding of her own heart.

"Mom doesn't eat much in the morning," Alex explained awkwardly.

Jaime focused on her son. Slowly, unsure of his response, she lifted her arms. Alex walked into her embrace without hesitation, and she pulled him close, the cold, hard knot of worry inside her easing at last.

"Don't take it out on Karl because you're mad at me, Mom." Alex stepped back to look at her. "Yesterday I just couldn't tell you in front of everyone else, but I'm sorry I put you through all that. I really was turning around to pay for the candy bar when the owner caught me. Before I even got to the door, I realized that I was acting like a spoiled little kid, throwing a temper tantrum because I couldn't have everything my own way. I guess I've been acting like that for a long time."

Jaime had thought she'd cried all her tears, but now she felt her eyes growing moist again. "Maybe I've been treating you like a little kid. Instead of appreciating you for what you are, I've been expecting you to conform to my idea of what you should be. And maybe deep down I *have* been seeing your father in you, afraid that somehow, someday, you'd get into trouble, too."

Alex shook his head. "I'm not my father, Mom. I figured that out yesterday. I promise I'll never steal anything again. I'll even think about going to college!"

Jaime smiled, knowing what that had cost him. "And I'll think about the part-time job you want to get." She hugged him close again. "You really scared me. You know that?"

"But it's okay now?"

"Yes, it's okay now."

"Then you'll have some breakfast?"

Jaime leaned back and ruffled her son's hair with a resigned sigh. "Yes, I'll have some breakfast."

Alex grinned and went to bring the food as Jaime sat down at the table. Within thirty seconds a glass of milk and a plate overflowing with eggs, bacon and biscuits was set in front of her.

She picked up her fork and took a tentative nibble. "It's good!" she exclaimed in surprise.

Karl had been touched and relieved by Jaime's reconciliation with Alex. Now he smiled as he sat down at the table with a full plate of his own.

"You didn't think Swedish men could cook?"

"Actually, I've never had an opinion concerning that subject one way or the other," Jaime told him truthfully.

This time she couldn't help returning his smile. Their gazes met and held for an embarrassing length of time. Finally Jaime broke contact and cleared her throat, searching for a safe topic of conversation. They ate in silence for several minutes before she happened to notice the steaming cup of coffee by Karl's plate.

"Oh, you found the coffee maker. It hasn't been used for so long that I'm surprised it still works."

"You want a cup?" Karl asked, already halfway out of his chair.

"No, I gave it up. My stomach..."

"If you put enough milk in it, it shouldn't bother you." He looked at her glass. "Or maybe I could just add a little coffee to your milk?" He raised his cup suggestively.

Jaime hesitated. "Maybe just a little bit."

Karl tilted his cup against her glass. They got lost in each other's eyes again, and suddenly the glass was overflowing.

Alex laughed out loud as Jaime ran to the kitchen for a sponge. "I know Mom's a klutz, Karl, but what's your excuse?"

A faint tinge of pink spread across Karl's face, and Alex stopped laughing. Then his eyes widened in sudden understanding, and he smiled. Maybe yesterday hadn't been a total loss after all.

Standing up, he carried his plate to the kitchen. "I've got to get going, you guys, or I'll miss my bus. Thanks for breakfast, Karl."

Alex gave his mother a quick kiss on the cheek, scooped his book bag off the couch and disappeared through the front door.

"I have to go, too," Jaime announced as she wiped up the last of the milk and returned the sponge to the sink. "I'm afraid I won't have time to finish my breakfast."

"Guess again."

Jaime followed his gaze to her plate. To her astonishment, it was empty. "I couldn't have eaten all that!"

"It's amazing what a little exercise can do for your appetite."

Jaime quickly took her dishes to the sink, hoping that Karl hadn't noticed the heightened color in her cheeks.

Then she discovered that that was the least of her worries when he came up behind her and turned her into his embrace. She shivered as he nuzzled her neck, his beard kitten-soft against her skin.

"Good morning, Jaime."

She closed her eyes and swayed against him. But a tiny remnant of reasoning ability remained. She knew she had to stop him. She had to stop him before he swept her away again. She pushed him back with trembling hands.

"Alex..."

Karl looked down at her in puzzlement. "What about Alex?"

"When Alex got home last night, you weren't...you weren't still..."

"Is that what's been bothering you? He doesn't know anything. He got home around eight p.m., and I was sitting on the couch watching TV. I told him you were sleeping and not to disturb you. He said Ted had already taken him to dinner, so we just talked for a while. Then I went back home."

"I still think he suspects that something's going on."

Karl smiled and traced her jawline with his index finger. "Does that mean I have to make an honest woman of you?"

The implications of his remark cut through the sensuous fog clouding Jaime's brain, and her fear of entrapment returned full force.

"Don't be ridiculous! I . . . I have to get to work."

With more strength than she'd thought she'd possessed, Jaime broke away from Karl and headed for the door.

She was halfway to her goal before Karl's voice stopped her. "Jaime, wait! I want to talk to you."

"What is there to talk about?" she demanded, her words sounding cold even to her own ears.

Karl could feel her deliberately distancing herself emotionally, drawing further and further away from him. What could he do, what could he say, to draw her back?

"Jaime," he began, "last night I didn't stop to consider the consequences of what I was doing."

Jaime gave him a cynical shrug. "Few men do."

He frowned and tried to catch her arm. "This man does—with every woman I've known except you."

Jaime moved away from his touch, her voice hard, her head held high. "Don't worry about me, Karl. I've taken care of myself for most of my life. If I have another child, I can certainly take care of him or her as well. And before you, I've always been careful to protect myself against other consequences, too. So you see, there's nothing to get upset about. You can forget last night ever happened."

"I don't want to forget it!" This time he succeeded in capturing her arm and drawing her stiff form into his embrace. Just as he had the very first time he'd touched her, he could feel the tension pulsing through her body as if it had a life of its own.

"I was talking about emotional consequences, not physical ones. You were so out of it, so upset that you didn't even notice, did you? I used a condom, Jaime."

Jaime was so surprised that she forgot to resist the tug of his arms. She was pulled against his chest to be held there gently, but firmly. "I . . . I guess that should have been obvious to me," she stammered. "I was just so distracted, so—"

"So sure that I'd fail the test?" Karl suggested.

"What test?" Jaime asked, confused.

"Think about it," he persisted. "You said that in the past you've been careful to protect yourself. But last night, with me, the thought didn't seem to occur to you. Doesn't that tell you anything?"

"It tells me that you're very bad for me," Jaime responded irritably.

"It tells me something different. I think that, unconsciously, you were setting me up to take a fall. You left everything up to me, assuming I'd prove what you'd suspected all along—that I was irresponsible, that I couldn't be trusted. But guess what, Jaime? I took responsibility. I protected you."

But Jaime wasn't ready to consider the possibility that he might be correct in his reasoning. "You're not a stupid man, Karl. You protected yourself—as I'm sure you always do. Don't make that sound like some noble sacrifice!"

Karl fought to hold his temper in check. Last night had been different from any encounter he'd ever had. Whether that was due to his long period of abstinence or the fact that he'd finally gotten Jaime to respond to him, he couldn't have said. He just knew that this woman was very special to him and that last night had been precious and beautiful. They had touched each other on a level that went beyond the sexual. Now she was trying to dismiss all that, to deny that it had meant more to her than simple physical pleasure.

But he wasn't going to reach her through anger. If he had to learn to muzzle his own feelings in order to liberate hers, then that was just what he'd do.

"Jaime," he said quietly, "I understand what you're feeling. You haven't let any other man touch you emotionally the way you let me touch you last night. I know that must be frightening to you."

Jaime wanted to yield to the warmth, the concern she heard in Karl's voice. Instead she wedged both fists against his chest, forcing space between them. "Why are you trying to glorify what happened last night, Karl? It's very simple. I was hysterical, and you took advantage of that fact to get what you've been after all along."

She dropped her gaze so she wouldn't have to see the expression in his eyes. But she couldn't help hearing his sharp intake of breath. He let her go and backed away.

"How can you stand there and say that?"

"Because it's true," Jaime retorted, still avoiding his gaze. "Just like it's true that I took advantage of your desire for me and used you to make it through one of the worst nights of my life. We used each other, Karl, and we both enjoyed it. So let's just call it even and forget it."

"Look at me!"

Jaime reluctantly lifted her gaze and felt ashamed as she saw the accusing expression in his eyes.

"I ought to walk out of here now and keep on going!"

Refusing to acknowledge the feeling of desolation his declaration aroused in her, Jaime answered him with a challenge of her own. "So why don't you?"

Karl tried to rise above his anger and choose his words carefully. "Because you matter to me, because last night mattered to me. And because I know why you're acting like this. You're trying to lower our relationship to a level where you can deal with it."

Jaime wanted to run from his words—words that were somehow more threatening than Karl's towering stature could ever be. But he held her prisoner with an intense stare that allowed no escape. She couldn't even force herself to look away again as he continued speaking.

"You can deal with a physical relationship of sorts, Jaime, as long as it doesn't touch the real you. It's caring that you can't handle. That's why you're trying to pretend you don't feel anything at all for me as a person."

A part of Jaime longed to admit that she did care. The desire to lay her head against his chest and just let him hold her was remarkably acute. But so was her fear.

In an agony of jumbled feelings, she shook her head. "Are you a businessman or a shrink, Karl? I've had it with your amateur analysis. I can't even think straight anymore!"

"Then don't think—feel." Karl pulled her back into his arms and kissed her with all the skill and depth of caring he possessed.

The burning heat of his lips and body brought back memories of an exquisite pleasure impossible to forget. But Jaime was fighting for her survival as an individual. She couldn't let herself be absorbed by this man.

She struggled with him, turning away from his mouth and hands. "No!"

Despite his resolve, Karl was about to lose the hold he had on his temper. He'd found something special, something he wanted to nourish so that he could watch it grow. Jaime was trying to kill it before they even had a chance to see what it might become.

"Jaime," he said, expending the last of his patience, "there's nothing to be afraid of. Not anymore."

"Yes, there is," Jaime contradicted him, her jaw set stubbornly. "You're trying to take over my life!"

Karl stared at her, amazed by her accusation. "I'm not trying to take over anything, Jaime. I thought I proved that to you in Mrs. Todd's house yesterday."

"You were fine at Mrs. Todd's house, but that was one isolated incident. You can't change your nature, Karl. Did you hear yourself last night? 'You're mine now.' That shows just how possessive you can be!"

Karl frowned down at her. "If I remember correctly, you seemed to share the sentiment. Have you forgotten what you said?"

Jaime hadn't forgotten the words, anymore than she'd forgotten the emotion that had evoked them. But she couldn't give in to that emotion. She couldn't allow Karl to make those words come true. She refused to live the life her mother had lived.

She lashed out in one last, desperate attempt to break free of the emotional hold he had on her. "People say a lot of things in bed that they don't mean!"

Karl released her so suddenly that she staggered before regaining her balance. The look on his face made her long to take back the words, to apologize. But she couldn't afford the cost.

Bitterness and anger drowned out Karl's understanding and regret. He saw now that there was no way he could reach Jaime. The harder he tried, the further she withdrew.

"Okay, Jaime," he said, resigning himself to the inevitable. "You win. Have it your way. I can't force you to share yourself with me if you refuse to allow it."

He strode to the front door, opened it, then paused with his hand on the knob. "Just one more thing. Don't come around to lecture my granddad about his attitude anymore, because you're just like him. I overheard what you told him at the door the other night about learning to bend or he'd break. Do yourself a favor and take your own advice—before it's too late."

Karl's comparing her to his grandfather was the last straw. "Last night's over, Karl," she declared fiercely. "I don't need you anymore. I don't need anyone!"

The expression in Karl's eyes would have intimidated the devil himself. "Keep repeating that until you convince yourself, Jaime."

The front door slammed with a finality that tore at her heart. She sank down onto one of the dining room chairs, vowing not to give in to the tears she could feel burning in her eyes.

"I don't need him," she quavered. "I don't!"

But you want him, the voice inside her whispered insistently.

And that was one truth Jaime couldn't deny.

Chapter Eleven

"Jaime! Wake up, will you? It's Friday, and I think you've dreamed the whole week away."

Jaime blinked and focused on Maria's face. "What?"

"I said, come out of your trance before you miss the weekend. Oh, darn! That's my phone ringing. I'll be right back."

Alone in her office once more, Jaime sank back into the reverie that her co-worker's voice had disturbed.

Friday. Karl had stormed out of her house on Tuesday. She hadn't seen him or talked with him since then. On Wednesday she'd caught herself glancing over at the Hallstrom house in the morning on her way to work and again in the evening when she'd arrived home. By Thursday it had become a ritual. It annoyed her and made her feel weak and foolish, but she couldn't seem to help herself.

And to make matters worse, she hadn't even managed to catch one glimpse of Karl. Maybe he was purposely avoiding her, purposely staying inside or making sure that he was away from home at the times he knew she'd be coming and going.

It seemed like Alex had been avoiding her, too. She'd thought that the worst of their problems were over. But she'd come home from work the Tuesday of the argument to find her son brooding and withdrawn. When she'd asked him what was wrong, he'd mumbled something about Karl and messing up her life. Then he'd disappeared into his room and closed the door. She'd hardly seen him since then, and he wouldn't respond to any of her efforts to discuss the subject.

Jaime knew that Alex was fond of Karl and that he was probably disappointed that things hadn't worked out between them. But Alex should have realized from the start that Karl was only a temporary fixture in their lives. He'd have to learn to accept that fact, just as she had.

But *had* she accepted it? The hearing was on Monday afternoon, only a weekend away. The thought of facing Karl in the judge's chambers filled Jaime with anxiety and apprehension. And somehow the thought of Ivar Hallstrom having to go through the hearing procedure bothered her even more. Ivar was going to be brought face-to-face with his own limitations—and this time there would be no avoiding the consequences.

Jaime didn't want to be there to see what the hearing would do to Ivar. Or what it would do to Karl. She had witnessed the radical effect that being declared incompetent could have on people's lives, but she'd always managed to insulate herself from their pain. The insulation was necessary if she was to continue to do her job. And, truthfully, most of the cases were clear-cut, the clients often so confused that they weren't even capable of understanding where they were or what was happening to them.

But Ivar Hallstrom didn't fall into that category. Besides, Jaime had gotten to know him too well. There was no way she'd be able to shield herself against his desolation— or against Karl's. And maybe Karl had been right after all.

Maybe she was more like that proud old man than she wanted to admit.

Night after night she'd lain awake, dreading what was about to happen, searching for a way out for all of them. So far she hadn't been able to find one.

"What's wrong, Jaime?" Sharon came in unannounced and carefully lowered herself onto a vacant chair. "You seem so distracted lately. Is it Alex?"

Jaime shook her head. "Not really." She quickly changed the subject. "I want you to know how much I appreciate what Ted did for us that day Alex was caught shoplifting. He's a great guy, Sharon."

Sharon beamed. "He is, isn't he?"

"Are you going to let her get away with that?"

Jaime and Sharon both turned their heads to look at Maria as she came into Jaime's office and leaned against the wall.

"What do you mean?" Sharon wanted to know.

"Jaime just changed the topic of conversation to your favorite subject—Ted—so you wouldn't ask anything more about *her*. Are you going to let her get away without telling you why she's been walking around like a zombie for days now?"

"I—" Sharon began.

"Well, *I'm* not!" Maria assured her. "Let's see now. The situation with Alex has been resolved, and everything's fine here at work. Mrs. Hunter is back in her ACLF safe and sound. And I heard from the administrator this morning that she even has a boyfriend there now."

Despite her own gloomy thoughts, Jaime was glad that Mrs. Hunter's placement was finally working out. "At least someone's love life is taking a turn for the better," she commented.

"Aha!" Maria exclaimed, causing Jaime to jump in her chair and Sharon to raise a hand to her rounded stomach. "So it's Karl!"

"I never said that!" Jaime retorted, her cheeks turning a telltale pink.

"But that's it," Maria insisted. "You haven't mentioned him in days, and you never would tell us what happened when you went out on that date with him."

"You're worried about what the hearing might do to your relationship, aren't you?" Sharon asked, her concern evident in her voice.

Jaime was suddenly too weary to be evasive. "I just don't know where my professional life ends and my private life begins anymore. I'm not sure what I want. The only thing I am sure of is that no man is worth going through all this."

Maria made a sizzling sound with her tongue and teeth. "Oh, Karl is worth it, amiga, or I don't know men."

"Maria!" Sharon protested. "Be serious!"

"I am being serious!"

Jaime frowned. "There's more to a relationship than just sex, you know."

To Jaime's surprise, Maria didn't deny the claim. "So what's wrong with Karl otherwise?" she asked.

Jaime groped for words. "He's too possessive, too protective, too...controlling."

"You mean you want a guy who'll leave you alone and let you live your own life, do your own thing and take care of everything by yourself?"

"Yes."

"You mean you want a man who doesn't give a damn what you do, who doesn't care enough to get involved in your life?"

"Don't try to twist things around!" Jaime responded. "I know what I mean."

"Do you?" Maria sighed. "Look, Jaime, is the man so protective that he won't let you do something by yourself if you really insist on it? So possessive that he'll lock you in your room to keep you all to himself? So controlling that he won't let you have opinions that differ from his?"

"Of course not!"

"Then what's the problem, my friend?"

Maria's questions had only confused Jaime more. "Me, him, the whole situation! And the idea of going through with that hearing is just tearing me apart."

Sharon looked thoughtful. "It would be so simple if Karl could just skip the hearing and take his grandfather back to Seattle."

Jaime was still pondering Sharon's words long after her two friends had returned to their own offices. There might be a way for her to help Ivar Hallstrom after all. But would she really be helping him? Was she absolutely sure that Karl could be trusted to protect his grandfather without the benefit of court supervision?

What she was thinking of doing violated all the rules of procedure that she'd respected and upheld for as long as she'd worked with HRS. It could even be interpreted as a betrayal of her professional responsibility. But maybe—just maybe—it was the right thing to do. Jaime picked up the receiver and dialed the Dade County courthouse.

"Probate/Mental Health. Brenda Hill speaking."

"Brenda, it's Jaime Mitchell. Will you answer a question for me?"

"I'll try," the young clerk responded cheerfully.

Jaime could picture the woman's characteristically sunny smile. "If a client we've filed on leaves the state before the day of the competency hearing, what happens?"

"This court has no jurisdiction outside of Dade County. If the client doesn't intend to return, we'd close the case."

Jaime leaned back in her chair. She had her answer. Now what was she going to do with it? "Thank you, Brenda."

She was about to hang up when the clerk spoke again. "You know, that's a very popular question, lately."

A cold chill inched its way up Jaime's spine. "Oh?"

"I had an older lady and then a man call me with the same question this week. I'd really like to meet the guy. He had the deepest, sexiest voice."

Jaime clutched the receiver. "Did he give his name?"

Brenda giggled. "Nope, and I didn't get his phone number, either!"

Jaime hung up with the sound of laughter ringing in her ears. But she didn't hear the woman's high-pitched giggle. She heard Karl's deep, sexy chuckle instead.

Jaime swung into the Hallstroms' driveway, jumped from her car and ran up to the front door. She pounded on the wood until her hand ached, but there was no response. But then she hadn't really expected there would be.

The sound of an approaching car caught her attention. Maybe she'd been wrong! Maybe... But her flash of optimism was short-lived. It wasn't Karl. It was an unfamiliar car driven by a short, dark man she'd never seen before.

"Good afternoon." The man smiled and climbed out of his car, carrying a long wooden stake with a For Rent sign attached. "Looking for a house to rent? This one's available next week."

Jaime's last glimmer of hope disappeared. "I'm Jaime Mitchell, Ivar Hallstrom's social worker. Has he moved?"

"Yup. Got a call on Monday notifying us that Hallstrom was leaving for Seattle on Wednesday. Let me tell you, these sudden decisions are costly. His lease runs until December. That means he lost his deposit and..."

But Jaime had already turned and was walking back to her car. She pulled it across the street and entered her own home.

Monday. Karl had already been planning to leave Miami the day he'd come to her office to beg her forgiveness. The day he'd made love to her.

She threw herself down on the bed where Karl had taken her into his arms and taught her the meaning of passion and fulfillment. After the tears she'd shed that day, Jaime had doubted she'd ever cry again. But now she began to sob quietly, the pain inside her so sharp and intense that she was sure it would never subside. Karl had given her so much, touched her so deeply. Had it all been a lie?

But a part of her refused to believe that Karl was capable of such calculated deception. Her sobs quieted as she began to consider alternative explanations.

She'd rejected him Sunday night after their date, and he'd gone home in a rage. Maybe he'd called the realty company the next day in a fit of anger. Then he'd thought better of his decision and had come to her office that afternoon sincerely intending to give their relationship one more chance. Maybe after they'd made love, he'd been ready and willing to stay.

Wincing, Jaime remembered the morning after they'd made love, the way she'd treated Karl, the ugly things she'd said to him. And she remembered what he'd said to her: "I ought to walk out of here now and keep on going!" If they hadn't argued that morning, would he still be in Miami? Or had he planned to leave even as he held her in his arms? Then again, maybe his decision to return to Seattle was something entirely separate from her, something motivated solely by Karl's desire to protect his grandfather—or to exploit him.

Jaime groaned and rolled onto her back. She was tormented by all those questions—questions to which she would never have the answers.

"Mom? Are you all right?"

Jaime saw Alex in the bedroom doorway and quickly sat up, rubbing at her eyes. "Are you home from school already? I . . ." Her voice trailed off when she met his gaze.

She remembered then that he wasn't a child anymore. He wouldn't be fooled by evasive chatter or sleight-of-hand. "The Hallstroms went back to Seattle."

"I figured that," Alex responded. "I just saw the sign on their lawn."

"Did . . . did Karl say anything to you about leaving?" Jaime asked, struggling to keep her voice steady.

"The last time I spoke to Karl was after school on Tuesday. He said that you didn't want to see him anymore and that you'd probably just get more upset if I kept hanging around him. I didn't go back over there again after that."

Jaime squeezed her eyes shut. "I'm sorry if all this has hurt you, Alex. I never meant for you to be hurt."

Alex sat down on the bed and put his arms around her. "I know that, Mom. And I know there's something weird going on here. It's just not like Karl to run out on either of us without saying goodbye."

Jaime pulled back and looked at her son. "You still believe in him, don't you?"

"Yeah, I guess I do."

The sound of a car horn in the driveway made Jaime jump. For an instant, she felt an irrational surge of hope. Could it be Karl?

Alex stood up. "That must be Mrs. Angelo." At the blank look on Jaime's face, he elaborated. "You remember, Mom. I'm going to Tony's house for the weekend to work on that history project we're doing together."

Jaime stared up at him, and slowly, realization dawned. She had spoken to Mrs. Angelo only last night to confirm the arrangements. How could she have forgotten?

"Are you sure you're all right, Mom? If you want some company... Well, I don't have to go to Tony's."

Jaime forced a smile. "You go ahead. I could use the peace and quiet. And I expect you to get some schoolwork done, you hear?"

Alex grinned and bent down to hug her. "I'll try to squeeze it in. And don't worry, I won't get into any more trouble. Promise."

The horn blared again, the front door slammed and he was gone.

After a few hours spent tossing in bed, trying to sleep, Jaime got up to confront a dark and drizzly day that was an exact mirror of her own mood. She tackled every household chore that needed to be done—and several that didn't. Anything to keep her hands busy, tire her body out, so she'd be too exhausted to think anymore. But it didn't work. The same unanswerable questions kept turning over and over in her mind until she thought she'd go mad.

"Time," she told herself. "It's just going to take time to get over him." But a part of her was afraid that even if she did succeed in getting Karl Hallstrom off her mind, she'd still hear his voice in her heart forever.

Unwilling to admit defeat, she grabbed some rags and the glass cleaner. She had just removed the screen from the front window, when her gaze strayed inevitably to the house across the street. The rag she was holding fell to the window-sill unnoticed. Karl's truck was in his driveway. And so was Karl!

As she watched, unable to believe her eyes, she saw that he wasn't alone. A petite and very pretty blonde clad in shorts and a halter was standing next to him, gazing up at him admiringly. A hot, burning sensation started in Jaime's stomach as she observed Karl's answering smile.

Unexpectedly her vision blurred and obscured her view. By the time she'd blinked the tears away, the woman was leaving the scene in a low-slung sports car and Karl had gone back into the house.

Jaime stood rooted to the spot, bombarded by so many conflicting emotions that she could hardly think. A few days ago she'd pushed Karl away because she was afraid of the feelings he aroused in her. She was still afraid, but now there was another emotion that was stronger than her fear. She had to see Karl again, to talk to him. The need to find the answers to her questions, to clarify what she felt and what she wanted, was undeniable.

As if from far away, she heard Sarah's voice. "I've taken more than a few chances. And that's brought me my share of pain. But it's brought me my share of happiness, also. That's what life's all about. Don't miss out on it. Don't let it pass you by."

The words echoing in her mind, Jaime stepped away from the window and let the curtain fall.

Chapter Twelve

Jaime stared up at Karl's unsmiling face and felt as if the ground beneath her feet were slowly giving way. "May I come in?"

After a second of hesitation that caused her heart to pound with dread, Karl swung the door wide.

Jaime sank onto the nearest chair, clutching its arms to keep her hands from shaking. Her need had driven her to seek Karl out, but she had no idea what to do now that she had found him.

"What do you want?" Karl asked bluntly, settling into an armchair across from her.

"We may not have parted on the best of terms," Jaime told him with a bravado she was far from feeling. "But you could at least be polite."

"How do you expect me to act after what you said?"

Jaime's control, weakened by frayed nerves and a sleepless night, was further taxed by his challenging stare. "I saw you with that blonde earlier. You seemed cheerful enough then."

Karl frowned. Was Jaime jealous? The possibility both intrigued and annoyed him. After the way she'd shut him out of her life and out of her bed, she had no right to question him regarding other women. He was angry about the way she'd treated him, and he wanted to stay angry. He didn't want to be glad to see her. He didn't want to remember the feel of her body arching beneath his, the look in her eyes when she'd gone over the edge of passion. He turned those memories away and concentrated on the cold and bitter things she'd said to him the last time they'd spoken.

He pushed Jaime a little harder, wanting to make her pay for the hurt she'd caused him, wanting to see her lose control. "She came to look at the house. But by the time she left, she was more interested in checking me out. I was tempted to take her up on her offer."

A tight feeling settled in Jaime's chest at the thought. "But you didn't?" The question was out before she could stop it.

"Not yet."

"Why not?"

Karl gave her a deliberate smile. "A little . . . anticipation can heighten enjoyment in the long run. Don't you agree?"

Jaime's hands tightened on the arms of her chair. "You talk as if making love is just one big game."

"Isn't it?"

"If you say so."

Karl was suddenly disgusted with the whole evasive, pointless conversation. "Are we going to continue playing verbal Ping-Pong with each other's feelings, or are we going to say something that matters?" He leaned forward in his chair, the expression in his eyes cold and dangerous. "You want the truth about my sex life, Jaime? I haven't slept with anyone since I left your bed. I haven't wanted to. You're the only woman on my mind. Now what the hell are you doing here?"

"I thought you'd left without saying goodbye!" The words burst out of Jaime as a high-pitched accusation. She continued more quietly. "I ran into the realtor, and he told me that your grandfather had gone back to Seattle. I assumed you had left without notifying me.''

"And that bothered you?"

"Yes, that bothered me."

Karl experienced a sense of satisfaction at her admission. "Why?" he pressed.

"Because..." Jaime took a deep breath. "Because you owed me a goodbye."

Karl's temper flared. "I don't think I owe you anything. The last time we spoke, I got the impression that you didn't want me around anymore."

Unable to deny the truth of what he'd said, Jaime sat in tight-lipped silence. Why had she even bothered to come over here? All it had gotten her was another unpleasant confrontation.

Something in her dejected expression touched Karl's heart and began to dissolve his hostility. He ran a hand through his hair with a muttered curse, finding it impossible to remain angry with the woman in front of him. "I didn't know that my grandfather was planning to leave Florida, Jaime."

"What?"

"Last Wednesday my granddad sent me halfway across Miami to pick up medication at a drugstore that didn't even exist. By the time I got back, he was gone. Wilma had left a note saying that she and my grandfather were on their way to Seattle. They didn't tell me beforehand because they were afraid I'd try to stop them."

"Wilma was behind all this?" Suddenly Jaime understood. "Then *she* must have been the older woman who called the court and asked what would happen if a client left town before his hearing."

"You've got to give the woman credit. The court, the realty company... She covered all the bases. She finally found a way to make things right for my grandfather."

It hadn't been Karl's idea after all! Jaime felt as if a heavy weight had been lifted from her chest. "But you called the court, too. Didn't you?"

Karl nodded. "After I discovered my grandfather had left, I wanted to find out the consequences of his action." He looked at Jaime, a hint of accusation in his voice. "Leaving the court's jurisdiction was one alternative you didn't bother to discuss with me."

"I came here to discuss it with you yesterday, but you weren't home. I thought you'd gone to Seattle, too."

"I drove down to Key West for a couple of days. After all that had happened, I needed time by myself, to—" Suddenly Karl realized what she had said. "You were going to suggest that I take my grandfather back to Seattle to avoid the hearing? But how could you justify doing that—professionally, I mean?"

Jaime told him the truth as she saw it. "I could justify it personally. And maybe that's the only way that really counts."

Karl was silent for a moment, weighing what she'd said. "That means you finally decided that I could be trusted to care for my grandfather without court involvement."

"Yes," Jaime admitted to Karl—and to herself. "But then when I thought you'd already left, it occurred to me that someone with nothing to hide would have stayed for the hearing—or at least called me to explain why he had to leave."

Karl resented her implication, but he couldn't fault her logic. "I explained what happened. Now let me show you something that should lay *all* your doubts to rest."

He retrieved a manila envelope from the coffee table and handed it to her. "I had my secretary get this stuff together and send it to me. There's the receipt for the repairs done on my grandfather's house, a copy of my cancelled check to the contractor and the papers my grandfather signed when he transferred the ownership of the company to me over ten years ago. And the deed to Granddad's house is in here, too."

"Does the lawyer you hired to represent you have copies of these?"

"Yes. I'll be on a flight back to Seattle early Monday morning. But my lawyer will be at the courthouse to present these papers to the judge—just to set the record straight."

Jaime felt a sudden chill go through her. She had expected Karl would be returning to Seattle soon, but that didn't make his announcement any easier for her to hear.

Karl looked at her expectantly, unaware of her distress. "Well, aren't you going to open it?"

Jaime hesitated, then handed the envelope back to him. "Professionally speaking, if you've already given copies to your lawyer for the court, then I don't have to look at these papers. Personally I already made up my mind about you before I called the courthouse yesterday. When I thought you'd left, the idea that you might be exploiting your grandfather did cross my mind again. But I just couldn't believe it was even possible anymore."

Their gazes met and held. "Karl, the contents of that envelope can't tell me anything I don't already know in my heart."

Karl was surprised by her admission—and more pleased than he was willing to admit. But he was still wary. What did this mean as far as their personal relationship was concerned? Had anything really changed?

Jaime was the first to look away, feeling awkward and self-conscious under his scrutiny. "Alex never doubted you," she told him, shifting the focus of the conversation. "I'm sure he'd want you to know that."

Karl couldn't hold back a smile. "I told him he ought to stay away from me. But somehow I'm surprised he didn't notice my car out front this morning and come knocking on my door."

"He's staying at Tony's this weekend."

Karl's smile turned into a frown. "Are you sure?"

"Yes. This time I talked to Mrs. Angelo myself."

Karl nodded his approval. "Good. Just so you'll know, I never intended to leave without telling Alex—or you—

goodbye. In fact, I was planning to bring these papers over to you tonight."

"You were?" Jaime exclaimed, extremely relieved to hear that one small bit of information.

"Yes, I was. And now that I've answered all your questions, Jaime, you can answer mine. Why did you come over here? And don't tell me it had anything to do with your job or my grandfather."

The words were so difficult for Jaime to say that they seemed to stick in her throat. "I just couldn't let it end the way it did," she whispered. "Not after what we'd shared. I've been carrying this awful feeling around inside me ever since I heard my front door slam behind you. I don't want— I refuse to go on feeling that way for the rest of my life."

Jaime's confession went beyond anything Karl had anticipated. She was telling him that she didn't want it to be over between them. His smile erased the last vestige of doubt as to her reception. "You missed me!"

Something in his voice, the expression in his eyes, seemed to dissolve all the barriers she'd erected. She returned his smile. "I guess I did."

"Well, that's a start. Now let me be honest with you. When I walked out of your house, I didn't intend to stay away forever. And when I planned to come over tonight, it wasn't just because I needed to talk to my grandfather's social worker." He looked into her eyes, his own bright with unexpressed emotion. "I'm very glad to see you, Jaime. I'm glad you're here."

Jaime's hands relaxed their grip on the chair. "So am I. I really don't know where all this is leading, but . . . until you leave, I don't want to think, I don't want to analyze, I don't want to worry about the future. I just want to be with you."

Karl wanted to capture the moment and hold it forever. He felt a surge of mingled tenderness and passion that threatened to propel him out of his chair to gather her in his arms and kiss her breathless. But he didn't want to take a chance on seeing that loving look replaced by one of wariness or fear. So he stayed right where he was and just en-

joyed the view. Jaime had managed to teach him the value
of patience and self-control. Sometimes he even succeeded
at putting his newly acquired knowledge into practice.

He had to clear his throat before he could trust himself to
speak. "It's dinnertime. Why don't we get something into
that poor, deprived stomach of yours?"

The tension that Jaime had been carrying with her for
days disappeared. She stood up, suddenly realizing how
hungry she was. "You don't fool me, Karl. It may be my
stomach you're talking about, but it's *your* stomach you're
thinking about!"

Karl came to his feet and paused, looking down into her
face. Slowly he lifted his hand and gently stroked her cheek.
She closed her eyes and sighed, and Karl's whole body reacted to that sigh. He barely restrained himself from covering those tantalizing lips with his own. But he knew he
wouldn't be able to stop with just a kiss. And even if she
were willing to let it go further, he wasn't. He intended to
take it slow, to make sure that Jaime felt secure and cher-
ished each step of the way. This time, there'd be no hasty,
impulsive act to remind her of past pain. There'd be no
doubts, no misunderstandings—nothing that could come
between them in the morning.

Reminding himself that patience was a virtue he needed
to practice, he gave her face one last caress. Then he let his
hand drop.

"I think I'll make some Swedish pancakes for dinner," he
said lightly. "How does that sound?"

Jaime murmured her assent, the thought of dinner the
farthest thing from her mind. She watched Karl turn away
and wondered why he hadn't kissed her.

"Those were the most delicious Swedish pancakes with
lingonberry preserves that I have ever tasted."

"Those were the only Swedish pancakes with lingonberry preserves that you've ever tasted."

Jaime pushed her chair away from the table with a sigh.
"You're right, but they *were* delicious. I have to admit that

the idea of having pancakes for dinner seemed kind of strange at first, but—''

"—they're not fish." Karl grinned and shook his head. "It was fate, you know. I intended to have salmon for dinner. But when that woman came to the door, I forgot to keep an eye on the oven. By the time I got back into the house after seeing her to her car, the smoke alarm was going off. My salmon was a smoldering lump of charcoal."

Jaime smiled at the picture. "Well, the way I feel about fish, I can't say I'm sorry. And you certainly did a great job on the pancakes."

Karl winked at her and bit into a slice of the apple cake that she'd helped him mix up before dinner. "If you think the pancakes were good, you should try this. Come on, have a piece. It's still warm."

Jaime couldn't resist the devilish gleam in his eye. "I'm sure it is. Maybe just a taste."

She opened her mouth and accepted the forkful of cake that he was extending toward her. "Mmm. You *are* a good cook, Karl Hallstrom."

"I'm a man of many talents."

And Jaime remembered in vivid detail just how talented he was. Her heart began to beat faster, but she avoided his questioning gaze.

She had come here to explore her feelings, yet now she was unsure of how to proceed. This time there was no crisis urging her toward intimacy, no emotional upheaval making her feel reckless enough to become the aggressor. If only Karl would take over, she could let his body persuade hers. But he seemed to be holding back, waiting for her to make the first move.

Karl sensed her uncertainty and changed the subject. "If I were at home, I would have used my own apples to make this cake."

Jaime raised an eyebrow. "You have an apple tree in your backyard?"

"My backyard's an acre of land, and there are several apple trees on it. A vegetable garden, too."

"In Seattle?" Jaime asked, picturing an isolated plot of farmland surrounded by concrete and urban bustle.

Karl smiled as though he could read her thoughts. "Actually, I have a rambling old two-story house on Vashon Island. It's only a fifteen-minute ferry ride across Puget Sound, but it's like entering a different world. Farms and orchards. Peace and quiet."

"It sounds perfect," Jaime said dreamily.

"Perfect?" Karl was fond of his home, but perfect wasn't one of the adjectives he would have used to describe it.

Jaime struggled to find the right words to convey her feelings. "It sounds so peaceful and old-fashioned and pretty. Like a . . . haven. A refuge from all the pressures and unpleasantness of the outside world."

When she put it that way, Karl knew exactly what she meant. He felt almost ridiculously pleased that Jaime shared his feelings.

"I have a workshop out back," he said, wishing she could see it. "I have it outfitted just the way I want it. Last year I bought a kiln, so I could do enameling."

"Enameling?" Jaime repeated with a frown. "Is that part of carpentry?"

Karl couldn't help chuckling at her question. "I get enough of wood at work! I don't do carpentry in my workshop, Jaime. I make jewelry."

Jaime stared at his hands. She tried to picture them doing the fine, delicate work she thought jewelry making might involve. She couldn't quite imagine it. But then she knew just how gentle those big hands could be when they were touching her.

A little embarrassed by her thoughts and by the way that she was staring, she forced herself to look away. "How did you become interested in making jewelry?"

"One of my great-great-grandfathers was a goldsmith in Sweden—or so the story goes. Back then a goldsmith was a craftsman who worked with all the precious metals. I like to think whatever talent I have comes from that ancestor. It gives me a feeling of . . . continuity, I guess."

"Can you show me anything you've done?" Jaime asked, intrigued by this unexpected creative streak in a man she had considered so practical.

"I give away everything I make," Karl explained matter-of-factly.

"You've never tried to sell anything?"

"A hobby is supposed to be strictly for enjoyment. It pleases me when my creations bring joy to others. Taking money for them would spoil that."

Karl looked into Jaime's brown eyes and suddenly realized that he didn't want to talk about jewelry. He didn't want to talk at all. He wanted to take Jaime into his arms and bring her all the pleasure her body was capable of feeling. But he held back, leery of frightening her with any sudden moves. Soon, he promised himself. Very soon.

Abruptly he stood up and began to clear the table. When Jaime tried to help him, he refused to allow it. "Why don't you go stretch out and relax for a few minutes?" he suggested, trying to give her a nudge in the right direction. "I'll take care of the dishes."

"But you cooked dinner," Jaime protested.

"It wasn't exactly a seven-course meal," he pointed out. "Besides, you're my guest. Go on now."

Retrieving her purse, Jaime walked down the hall to the bathroom. She combed her hair and freshened her make-up. She prepared herself for the lovemaking she had been both anticipating and dreading since she'd first decided to come across the street. But when she finally emerged, she didn't feel any more at ease.

Passing Karl's bedroom, she paused indecisively. What if she slipped into his room, took off her clothes and waited for him in his bed? A flush rose in her cheeks at the thought. Why not? Her bolder half demanded. Karl wasn't exactly a stranger! Yet, in a way, he was. She hadn't known him for very long, and part of her was still wary, still apprehensive.

With a sigh, she walked by the open doorway and continued down the hall. Why did relationships between men and women have to be so complicated?

She found Karl in front of the refrigerator, holding two empty wineglasses in one hand and removing a bottle of amber-colored liquor from the freezer with the other.

He turned to look at her, surprised to see her back in the kitchen. He had been having pleasant visions of her lying in his bed, waiting for him.

"You keep your wine in the freezer?" Jaime asked, breaking into his thoughts.

Karl heard the nervous squeak in her voice, and his heart went out to her. He was trying his damnedest to be considerate and take things slowly. But that only seemed to be making her more uncomfortable.

"This isn't wine," he said as he wrapped a towel around the bottle. "It's a Swedish liquor called aquavit. It's supposed to be served ice-cold—and it's supposed to be served *with* the meal. But, with your delicate stomach, I thought it would go down better after dinner."

"It's Swedish?" Jaime quavered as they walked into the living room. Her mind wasn't on the drink, but she really didn't know what else to talk about. "It sounds Latin."

"The Swedish name is *brännvin*. That means 'burnt wine.'"

"Sure sounds tasty."

"Don't worry, it is." He continued talking, trying to put her at ease. "Regular aquavit is colorless. This kind here is aged and a little smoother."

"Almost safe for human consumption."

"Almost." That was his Jaime. So scared that she was practically shaking, and she was still trying to make jokes.

Karl came to a halt in front of the sofa and set the bottle and the glasses down on the coffee table. He began to throw the pillows from the couch onto the floor. "We can have our drinks out here and relax in front of the fireplace. The logs aren't real, but I can turn on the flame effect, and we can pretend."

There was such relief in Jaime's smile that Karl had to look away. He wanted her so much he couldn't think straight. But she was making him feel like the villain in a melodrama. He almost decided to send her across the street to sleep in her own bed, but one thought stopped him. He'd be leaving Monday morning. And when would he see her again? When would there be another chance for them?

Determined to follow through with his original plan, Karl crouched down and concentrated on finding the correct switch.

Jaime stood watching him. She was used to this part of the house, and gradually she began to relax. The furniture was colonial, the colors earth tones. It was almost impossible to feel ill-at-ease in a room like this. She wondered if Karl's home on Vashon Island had a similar look about it. The way he had described it, it had sounded like everything she'd always dreamed of having: the land, the house . . . the man? She still wasn't sure about the man.

She contemplated Karl as he squatted in front of the flickering light. He seemed larger than life, primitive, frightening. How was it possible for her to be so fearful of all he represented, and so attracted by it, too? She caught herself wondering what he'd look like with the orange light playing over his bare skin. But she already knew—all rippling muscles and classic lines, like a Greek statue come to life.

At that moment, Karl turned and looked into her eyes. He read the desire there, and his heartbeat accelerated. The woman he'd been waiting for so patiently was here at last. The real Jaime, the Jaime he'd held in his arms and loved so well. This time her gaze didn't waver from his, and Karl suddenly knew without a doubt that neither of them would be sleeping alone tonight.

He got to his feet and crossed to her side. Picking up the bottle, he filled the two wineglasses. Then he set the bottle down again and reached for one glass.

Looking directly into her eyes, he raised his glass to chest level. "I'm so glad to have you here to share this night with me, Jaime Mitchell. Skoal."

He tossed back the liquid in one swallow, then set the glass down beside the bottle.

Jaime took a deep breath and raised her glass as she had seen him do. "Skoal."

When the ice-cold liquor hit the back of her throat, it was miraculously transformed into a fiery warmth that spread throughout her chest and then sank lower to suffuse her stomach with its heated glow.

She cleared her throat discreetly, her cheeks flushed. "That was very . . . interesting."

Karl smiled and lightly traced the curve of her neck with one finger. "Ice-cold outside, liquid fire inside. Reminds me of a Miami lady I know."

Jaime felt the warmth generated by the aquavit move outward until it seemed as though every cell of her body had been invaded and inflamed. Or had Karl's touch been the catalyst?

Then his mouth found hers, and her empty wineglass dropped from nerveless fingers to land against the carpet with a dull thud. The burning liquor that she had consumed and the warmth of the man in her arms combined to ignite Jaime's passion as Karl continued to explore her mouth, caressing her tongue with his own.

She lost all sense of self as she entered a world where Karl's heartbeat, his breath, his desire were one with hers. Her lips swelled and blossomed under his as he lifted the hem of her blouse to cup one small breast. He massaged the sensitive tip until it peaked against its white lace covering, and Jaime shivered in his arms.

Karl murmured an endearment against her lips, his hands working frantically to free her from the barrier of her clothing. He wanted her even more than he had the first time. But when he finally looked down at the pink-and-white perfection that he'd uncovered, he was afraid to even touch her—afraid that he'd be overcome by the urge to lower her to the floor and slide his body inside the snug warmth of hers. If the intensity of his passion frightened him, what would it do to her? She might turn away from him again. And he wasn't sure he'd be able to stand that.

Taking her hands, he drew them toward his mouth, pressing a kiss on each before he brought them to rest against his chest. "Touch me," he whispered, his voice husky with wanting.

Her hands trembling, Jaime fumbled with the buttons on his shirt. She had always been a passive recipient, never an initiator. But by the time the material parted, she was as eager to touch Karl as he was to feel her touch. Slowly she slid the garment down his muscular arms, her fingers caressing his skin in its wake. When the shirt fell to the floor, Jaime pressed her hands against his warm flesh. Then, impulsively, she followed them with her lips.

With unsteady fingers, Karl unbuckled his belt and shed the remainder of his clothing. At last he stood revealed to her as she had seen him in her imagination, the light flickering over his body like a lover's caress.

The sight of his arousal inspired no fear in Jaime, only a desperate longing to feel him deep inside her. "I want you," she whispered, amazed that it was true.

Reining in a feeling of wild exhilaration, Karl gathered her into his arms and kissed her gently but thoroughly.

Jaime felt his velvet-skinned hardness press against the length of her stomach and watched as his mouth moved down to her breast. Moaning at the tantalizing sensation, wondering that any man's touch could arouse her so, she buried her fingers in his hair.

Karl felt her response, and suddenly he could wait no longer. "Do I need to—"

"No, it's taken care of. I was hoping this would happen. I..."

Karl's mouth covered hers, absorbing her words and her will. Jaime closed her eyes and let her head fall back, all her doubts fading away to nothingness. She craved Karl's caress as she had craved no other man's, trusted him as she had trusted no other man. There was no pain-filled yesterday, there was no uncertain tomorrow. There was only the present and Karl.

She felt his hands gripping either side of her waist, then suddenly she was being lifted.

"Put your legs around me."

Jaime complied, clutching his shoulders in reaction to the deepest, sweetest penetration she had ever known.

Karl's breath was hot against her neck. "I missed you, Jaime. I missed you so damned much."

He slipped his hands beneath her to squeeze her bottom, to lift her and let her slide back down again. His words were breathless, disjointed whispers, interspersed with sighs. "Been thinking this . . . since I . . . pulled you . . . over that fence."

Jaime smiled as she slid against him, a little breathless herself. "You are . . . a pervert."

He squeezed her again, kissing her forehead, her eyelids, her lips. "Where you're . . . concerned . . . guess I am."

Karl fought the rush of ecstasy that threatened to overtake him, suckling Jaime's breasts, caressing her, using his mouth and hands to bring her pleasure as intense as that which he was feeling.

Jaime's body remembered the satisfaction he'd brought her in the past, just as her heart remembered his gentleness and caring. This time there was no inner struggle, no hesitation. Her lips sought his as she took over the rhythm, increasing the depth and force of his penetration. Her face flushed, she moved against him until a molten core of feeling erupted inside her, and she gasped out his name.

When Karl felt her contractions and the accompanying rush of moisture, his tenuous restraint vanished as if it had never existed. Making a growling sound deep in his throat, he laid her down against the pillows and drove into her for all he was worth. She arched toward him, wrapping her trembling legs around him, drowning in one long continuous wave of feeling.

"Jaime..." He grabbed her hips, forcing her closer, plunging in as far as she could take him.

Jaime gave him all she had until he collapsed against her, still murmuring her name.

For a long moment, she drifted in the twilight world between sleep and wakefulness, too caught up in the afterglow of lovemaking to notice anything else. Then she gradually became aware that she was having difficulty drawing a breath.

She pushed against Karl's shoulder, barely managing to suppress a giggle. "Karl, you're crushing me!"

Karl lifted his head and focused on her face as her words finally registered. He rolled to the side immediately, and Jaime turned to nestle against him.

She mumbled a protest when he set her away from him to look into her face. "Are you okay?" he asked, and Jaime heard real fear in his voice.

She reached up and touched his cheek, smiling to reassure him. "I'm more okay than I've ever been in my life before."

"You're really not hurt?"

Jaime shook her head, puzzled by his reaction.

Exhaling the breath he'd been holding, Karl drew her close again. "Oh, Jaime, you scared me! I scared myself. I've never let myself go like that with a woman before. I've always made sure that part of me was watching out, holding back. This time, I lost it. I didn't even realize what was happening."

Jaime smiled and kissed his chest, draping one leg over both of his. "If I had been in pain, believe me, I'd have gotten your attention. But it felt good, Karl. It was... beautiful."

Karl kissed her and wrapped his arms around her again. When he got to his feet a moment later, she was already half-asleep.

"Come on, sweetheart," he urged, pulling her up to stand beside him. "Let's go to bed."

Jaime leaned against him and brought one hand to her mouth to smother a yawn. "Bed?"

To Karl, she looked like a cross little girl who'd been awakened from her nap too soon. He wanted to hold her and comfort her and spoil her.

Smiling indulgently, he kissed the top of her head and lifted her into his arms.

When he laid her down on his bed she sighed, burrowed under the covers and fell into a deep sleep.

Karl lay down beside her and put one arm around her waist. Instinctively Jaime snuggled against his warmth. Karl pressed a kiss on the soft skin of her shoulder, then rested his cheek where his lips had lingered seconds before.

Asleep, she gave him her complete trust, but what would happen when she woke? His arm tightened around her as he remembered their prior lovemaking and the argument that had followed. Had the ice princess been banished for good this time or would she return again, stronger than ever? And how would he react if she did?

Drifting toward sleep, Karl wondered what tomorrow would bring.

Chapter Thirteen

Jaime smiled and stretched luxuriously. She could have stayed snug beneath the covers all day. But it was full light, and Karl had been gone when she awoke. A nagging little voice inside kept urging her to go to him. The longer she lay in bed, the louder and more insistent the voice became.

With a sigh, she sat up and drew the quilt around her shoulders, taking it with her as she padded barefoot to the bathroom. Then she headed for the kitchen. Knowing Karl as she did, the kitchen was where she had the best chance of finding him.

She pushed open the swinging door and saw the object of her search seated at the kitchen table munching contentedly from the plate in front of him.

Karl looked up and saw Jaime bundled inside the quilt, looking like an explorer about to embark on an arctic expedition. She raised one hand to rub the sleep out of her eyes, then tried unsuccessfully to smooth her tousled hair.

Karl smiled a good-morning. He couldn't understand why he thought this thin little waif was the most appealing, most desirable woman he'd ever seen. But he couldn't seem to stop thinking so, either.

Jaime returned his smile and came to sit at the table with him, the quilt trailing behind her like a royal train. Karl reached for her hand, then leaned across the small table to kiss it.

"Did you sleep well?" he asked.

Jaime couldn't help but laugh at that question. Karl held his breath at the pure exuberance of the sound. He'd never heard Jaime laugh before, and he was enchanted. But he was also puzzled because he didn't know the cause of her laughter.

"When I slept, I slept well," she told him archly.

"What does that mean?"

It was Jaime's turn to look puzzled. "Well, you...reached for me so many times last night that I lost count."

Karl looked at her, surprised and a little embarrassed. "And I thought I was dreaming of you." He rubbed his eyes with both hands. "I must be losing my mind! I'm sorry, Jaime. If I remember right, you couldn't have gotten much out of it."

Jaime smiled again, recalling the sweet bondings that had occurred in the wee hours before dawn. They really had seemed more dream than reality. But they had etched Karl's touch and taste and scent indelibly in her memory. And in her heart.

"I was more asleep than not, but I enjoyed the touching, the holding. It was ... nice."

It had been more than nice. It had been the first time in her adult life that she had felt content, secure, cared for.

"Come here, Jaime."

Karl took her face in his hands and leaned forward to kiss her. Jaime closed her eyes, then quickly opened them as the smell of vinegar, onion and another, sickening odor assailed her. She pulled back before Karl's lips touched hers.

For the first time, she noticed the open jar on the table. It was half full of onion and carrot slices mixed with shiny, silvery chunks of another substance she didn't recognize.

"What's that?" she asked in a small voice.

Karl looked at the jar then back at her. "That? That's just pickled herring."

Jaime quickly pushed away from the table. "I'm sorry, Karl," she mumbled as she backed toward the door. "But I have to...take a shower."

She beat a strategic retreat to the downstairs bathroom and shut the door. How could he eat that stuff? And for breakfast?

Shuddering, she let the quilt drop to the floor and adjusted the water temperature. Then she stepped into the spray, pulling the opaque shower curtain closed behind her.

She was just rinsing the shampoo out of her hair when she heard the bathroom door open. Jaime was so startled that she managed to get lather in her eyes. It stung like crazy, but she hardly noticed.

"What are you doing in here?" she asked shakily.

"Bruthing my teeph," Karl responded, his words slurring around the toothbrush in his mouth. "And using mouthwash."

Then the shower curtain was pushed aside, and he stepped into the tub.

Jaime shifted her hands, trying to cover herself, although she knew it was a ridiculous and futile gesture. "What do you want?"

Karl's feeling of apprehension deepened. First Jaime had fled the kitchen, now she was pulling away from him in here. Was she withdrawing emotionally as well? He had to bring her close again.

"Can't you guess what I want?" he asked, forcing himself to smile.

When she still didn't respond, he trailed one finger down her cheek, wiping away a stray trace of shampoo. "Is all this because of that jar of fish?"

Jaime's whole face seemed to crinkle up in revulsion. "That wasn't just fish. It was cold, disgusting, smelly fish!"

This time Karl's smile was genuine. He purposely made the tone of his voice light and teasing. "Well, you don't have to hide in the corner. I told you I even used mouthwash."

Jaime couldn't quite meet his gaze. "I know it's foolish after last night, but I've never shared a shower with a man before."

"Then you've been missing one of life's great experiences."

He bent to kiss her, and after a moment her arms rose to circle his neck. Karl breathed a mental sigh of relief as he brought her wet body snug against him. Jaime was his again.

When he lifted his head, they were both breathing hard.

"Is this what makes sharing a shower one of life's great experiences?" Jaime asked coyly.

Karl picked up the soap and began rubbing it between his hands, building up a rich lather. "It's a start."

"I think I get the idea."

He was a little startled when she took the soap from him and followed his example. When he felt her touching him, he couldn't quite believe it.

Holding him tightly, Jaime slid her hand up, then down the hard, soap-slicked length of him.

Karl closed his eyes and tried to retain some measure of control. His shy little Jaime had turned the tables on him with a vengeance. "That feels so good," he whispered.

Jaime was surprised to find that she was actually enjoying herself. She'd never enjoyed this aspect of life before she'd met Karl.

She released him and picked up the soap again, observing Karl's reaction as he watched her working the bar back and forth between her fingers. "I think I need two hands for this job," she decided, her voice low and as deliberately provocative as the expression in her eyes.

Karl thought his heart would leap out of his chest. Was this sexy, audacious woman really Jaime Mitchell? It didn't seem possible.

Unable to hold back any longer, he took her in his arms and kissed her, running his soapy hands over her breasts and buttocks, then down between her thighs.

The bar of soap fell to the floor of the tub unnoticed as Jaime quivered in Karl's arms. The sensations he was evoking were even stronger than those she'd felt the night before. Then he slipped a finger inside, and she stiffened at the uncomfortable feeling it caused her.

Karl immediately withdrew. "What is it?"

She tried to smile, but it turned into an unconvincing grimace. "Nothing major. Just a little twinge."

But Karl was already frowning darkly. "I *was* too rough with you last night!"

The idea seemed so absurd that this time Jaime gave him an honest smile. "My body just has to stretch a little to adjust to yours."

Karl's frown only deepened. "So much that it hurts you?"

"It certainly didn't hurt while you were making love to me. It doesn't really hurt now. It's just that I definitely know that I've been . . ." She paused awkwardly.

"Loved?" Karl supplied.

As soon as he said the word, Jaime knew that was exactly what she'd meant. "Yes. Loved."

He kissed her again, and she leaned against him, caught up in a desire that went beyond physical boundaries.

Karl pulled away first. "You said that you were sore," he reminded her, his eyes twinkling.

"It doesn't matter," Jaime told him, trying to draw him close again.

"It matters to me," Karl said as he sank to one knee on the shower mat.

Jaime was startled when he lifted her leg and casually hooked her knee over his shoulder. She was left trying to balance herself on one foot, while the other dangled down Karl's back like the trailing end of a long scarf.

"What are you doing?" she demanded, clutching his head for support.

Cupping her buttocks, he smiled up at her and tilted her pelvis forward. "I'm just making it all better."

Jaime woke from a sound sleep to the feel of Karl's lips on hers.

She groaned and pushed him away even as she felt her body beginning to respond to his nearness. "Oh, please, Karl, not again!"

She heard him chuckle, then opened her eyes and saw his smiling face above hers.

He stroked her cheek and kissed the tip of her nose. "No, not again. I just wanted to wake you. It's getting late."

Jaime's feeling of well-being vanished as she realized why he'd awakened her. This was their last day together. By this time tomorrow, Karl would be back in Seattle. Tomorrow night she'd be sleeping alone.

She made an effort to put those considerations out of her mind for the present. She'd have plenty of time later to think things over, to sort out her feelings. Now she wanted to live for the moment, and she wanted to share every moment with Karl until it was time for him to leave.

She smiled up at him, caressing his fiery beard. "Did I tell you that you're very good at making it all better?"

"And you certainly know how to get a man all lathered up."

Jaime giggled, and Karl hugged her, running one hand over her breasts, then down to her stomach. Absently he let his fingers trace the healed-over, faded marks that her pregnancy had left there. He tried to imagine her flat little belly rounded with child, her small breasts swollen with milk. He found it very difficult.

"Did you nurse Alex?" he asked curiously.

His question stirred up an old feeling of inadequacy in Jaime. She was suddenly acutely aware of her tiny breasts and the disfiguring marks on her stomach. She fumbled with the sheet, trying to pull it up, to cover herself.

Karl felt a surge of anger. He'd never met a woman who wasn't self-conscious about some part of her body. They'd all been intimidated by the airbrushed perfection of center-folds, the beautiful—and, in many cases, surgically enhanced—models and actresses they saw on TV. And by the men they'd known who had bought into that same fantasy.

But Karl wasn't one of those men. He loved women just the way God had created them. He found the female form, in all its glorious diversity, inately desirable and attractive. Especially the slight, precious body he was holding in his arms. It had given the gift of life to a beautiful son, and in the past twenty-four hours it had given Karl unequaled pleasure. Now Jaime was trying to hide it from him as if it were something to be ashamed of.

In an uncharacteristic show of force, Karl tugged the sheet from her grasp and threw it off the foot of the bed. Then he looked down into her startled eyes and smiled reassuringly.

"I won't let you hide from me, Jaime," he said softly. "It's too late anyway. I've seen all there is to see—and it's beautiful."

He kissed her tenderly, then drew her close against him, determined to find out what was upsetting her. "You didn't answer my question. Did you nurse Alex?"

Jaime buried her face in his shoulder. "I tried, but I just couldn't. My milk never came in. The nurses told me it was because I was so tense, so nervous. I felt like such a failure."

Karl let one hand drift over her hair, longing to comfort her, but not knowing quite how to go about it. The pain in her voice was so fresh, as if it had all happened yesterday.

He pulled back and let her see his smile. "Well, I don't think it stunted his growth any. He's as tall as you already and still growing."

Jaime smiled, too, a little embarrassed. "You're right. I guess I'm just being silly."

"No, you're not being silly. You just have an amazing capacity for carrying around guilt. But I'm not going to let you get away with it. If you have to blame yourself for something, take the blame for how well Alex has turned out."

Jaime thought that over. "He has, hasn't he?"

"Uh-huh. Now if you don't get up and get dressed, you can blame yourself for making us late for lunch—brunch in your case. I know this great seafood restaurant . . ."

Jaime socked him in the arm and only succeeded in hurting her hand. Karl kissed it tenderly, his expression suddenly serious. His mouth was slowly moving toward hers when the phone rang.

Without giving the action a second thought, Jaime reached over and picked up the receiver. "Hello?"

There was a long moment of silence, and then Ivar Hallstrom's voice came crackling over the line. "Jaime Mitchell? What are you doing there?"

Jaime sat straight up in the bed and pulled the covers up to her chin. "I—"

"Are you still checking up on me?"

"Of course not, Mr. Hallstrom," Jaime assured him, watching as Karl bounded off the bed and out of the room. "Since you decided to leave town and avoid the hearing, I'm not—"

"I never ran away from anything in my life!"

Jaime had expected Ivar to be a happy man now that he no longer had to face the prospect of a competency hearing. But he seemed more irritable and dissatisfied than before. It was with a profound sense of relief that she heard Karl's voice in her ear and realized that he'd picked up the kitchen extension.

"Jaime isn't here because of the hearing, Granddad. She came to see me."

Jaime could hear Wilma talking in the background. "When I suggested coming back to Seattle, Ivar Hallstrom, you thought it was a grand idea. But ever since we got here, you've been nothing but miserable!"

"I'll be damned if anyone's going to call me a coward!"

Wilma's sound of exasperation reached Jaime's ears. "No one's calling you a coward, Ivar. That's just your own conscience talking. And it's all foolishness. The decision has already been made."

"*You* made the decision," Ivar told Wilma. "*You* engineered this!"

"Now just a minute!" Karl interjected. He took a deep breath, bracing himself. What he was about to say was difficult, but necessary. "Granddad, you always told me that a man takes responsibility for his own actions, right or wrong. And I know for a fact that nobody carried you onto that plane."

There was a moment of tense silence. Then Ivar sighed. "You're right, Karl. Running just sticks in my craw is all. I guess I *was* looking for someone to blame. And, as usual, Wilma was handy. I'm sorry I took it out on you, Willy."

Jaime swallowed hard, her eyes a little too moist. "I want to apologize, too. I didn't mean to upset anyone."

Suddenly Wilma was on the line. "Jaime? I'm glad you're there! I want you to know that I'll be staying with Ivar in his house from now on. He's agreed to let me supervise his medication and the bills and all." She paused and then continued, her voice uncharacteristically husky. "I feel badly about leaving the way I did, Jaime, not being able to say goodbye to you or to Alex. But, you understand, I had to make things right for Ivar again."

An awkward silence followed, and Jaime realized she wasn't the only one who knew things still weren't "right for Ivar."

"I understand," Jaime ventured finally. "And I think Ivar Hallstrom is very lucky to have two people who love him so much. I know that you and Karl will take care of him."

Wilma yielded the phone to Ivar, and Jaime listened as Karl began to tell his grandfather about the burned salmon and the smoke detector. Suddenly Ivar laughed, and the tension was broken.

"Remember when you were ten, Karl, and you insisted on being the one to cook that big fish you caught? Only you forgot to clean it first! Sounds like you haven't changed much."

As Jaime listened to their conversation, she felt a warm glow building inside, a sense of family that she'd never known before—even when her mother was alive.

But all too soon it was over, and Wilma got on the phone again to say goodbye. "Give Alex my love," the older woman told Jaime. "And write!"

"Tell the boy I miss him!" Ivar added.

Karl hung up the extension and walked back into the bedroom. The look on Jaime's face told him how she felt. "Now you understand why I was so angry when I came into your office that first day," he said quietly. "Now you know what I was fighting to protect."

"Yes," Jaime agreed. "Now I know." And she knew that she wanted the same sense of caring and belonging that Karl and Ivar shared—the sense of caring and belonging that she'd felt sleeping in Karl's arms. But was she willing to sacrifice her independence in order to have it?

The phone call from Seattle seemed to cast a shadow over the rest of Jaime's day.

Karl took her to lunch at a nearby Italian restaurant, then they came back to the house to finish packing up Ivar's few remaining belongings. They talked and joked with each other as they worked. But somehow the sense of closeness that had been theirs earlier seemed to dissipate as the fact of their impending separation became harder and harder to ignore.

"This is the last one." Jaime finished taping the box and straightened up with a sigh.

Karl looked up from the papers he was sorting and noticed that it was dark outside. He felt a growing sense of alarm. Alex was due home any minute, he'd be flying back to Seattle in a matter of hours, and he hadn't really resolved anything with Jaime.

He wanted her to come to Seattle where he could see her, hear her voice, hold her in his arms. But was he prepared to offer her marriage in order to make that possible?

Karl had considered marriage a few times over the years, but he'd never actually proposed to a woman. He'd held back, waiting. Waiting to fall in love. Was he in love with Jaime? He couldn't seem to get enough of her physically, and he would give his own life to protect hers. But was that what love was all about?

The love he'd seen between his grandfather and grandmother in the years before she'd died had been steady, satisfying, comfortable—not at all like the tumultuous, argument-prone, up-and-down relationship he had with Jaime. With her, the pleasure and the pain were both so extreme that sometimes he thought he was losing his mind.

Love was something shared by two people with a common outlook, and personalities that meshed together like the gears of an efficient machine. Jaime's personality was so different from his that he felt continuously off-balance and out-of-synch.

But, despite their differences, he wasn't ready to give her up. He'd really missed her during the few days they'd been apart, and the thought that he might never see her again was actually painful. How could he let her walk out of his life for good?

"Jaime, I don't want to say goodbye."

Jaime looked up at him, startled to hear her own thoughts spoken aloud. She didn't want to say goodbye either. Maybe . . . maybe she was even in love with Karl Hallstrom! But then she had thought she was in love with Alex's father, too. Her mind and her experience told her that love was rooted in physical attraction and self-delusion. It was a temporary emotional state that just couldn't survive the test of time, the test of day-to-day living. But somehow, as she looked up at Karl, her heart refused to accept that line of reasoning.

"I wish we didn't have to say goodbye!"

Suddenly, looking down into Jaime's face, Karl knew exactly what he wanted. He put his hands on her shoulders. "Come to Seattle with me, Jaime. Marry me."

Jaime was surprised to find a thrill of joy mixed in with the familiar fear. She was actually considering his proposal! What was wrong with her? Marriage was the last thing she wanted—wasn't it? No, the last thing she wanted was for Karl to walk onto a plane and put the length of the country between them.

If only he lived in Miami. But even the thought seemed incongruous. Karl belonged in Seattle with his rambling house, his workshop and his apple trees. Then there was his business. The company meant much more to him than just a way to earn a living. It was his family's heritage and a job he loved.

Jaime felt tied to her job, too, but she couldn't claim to love what she did for a living. It provided her with security, independence and a sense of self-worth. Those were the things she was afraid of losing, not the job itself.

"I don't know, Karl," she said finally. "The whole idea of marriage frightens me. And then there's my house, my job. I need time. I have to think this over."

Karl had never laid his heart on the line for any woman the way he just had for Jaime. He'd offered her all he had to give and found out that it wasn't enough. After the love they'd shared this weekend, he'd thought she cared for him. Had he been wrong?

"Forget your crummy job and that rundown house! I can take care of you and Alex, Jaime. I can give you everything you need. You'll never have to worry about anything again."

He knew he'd said the wrong thing even before the sound of the last syllable died away. His sudden, desperate need to wrest some kind of commitment from her had made him forget to screen his words. He'd said exactly what he felt.

The wariness and hurt pride in Jaime's eyes told him what her reaction was even before she spoke. "I don't need you to give me things, Karl!"

"Why do you see my offer to provide for you as some kind of threat?" Karl demanded, frustrated by her attitude.

The words Jaime had been holding back for so long finally burst out as if they had a will of their own.

"I'm afraid I'll lose my control, my independence, my self-confidence," she told him, her voice rising. "I'm scared I'll lose myself in you, Karl. You'll wrap your strength around me and do everything for me, and I'll never have the courage to face the world on my own again!"

Karl stared at her for a long moment, truly shocked by what she'd said. She couldn't be serious! But then he looked into her eyes and saw that she'd meant every incredible word. Is that what Jaime thought of him?

"You make me sound like some kind of monster! Do you really believe I'm capable of doing that to a woman? Do you believe I'd want to? What does it take to earn your trust?"

"I trust you more than I've ever trusted any man!"

"And that's not a heck of a lot! Well, I'm sick of taking the rap because of how your mother ruined her life and what Alex's father did when you were eighteen. You're thirty-two now, and those people are dead. You're alive, Jaime. Start living for the future instead of just reacting to the past!"

Jaime shook her head. She'd just taken her first tottering step, and now Karl expected her to run a marathon! "Don't you see how far I came toward living for the future when I came to you yesterday, Karl? I just can't do it all at once. I need more time."

"How much time?"

"I don't know," Jaime told him truthfully. "As long as it takes."

"I deserve a better answer than that!"

"I don't have a better answer than that!" Her emotions in turmoil, Jaime felt her fear escalating in response to Karl's demands. Suddenly she felt like she was suffocating. She had to get away from the anger and the accusation in his eyes.

"I'll call you," she told him, reaching blindly for her purse.

Karl watched her moving away from him, battling his own unexpected fear. If he couldn't persuade Jaime to come with him now, when the impression of their lovemaking was still fresh in her mind, how could he hope to do it once he'd returned to Seattle? Then he'd be nothing but a fading memory. He was suddenly sure that if he left without getting a commitment from her, he'd never see her again. His every instinct was pushing him to go on the offensive, to fight for her. And there was no one to fight but Jaime, herself.

Without thinking, he reached out and grabbed her by the arm. "You're not going anywhere yet, lady. Not until this is settled between us!"

Jaime saw the determination in his eyes and felt the overwhelming strength of the big hand that had her imprisoned in a viselike grip. When she felt herself being hauled toward him, she reacted in a blind panic.

The impact of her palm against his cheek seemed to echo in the quiet house. Karl's hand fell away from her arm. They stared at each other, stunned.

"Oh, Karl," Jaime said in a horrified whisper. "Why did you try to force me?" Tears blurring her vision, she whirled around and fled.

Stung by her accusation, Karl watched her cross the street and felt as if a part of him were being ripped away. Instinctively he started after her.

Suddenly the sights and sounds surrounding him faded into the background, and he found himself replaying an old, half-forgotten memory.

He was a boy of eight again, running down the steps and out to the driveway, tears streaming down his cheeks.

"Don't leave, Mama! Please don't leave! I'll be good, I promise!"

His mother pulled open the door of the car and threw her suitcase into the back seat. "I have to leave, but I'll be back."

"When? When will you be back?"

"Soon." She pushed at the small hands that were clutching her dress, her blue eyes filled with a pain and a desperation that exceeded his. "Let go, Karl! You can't stop me!"

"I won't let you go!"

He heard the roar of the car engine. He felt the sting as his mother's palm cracked against his cheek. Stunned, he released the material of her dress. The car door closed. And she was gone.

The door of Jaime's house slammed, recalling Karl to the present. He could go across the street and knock on that door. But what was the point? He'd learned a long time ago that no love was strong enough to hold someone who didn't want to stay.

Feeling more alone than he'd ever felt before, Karl turned and slowly walked back into the empty house.

Chapter Fourteen

"Why do courthouses have so many steps?" Sharon asked with a sigh.

"Personally I've always thought it was a matter of deliberate intimidation." Jaime shaded her eyes against the glare of the afternoon sun and peered upward. There did seem to be way too many steps between the sidewalk and the entrance of the courthouse. And, unlike Sharon, she wasn't almost nine-months pregnant.

For some reason, that thought brought an image of Karl to her mind, his hand pressed against her abdomen, asking if she'd nursed Alex.

When she remembered the warmth they'd shared, her heart came close to breaking. She could hardly bear the thought of not seeing him again. But she knew that she could never survive emotionally living in the shadow of a man that strong, that dominant. She ought to be glad that he had gone back to Seattle. She ought to be, but she wasn't.

"Come on," Maria urged. "We'll be late for the hearing."

For once, Jaime wasn't concerned with punctuality. All day she'd been expecting a call from the judge's secretary telling her that Karl's lawyer had had the hearing canceled. Ivar Hallstrom was in Seattle beyond the court's jurisdiction. Under those circumstances, there was really no reason for the hearing to be held. But then, Jaime had never had a case like this one before, and she didn't pretend to understand all the ins and outs of the legal system.

The bottom line was that the hearing was still scheduled, so she was obligated to appear. It was the last thing she had to do before closing the Hallstrom case. But it wouldn't be so easy to put her memories of Karl to rest.

Sharon sighed again. "Okay, let's get this over with."

Agreeing with the sentiment, Jaime took Sharon's arm, and the two of them followed Maria up the steps.

Ron Martinez, Ivar's court-appointed attorney, met them on the third floor as they stepped out of the elevator into the large public waiting room. "Hi, guys! Let's hustle. Judge Harrison is ready for us, and I'm told the private attorney Karl hired is here, too. Is the HRS lawyer coming?"

"No, he isn't," Jaime replied as they followed Ron through the smaller waiting area reserved for lawyers. When the bailiff there had finished checking them in, Jaime turned back to Ron. "The HRS attorney decided that there was no reason for him to be present since the client isn't even in town."

"What do you mean he's not in town?"

"I thought you knew!" Jaime exclaimed. Quickly she gave him a rundown of the situation. She managed to avoid any mention of her personal involvement with Karl while communicating her belief in his good intentions and outlining the documents he had given to his attorney. " . . . and I don't understand why the hearing hasn't been canceled," she concluded. "Do you?"

Ron shrugged. "Maybe Karl's lawyer didn't even contact the judge to request a cancellation. He certainly didn't call me."

"And neither did I. I'm sorry, Ron. I assumed you knew."

"No big deal. Let's go on in and see what happens."

Judge Harrison's secretary nodded to them as they moved through her office and on into the judge's chambers.

Of the four judges who presided over competency hearings, Judge Harrison was Jaime's personal favorite. He exuded authority without being the least bit pompous. Competency hearings in Dade County tended to be less formal than other court proceedings at any rate, conducted in chambers without judges' robes or other frills. But Judge Harrison was special. He always made Jaime feel like she was coming to visit a favorite uncle.

"How are my girls?" the judge boomed, coming out from behind his desk to greet them. "Are you still working, Sharon? When's that baby due?"

Jaime took a seat at the large rectangular table that had been set against the front of the judge's desk in a perpendicular, T-shaped arrangement. She reached across the table to shake hands with Glen Tarver, the attorney Karl had hired, forcing a smile as she introduced herself.

Karl. Why did she have to be continuously reminded of Karl? She was impatient for the hearing to be over so that she could be finished with the Hallstroms once and for all. So that her life could resume its familiar, comfortable routine. But her inner voice was laughing, mocking her. Deep down she knew that, after Karl Hallstrom, her life would never be the same again.

A flicker of movement in her peripheral vision disturbed her thoughts, and she turned her head to glance toward the doorway. Her whole body stiffened in reaction to what she saw. "No!" she exclaimed, springing to her feet.

Ivar and Wilma came to a halt just inside the room, and Jaime's gaze locked with Karl's. She felt the same confused emotions she always felt when she saw him: joy, hope, desire, despair. But now her predominant emotion was fear. Ivar had been safe in Seattle. How could Karl let his grandfather come back to Miami? To this?

But Jaime could guess the answer to that question. She could still hear Ivar's defiant declaration: "I never ran away from anything in my life!"

Karl looked at Jaime, longing to go to her, to explain. But there was no way he could do that right here, right now. It would have to wait until after the hearing.

"Jaime, sit down."

A hand gripped her arm, and Jaime looked down into Ron's concerned face.

Suddenly aware that all eyes were on her, Jaime slowly sank into her chair. Ivar had come back of his own free will, and there was nothing she could do to help him now. Pain clutching at her stomach, she watched Karl take a seat directly across from her.

Ivar and Wilma settled to his left. Wilma was dressed in a typically flamboyant turquoise dress with a gold lamé jacket. Both men wore well-tailored suits, and ties. Jaime realized that Karl had worn the same suit for their date at the seafood restaurant. Just thinking of that night brought back memories that made her throat ache with suppressed tears.

Wilma gave her a discreet wave, looking every bit as dejected as Jaime felt. Ivar nodded, and Karl smiled. Jaime was too anxious and upset to even consider returning that smile.

She jumped at the sound of Judge Harrison's voice. He stated the purpose of the hearing, then asked Ivar if he understood. Ivar answered in the affirmative, and the judge continued.

"Will all those who plan to testify at this hearing please raise their right hands and repeat after me..."

After they'd all been sworn in as a group, Judge Harrison addressed Ron and Karl's lawyer. "Since the HRS attorney isn't present today, and in the interest of time, I'd like to keep these proceedings as simple and as informal as possible. Do you agree, Mr. Tarver? Mr. Martinez?"

"Agreed," Ron responded.

Tarver conferred briefly with Karl. "Agreed, Your Honor."

"All right, Jaime. Tell the court why you filed."

Jaime opened Ivar's case record and referred to her notes. With clinical detachment, she related the circumstances of the referral and described her initial assessment, running through the list of competency questions and Ivar's responses.

"In your professional opinion, is Ivar Hallstrom able to handle his own affairs?" Judge Harrison asked.

Jaime looked at the three tense faces across the table and no longer felt any detachment. "No," she replied only a little above a whisper. It was the single hardest syllable she'd ever had to say.

"And this neighbor," the judge pressed, "the one who alerted you to the alleged medication problem and the possibility of exploitation—is she here to testify?"

Wilma burst into tears, and Jaime prayed that she'd have the strength to refrain from joining her.

Ivar pulled the weeping woman close and stroked her bright red hair. "Stop that now, Willy. Pull yourself together and answer the judge's questions. I came back here to face up to this thing—to face my limitations, as Jaime's so fond of calling them."

But Wilma only sobbed harder than before. "Dammit, woman," Ivar said, his voice a soft rebuke. "There's nothing you can tell the judge that I don't already know. It just took a while for me to accept the truth."

Jaime felt humbled by Ivar's courage and strength of character. If only those were the qualities being judged here today.

"Let me talk!" Karl shook off his attorney's restraining hand and shot to his feet. "Does this hearing need to go any further?" he asked the judge, his voice cracking with emotion. "My grandfather had returned to Seattle where he has a home and people who care for him. He voluntarily came back to Miami to face this court because he felt it was something he had to do. But it's all unnecessary, Your Honor! He doesn't need a court-appointed guardian. He already has me and Wilma. Jaime knows how things are. Just ask her!''

"Young man," Judge Harrison said sternly, "I'll decide what's necessary here. And I can hear you just as well when you're sitting down.''

Karl returned to his chair, looking a little abashed.

Judge Harrison handed Wilma his handkerchief, then turned to Jaime without missing a beat. "Do you have something to say, Jaime?"

Jaime wasn't sure how to answer. "Well, the client does have his own home in Seattle. His grandson, Karl, lives a few minutes away. And Wilma Woodruff, the neighbor who originally called in the referral, is now residing in the home with Ivar on a full-time basis.''

Judge Harrison looked at Wilma who was still sniffling, and at Ivar who was patting her hand. "I won't even venture to ask how that set of circumstances came about. Do you believe that this arrangement meets the client's needs, Jaime?''

"Yes, Your Honor. Wilma is continuing to help Ivar by managing the bills, monitoring his medication and making sure that he keeps his doctor's appointments.''

"And you found no evidence of exploitation?"

"None whatsoever, Your Honor. I find family and friends to be supportive, loving and protective of the client's best interests." Jaime hesitated, knowing she was pulling the foundation out from under everything she'd just said. But it was her job to give the judge a true picture of the situation.

"I also feel you should know, Your Honor, that I became personally involved with Karl Hallstrom while working on this case.''

Ron cleared his throat, and Judge Harrison frowned. Jaime didn't dare look in Karl's direction. She continued talking, determined to make her point. "I know this casts doubt on my objectivity as well as my professional ethics. But, Your Honor, I swear to you that if I had found any evidence to indicate that Karl Hallstrom was exploiting his grandfather, no personal considerations would have prevented me from bringing it to this court's attention."

Judge Harrison turned to Sharon and Maria. "Do you two ladies concur with Jaime's assessment of the situation?"

Both social workers answered in the affirmative.

"Mr. Martinez?"

"As my report reflects, Your Honor, I agree with Jaime. But, unlike her, I'm undecided on the question of Ivar Hallstrom's competence."

Silence reigned as Judge Harrison leaned back in his chair and pondered the testimony. "I've reviewed the documents submitted to me by Mr. Tarver concerning the Hallstrom Lumber Company and the five-thousand-dollar check written by Ivar Hallstrom to Karl Hallstrom. I find no evidence of exploitation."

Jaime returned Karl's smile with a tremulous curve of her lips.

"Further, I have reviewed the reports submitted to me by the court-appointed attorney, the layperson and the two psychiatrists. Mr. Martinez and the layperson are undecided on the matter of Ivar Hallstrom's competence. One psychiatrist says Mr. Hallstrom is incompetent; the other believes that he is competent."

Jaime held her breath, her fists pressed against the tabletop. She knew from experience that it was now possible for the ruling to go either way. For the first time, she was hoping that it would be decided in the client's favor rather than her own.

"Considering the client's current situation and the conflicting nature of the psychiatrists' reports, I am not going to declare Ivar Hallstrom incompetent at this time. The petition is dismissed."

Jaime sagged back in her chair, watching misty-eyed as Karl pulled Ivar and Wilma into his embrace.

"You're slipping, Jaime," Ron told her with a grin. "How many have you lost altogether now? Does this make four or five?"

Jaime smiled. "I can't count this one as a loss, Ron."

"Karl Hallstrom."

All eyes turned back to Judge Harrison, and the room fell silent once more. "Now that this is all over, are you going to do right by my girl?"

Jaime blushed scarlet, but Karl only smiled. "I've already asked her to marry me, Your Honor. But she hasn't given me an answer yet."

Attention shifted to Jaime as she sat fidgeting in her chair. She was more relieved than she would ever admit to learn that Karl hadn't withdrawn his proposal. But she also felt thoroughly humiliated by the fact that her private life had suddenly become public domain. "Your Honor," she began. "This is a personal matter—"

Ivar snorted. "'A personal matter,' she says. A blind man could see that you two are crazy in love."

Suddenly it didn't matter to Jaime that she was making a spectacle of herself. She had to respond to what Ivar had said. "Loving someone and being able to live with them are two different things."

"That's what Karl said to me last night when I called him back to tell him I was flying to Miami. He seemed to be under the misapprehension that love was perfect harmony and understanding. I told him he wasn't going to find any woman this side of heaven who could give him that—and it sounded mighty boring to me anyway."

He clapped his grandson on the back and smiled. "Karl figured from watching his grandma and me that love was a smooth ride. What he didn't realize was that we'd been working hard for twenty years before he was born to level out the bumps. Willy and I still have a long way to go in that direction, but I know we're going to make it."

Jaime watched as Ivar clasped Wilma's hand, and her heart warmed at the sight of the other woman's radiant smile.

"Time for the next hearing, Your Honor," the judge's secretary prompted from the doorway.

Jaime sensed Karl's gaze on her as she got up and left the judge's chambers, but it was Ron who came up behind her in the public waiting room and planted a kiss on her cheek.

"I never thought it would happen for you, Jaime. But *damn* I'm glad it did! I only hope that you and Karl will be as happy as Ginny and I are."

Before Jaime could respond, Ron had latched on to Mr. Tarver, and both lawyers disappeared in the direction of the Law Library.

Suddenly Karl was at her side. "Can I talk to you in private for a minute? Please."

Jaime turned toward Maria and Sharon. Maria waved her on with a smile. "Go ahead, we'll wait for you."

The two social workers took seats on one of the high-backed wooden benches that were lined up like church pews in the large rectangular room. Jaime noticed Ivar and Wilma heading in the same direction.

Then Karl spoke, claiming her full attention. "If you don't mind, I think we can be alone in here."

Both eager and apprehensive, Jaime allowed herself to be drawn into a small unoccupied office. Then Karl closed the door behind them, and Jaime was no longer conscious of her surroundings. She was only aware of the man who was sharing the limited space with her.

He was standing so close to her that she was having trouble forming a coherent thought. All she could seem to concentrate on was how she'd felt when he'd made love to her and how much she wanted him to make love to her again.

Desperately she tried to focus on the way he'd acted yesterday, the way he'd tried to force a decision from her. Had he brought her in here just to restate his demands?

But to her surprise, Karl's eyes held understanding instead of anger. "I'm not here to demand an answer, Jaime. I'm here to rephrase the question. And to share some things that I've come to understand better since the last time we talked."

"What things?" Jaime asked curiously.

"Yesterday I was too busy worrying about my own feelings to really listen to what you were saying. But later on, when I had a chance to play back what you had said, I realized something important."

He paused and lifted one hand to touch her cheek. "There's someone you trust less than you trust me, Jaime. And that's yourself."

"What are you talking about?" Jaime demanded in sudden dread.

"Those things you said to me about losing your control, your independence, even your self. When I thought about it, I realized that you're not afraid of my being strong enough to take them away from you. You're afraid that you'll be so weak you'll want to give them up."

Jaime stared up at him, shocked to hear her innermost feelings put into words and spoken aloud by another person. Karl had uncovered her deepest secret. But instead of feeling threatened or humiliated, she felt almost relieved.

"So now you know the truth, Karl. It's all a charade. All the time I'm pretending to be strong, I'm really scared to death."

Karl shook his head. "Jaime, you *are* strong, you *are* self-sufficient. You work at a job that *I* wouldn't be strong enough to do. You've done it for years and done it well. You've raised a child all by yourself and done a hell of a good job at that, too."

Jaime opened her mouth to protest, but Karl wouldn't allow it. "You have, Jaime. And you don't do all that by just pretending to be strong. Somewhere along the way you bought the idea that being strong means not having any doubts or fears or needs. That's just like saying that courage is a lack of fear. It isn't. It's being afraid, but going ahead despite that fear. That's what you do, Jaime. You're as brave, strong and independent as anyone I know."

Jaime stood very still as she let his words settle in her mind. "But I couldn't even handle what happened with Alex and Sarah. I fell apart!"

Journey with Harlequin into the past and discover stories of cowboys and captains, pirates and princes in the romantic tradition of Harlequin.

Printed in Canada

"You look pretty together to me right now. And—although I hate to admit it—you would have come out of it fine even if I hadn't been there. Listen, lady, having deep feelings, needing someone else, doesn't make you weak. It makes you human. And like I tried to tell you before, there's nothing wrong with that."

"When you put it that way, Karl, it sounds wonderful. But the reality of it is, I don't think I'm strong enough to live with someone like you. Someone who knows exactly what he wants and is determined to get it, who isn't afraid of anything."

Karl chuckled softly. "We're more alike than you think we are, Jaime. I'd really love to be able to agree with your assessment of me. But the way I acted yesterday raised a lot of doubts and questions in my mind. I wondered why I pushed you so hard for a decision when I knew all the time that that kind of pressure would only make you pull farther away. The answer was buried so deep inside me that I almost didn't find it in time."

His eyes shifted away from hers, and suddenly he was reliving events only he could see. "I've always made a big show of being open with my feelings, Jaime. But I realized last night that, until I met you, that's all it was—a show. I guess I was real anxious to prove to myself that my mother's leaving hadn't hurt me, hadn't closed me off to other people. Except that no matter how hard I tried, no matter how much I talked about it, I couldn't trust another human being enough to fall in love. Until I met you."

He turned to look at Jaime, and his words and the warm feeling she saw shining from his eyes nearly destroyed her last defenses. "But I was still afraid, Jaime. Afraid of the power love had over me, the power you had over me. You made me lose control the way no woman ever had before. You made me feel an emotional hunger I didn't know if I could ever appease."

He smiled wryly. "Not that I didn't try. I made love to you over and over again, trying to cram a lifetime of intimacy into a single weekend. But it wasn't enough. I still wanted more. I finally laid it all on the line and offered you marriage, and you decided to leave anyway—just like my mother had years before.''

"Your mother?" Jaime frowned in concentration. "I know she left when you were eight. But what does that have to do with how you acted last night?"

"I told you to let go of the past, Jaime. But I didn't realize until yesterday how my own past was affecting my present. Somehow, emotionally, without ever being conscious of the fact, I equated your rejection with her desertion. I was convinced that I'd never see you again, either. That's why I tried to push you into making a commitment even though I knew I was putting too much pressure on you. But I've had a chance to think things over, and I—"

There was a knock on the door, then it flew open to reveal Maria's anxious face. She gripped Jaime's arm hard. "I'm sorry for breaking in on you guys, but it's Sharon. She's in labor!"

"But she still has two weeks to go until her due date!" Jaime protested.

"Apparently the baby doesn't know that!"

"How far apart are her contractions?" Jaime asked, trying to recall details from when she'd given birth to Alex. All she remembered was a pain-filled blur.

"Five minutes," Maria responded. "We timed two contractions while you and Karl were talking, and Sharon timed several during the hearing."

Jaime and Karl both looked at Maria in frank disbelief. "Hey," Maria protested, "don't blame me! Sharon said she wasn't sure if the pains were the real thing or just a false alarm. She wanted to time a few before she told anyone."

"I don't believe she could be that cool," Jaime murmured.

"With labor pains five minutes apart, we ought to get her to the hospital," Karl said.

Both women stared at him suspiciously.

"I play poker with an obstetrician," he hastened to explain.

"Excuse me."

Jaime, Karl and Maria turned in unison to look at a smiling Sharon. "I just called my doctor and my husband. They're both going to meet me at the hospital. Maria, do you think you could bring your car around to the front of the courthouse so I won't have to walk so far?"

Maria gaped at her friend in astonishment before recovering herself. "Sure. Of course."

They walked Sharon over to the elevator where Ivar and Wilma were already waiting. Jaime impatiently pressed the Down button. The first car that stopped was full.

"Move over, honey," Maria said as she forced her way into the crowded elevator. "I'll go first, Sharon. I'll get the car. Tell that baby to wait for me!"

The doors closed on the picture of Maria squeezed between two attractive men who looked like they weren't at all adverse to the idea of sharing their limited space.

"I'll bet she has both their phone numbers before they get to the first floor," Jaime ventured, expressing her confidence in her friend's prowess with the male gender.

"Absolutely," Sharon agreed.

There was room for all five of them in the next car. They reached the first floor and passed through the revolving door without incident. But when Sharon stood outside and looked down the courthouse steps to the street below, she balked.

"Oh, Jaime! How am I going to make it down all those stairs! What if I have a contraction on the way down? I might fall!"

Before Jaime had time to suggest an alternative, Karl had lifted Sharon into his arms and was negotiating the stairs as swiftly and surely as if they were level ground. Jaime hurried after him, Ivar and Wilma following at a slower pace.

Maria pulled up with the car just as they reached the sidewalk. Jaime opened the front door, and Karl deposited Sharon on the passenger seat.

Jaime was about to climb into the back when Karl's voice stopped her. "I hope I'll be seeing you again, Jaime."

"Seeing me?" Jaime echoed in confusion.

Karl was more afraid than he'd ever been in his life. He was leaving himself open for more hurt than he could handle. But he knew it was something he had to do. "Ever since I met you, I've been trying to figure out what it was that you needed from me. Now I finally know: love, respect, trust. And the freedom to make your own choices without any pressure or interference from me."

He touched the ring finger of her left hand. "I still want you to come to Seattle, marry me and stay with me forever. But if you can't make that kind of commitment, I understand. You can come for a year, a month or a weekend, instead. And if you decide not to come at all, all I ask is that you let me know."

Jaime could hardly believe it. He was giving her the time she'd asked for. And after what he'd told her moments before, she understood how much that gesture cost him. "Thank you, Karl. I'll . . . I'll think about your offer."

"You do that. And stop telling yourself that if you come to Seattle, I'll try to take over your life. It's just not true. And even if it were, you wouldn't let me get away with it. You're too strong for that."

He took her face between his hands. "I don't want to carry you through life, Jaime. I just want to walk beside you and share the trip."

Torn, Jaime threw a guilty glance in Sharon's direction. "I have to go now, Karl. Can we meet later?"

"Wilma and Granddad are staying in Miami for a few days at Wilma's house. But I'm flying home today. If I stayed, I might be tempted to start pushing for an answer—and that's the last thing you need."

Unexpectedly he drew her close for a quick, desperate kiss, then pulled back to look into her face. "I won't call or write until I hear from you, Jaime. No pressure. You have my word."

He gazed at her intently, his lips warm as they brushed hers one final time. "And you have my love."

Dazed, Jaime climbed into the back seat, and Karl shut the door behind her. As Maria sped away from the curb, Jaime called out goodbyes to Wilma and Ivar. Then, unable to resist the impulse, she turned to watch Karl through the back window. His figure became smaller and smaller as they got farther away, until finally it was no longer distinguishable.

But his words still filled her mind and heart, his taste still lingered on her lips. Was he right? Was she really strong enough to share her life with him?

Unsure of the answer to that question, Jaime faced forward again.

Sharon turned and looked back at her with a smile. "I wouldn't have missed eavesdropping on that conversation for anything in the world. It was so romantic!"

"Are you sure this woman is in labor?" Jaime asked Maria.

"*She's* sure," Maria responded, her gaze glued to the road. "And that's good enough for me."

"It *is* romantic," Sharon insisted. "You have to go to Seattle, Jaime. You have to at least *try* staying with Karl for a while."

Jaime wasn't so certain. "I have Alex to think about. Besides—"

Maria interrupted her, obviously exasperated. "Don't tell me, let me guess. You don't want to feel obligated to the man. Well, then why don't you just move out there and get your own place? That way you could keep seeing Karl without having to make a commitment right away—or at all if you decide against it."

Jaime shook her head. "Even if I sold my house, I'd be lucky to clear anything after I paid off the mortgages. So, basically I'd be dependent on Karl until I found a job and a place to live. And what if I gave up everything I have here to go to Seattle and then it didn't work out between us?"

"What do you have here that's so wonderful?" Maria scoffed. "Your job? You'll get a better one in Seattle."

"I don't know that for sure. Besides, how can I walk out on my responsibilities here? Especially now, with Sharon leaving?"

Maria made a derisive sound. "Do you think you're indispensable? Don't pass up a chance at happiness with a man who really cares about you. I heard what he had to say about sharing the trip, and it sounded like a good deal to me. What's the matter, don't you trust him to keep his word?"

"If I hear the word trust one more time..." Jaime muttered. It was her own fear, her own inadequacy that she couldn't come to terms with. But she didn't want to admit that to her friends. She was scarcely able to admit it to herself.

It would be too easy for her to become dependent on Karl. And she knew she couldn't count on him or any other man to fulfill her needs. In Miami she had her own home and the promise of a raise and a promotion in the near future. Add Alex to the list and she already had everything she needed. Or did she? Didn't she need the warmth and caring she'd found in Karl's arms?

Another contraction raced through Sharon's body and, though she practiced her breathing technique, Jaime could see the pain in her friend's face. "Are you all right?" she asked anxiously.

"That one really hurt," Sharon said shakily.

Reaching between the bucket seats, Jaime grabbed the other woman's hand and squeezed. "Hold on, we're almost at the hospital. Soon you'll have a beautiful baby to show for all this trouble."

Sharon squeezed back and turned her head to look at Jaime. "When you had Alex, was it...did it hurt a lot?"

Jaime thought of the shame, the fear and the pain her son's birth had cost her, and sighed. "I was alone, I was unprepared and I was scared to death. So for me there was a lot of pain. But even so, I kept telling myself that it was a good kind of pain because it was pain for a reason—the best reason in the world. It was worth it to me, Sharon. And that's the truth."

"Would you do it again?"

The image of a smiling, red-bearded giant with twinkling blue eyes flitted through Jaime's mind. "I don't know, Sharon," she said softly. "I honestly don't know."

Chapter Fifteen

Karl scanned the road ahead of him, squinting against the glare of the afternoon sun. Another day without Jaime. She hadn't called or written since she'd left him at the courthouse four weeks before. And he hadn't had a decent night's sleep for weeks wondering why. Unless he counted last night when he'd conked out on his grandfather's couch from sheer exhaustion.

"How could she do this to me?" he whispered, unaware that he'd spoken aloud.

A phone call—even a letter—telling him that she was staying in Miami would have been preferable to this endless waiting and wondering. It was a cruel and cowardly way to end a relationship. Had the warmth and courage he'd seen in her been just an illusion? No, he'd held that warmth in his arms. Her caring had touched his heart.

Then what was the explanation? His hands tightened on the steering wheel. Maybe something had happened to her. An accident, a mugging. Some referral she'd gone out on when he hadn't been there to back her up. The possibilities were enough to threaten his sanity. And if something had happened to her, would anyone think to notify him? He was nothing in her life. He had no claim on her at all.

The short ferry ride across Puget Sound had its usual soothing effect on Karl. By the time he drove his car onto Vashon Island, he'd managed to attain a degree of calm. He'd resigned himself to the fact that Jaime wasn't here because she didn't want to be. She hadn't called because she was afraid if he talked to her he might be able to convince her that there was a chance for them. And that possibility scared the hell out of her. She was safe now, wrapped up tight in her impenetrable cocoon of ice once more. As if they'd never met. As if there had never been a man in her life named Karl Hallstrom.

Karl swung into his driveway, tires screeching, his brief interlude of serenity a fast-fading memory. He entered the sprawling two-story house and slammed the door behind him. There was no reason to try to control his temper anymore. Jaime wouldn't be here to see him. He crossed to the liquor cabinet and removed a bottle, not bothering with a glass. Slumping down into his favorite armchair, he unscrewed the cap and took a long swig of the contents, grimacing as the fiery liquid burned its way down his throat.

He'd been stupid to think that he could get a woman as scarred as Jaime to trust him enough to pull up stakes and come all the way across the country to start a new life. He'd expected too much; he'd moved too fast. But damn, he'd wanted her so. He needed her. He still loved her.

All his life he'd gone after what he'd wanted, taken what he'd needed. Waiting for someone else to take action was the hardest thing he'd ever done. And what had it accomplished? She wasn't here, was she?

A grimly determined look came over his face, and he reached one large hand out to grab the phone. He'd fly back to Miami and lay siege to her home and her office if necessary. But first he'd call her and tell her exactly what he thought of the way she was acting.

He picked up the receiver, then returned it to the cradle without dialing. No, he had given her his word. He had to wait for Jaime to come to him—no matter how long it took. It was the only way he would ever earn her trust. Without that trust, there could never be anything real between them. And if she chose not to contact him at all, he had to respect her right to make that decision.

He was still sitting, staring morosely into space when he heard the sound of a car pulling into the driveway. Hastily setting the all-but-forgotten whiskey bottle aside, Karl jogged to the door and threw it open.

As nervous as a child on the first day of school, Jaime was just raising her hand to knock. Then the door was suddenly wrenched open, and Karl filled the doorway, his eyes wild, his flaming hair in disarray, looking like some Nordic god about to smite an offending mortal.

Startled, Jaime took a step backward and almost fell off the porch.

"What are you doing here?" Karl demanded, torn between anger and a wild, soaring joy.

Jaime gazed up at the frowning hulk confronting her and wondered the same thing. "I... you asked me to come. Didn't you?"

Karl saw the uncertainty in her eyes and was ashamed to be the cause of it. No feelings of anger or hurt pride were going to prevent him from giving his woman the acceptance and reassurance she needed.

He stepped forward and gently gathered Jaime into his arms. "Yes, I asked you to come. And, believe it or not, I'm glad to see you."

She relaxed against him with a sigh, and he tightened his arms around her. His voice was soft as his big hands smoothed her hair. "I'm sorry, sweetheart. I know how I must have looked just now."

Jaime pulled back and stared up at him with mischief in her eyes. "You looked just like you did that first day you came into my office. As if you were going to tear me to shreds and scatter the remains to the four corners of the earth.''

Holding her in his arms like this, it was an effort to recall what he'd been mad about. But he was determined to discover just what was going on. ''You drove all the way up here?''

''I decided it was the best thing to do,'' Jaime told him. ''That way I could bring my car and take along a lot of my things in a rented trailer. And, well, driving gave me time to make the transition between there and here—between my old life and this new life I'm starting. I needed to take it slow, to have that time to adjust.''

Just when he thought he had the woman all figured out, she'd thrown him another curve. ''You brought your things? You're really moving up here? That's great, but I thought for sure you'd come for a visit first before you decided to move.''

Jaime smiled, a little embarrassed by her own impulsiveness. ''I decided it wasn't necessary. I already knew everything I needed to know.''

The warm light in Jaime's eyes dissolved the last remnants of Karl's resentment. Did this mean that she was ready for marriage and a life together? He was afraid to ask the question, afraid he'd scare her away again. He'd take things slow and let her tell him when she was ready. She was here, and that was the important thing. Now they had all the time in the world to work out the details.

With an effort, he gathered his thoughts together and asked the question that had been on his mind when he'd first seen her on the porch. ''Why on earth didn't you call and let me know that you were on your way?''

Jaime read the hurt in his voice, and her expression softened in understanding. Sometimes it was difficult for her to remember just how vulnerable this mountain of a man really was.

''I didn't call before I left Miami because I was afraid you'd try to talk me out of driving up here in this old car of mine. I even had a nightmare about a big argument that ended with you telling me not to come. But I never intended to burst in on you like this. I tried to call you several times last night, and again this morning, but there wasn't any answer.''

Karl nodded as he realized what had happened. ''I fell asleep at Granddad's house last night. So of course I wasn't home when you called.''

A voice that was a study in affected boredom broke into their exchange. ''Hey, you guys, you think you could finish this conversation inside? It's *freezing* out here!''

Karl and Jaime both turned to face Alex. He was leaning against a pillar of the porch, the picture of nonchalance. But he couldn't quite hide the sparkle in his eyes when Karl extended his hand for a formal shake, then unexpectedly drew him close for a brief hug.

''Welcome to Seattle, buddy. You're right. It must be at least sixty degrees out here. We'd better get inside before you turn into an icicle.''

Alex grinned sheepishly, more pleased than embarrassed by Karl's teasing. ''Well, it's cold compared to Miami!''

''Already sorry about the move?'' Karl inquired.

Alex shook his head. ''No way. It's the smartest thing Mom ever did. The only hard part was waiting around for her to realize what I knew all along.''

''Alex!'' Jaime exclaimed, surprised by his comment.

''Come on, Mom! It's obvious how you feel about Karl.''

Karl examined Jaime's face closely. Was it obvious? She was here, but she still hadn't agreed to any permanent commitment.

''Did Mom tell you about the baby?''

Seeing the expression on Karl's face, Jaime hastened to explain. ''*Sharon's* baby. She had a beautiful eight-pound-three-ounce girl. Sharon named her Karla Michelle.''

''*Karla?*'' Karl exclaimed, laughing incredulously. ''That trip down the courthouse steps must have made a lasting impression on your friend.''

''Actually, I think it was one of Sharon's attempts to nudge me in the right direction.''

All at once, the door of the house next door opened and a pretty teenaged girl in shorts and a T-shirt came down the steps. "Hi, Karl!" she called. She smiled, and Jaime caught the glint of braces in the afternoon sun.

Alex snapped to attention with miraculous speed. "Who's that?" he asked curiously.

One corner of Karl's mouth lifted. "Her name's Julie Delaney. Why don't you go on over and say hello—if you think you'll be able to stand the cold out here for a little while longer."

"Oh, Karl," Jaime whispered as she watched her son casually amble down the steps and across the yard. "I don't think I'm ready for him to discover girls yet."

Karl put an arm around her shoulder in sympathy as he watched Alex introduce himself to a shyly smiling Julie. Then both young people disappeared into the home next door. "Well, it looks like *he's* ready. But don't worry, Julie's mom is home, so they'll have a chaperon."

He looked down at her, still trying to absorb the reality of her presence. "I can't believe you're really here, Jaime. I thought I'd never pry you away from that job of yours."

"I got that promotion I was after, you know."

Karl caressed a strand of her hair. "And you left anyway?"

"When I thought it over, I realized that no job could be the center of my life anymore. You had taken over that position. And I had to come to Seattle to be with you."

Karl considered her statement. Not to *marry* him, to *be* with him. It was less than he had hoped for. But just the fact that she was here seemed like a miracle. He'd take her, whatever the terms.

He bent to kiss her, his mouth slowly drawing closer to hers.

"Mom?"

Starting in surprise, Jaime pulled away from Karl to see that Alex was back on the porch with them.

"Mom, is it okay if I go to the movies with Julie and her mother?"

"I'm not sure," Jaime said hesitantly.

"I've known the Delaneys for years," Karl told her. "Julie's dad is the obstetrician that I play poker with."

"Then I guess it's all right." Jaime pulled a ten-dollar bill out of her purse and handed it to Alex. "But you're the one who's paying for it. This is just an advance on your allowance."

"See you two later," Alex said, bounding down the steps.

"Not too much later," Jaime warned.

"Have fun!" Karl called after him. He turned back to Jaime, a serious expression on his face. "The boy's getting too old for an allowance. I can find a part-time job for him at the company—if you approve."

Jaime's first impulse was to say no. Then she reminded herself that she had to consider what Alex would want, too. "Maybe just on Saturdays to start. Then we'll see how he settles in at school. Right now, I'm the one who has to worry about finding a job."

"I thought that you might want to go back to school full-time to get your master's degree," Karl said in a roundabout offer of financial support. "I even checked into the program at the University of Washington. You can get a Ph.D. in social work there if you want to."

Jaime smiled at him, appreciating his unspoken offer and rejecting it. "I do want to get my master's, but I need to get a job to pay expenses while I'm doing it. I've decided that I want to go into substance-abuse counseling. I'm especially interested in counseling pregnant women and mothers who are on drugs."

"Weren't you the lady who wanted a job with less client contact?"

"Weren't you the man who told me how good I was with people and how trying my best was good enough? Well, it took me a while. But I thought about the clients I'd had and what I'd accomplished over the years. And I realized that you were right."

"I'll bet Charlene Todd had something to do with this decision."

Jaime nodded, pleased by his perceptiveness. She had taken the risk of reaching out to Charlene and, despite her fumbling and her lack of training, she'd actually made a difference. It was a good feeling.

"Don't tell me she decided to give up drugs and move back in with her mother?"

"Yes, believe it or not. And she's doing fine so far. Her little boy is still in the hospital."

"She had her baby already?" Karl asked, surprised.

The sad look in Jaime's eyes told him the rest of the story even before she spoke. "He was born prematurely with some serious medical problems. And he may be mentally impaired as well."

"And Charlene? How does she feel now?" Karl asked with a hint of sarcasm.

"There's no way Charlene can change what's already happened," Jaime reminded him gently. "But if she stays off drugs, she can give her baby the love and the care he needs. And right now, that's all that matters."

"But she could go back on drugs again," Karl warned. "And you'll have to face similar situations everyday if you go into that kind of counseling. It's a sure thing that you're going to lose more than you win."

"As a very smart man once observed, that won't stop me from trying."

Karl conceded the point, amused to find his own words used against him. "I guess I can't argue with that."

"Somehow, I didn't expect you to," Jaime told him teasingly. Then her tone grew more serious. "I'd like to give it a try, despite the odds. I'd like to try to help."

Karl plunged into the opening, determined to offer her something she might be willing to accept. "Speaking of help, one of my assistants just quit. You'd be doing me a favor if you'd help me out at the company—just until you complete your degree, of course."

Jaime smiled up at him. "I'm looking for something in social work. Besides, if I'm one of your employees, a personal relationship would be a conflict of interest."

Karl caught the gleam in her eye, and his pulse rate accelerated. It had been a long four weeks. "Somehow, I don't think that would stop me."

"In that case, we can discuss it."

"Let's discuss it some other time," Karl said huskily. "When we don't have a whole afternoon alone. By ourselves. Just the two of us."

Maneuvering her into the house, Karl swung the front door closed behind them. Jaime suddenly found herself pressed up against the entryway wall by a very large, warm, hard body. For just a second she felt suffocated, trapped. Then she relaxed and let herself respond to the love and caring Karl was offering her. Raising her lips, she invited his kiss.

Karl lowered his mouth to cover hers with a desperate yearning that told her better than any words how much he'd missed her. "I thought I'd lost you," he whispered. He parted her lips with a gently persistent tongue, and Jaime's passion rose to match his.

When Karl felt her tongue seeking access to his mouth, he made a wordless sound of welcome deep in his throat. His hands rose to capture her face between them and mold her lips more firmly against his own.

Jaime's hands roamed over his shoulders, tracing the taut ridges of muscle down the curve of his spine to the small of his back. All thought of restraint fled as her hands surrendered to temptation and strayed even lower. Cupping his firm buttocks, she pulled the unyielding hardness of his body against the softness of her own.

"Jaime..." he breathed, tortured beyond endurance by the unexpected fervor of her response.

Karl stooped and swung one arm behind her knees. Instinctively Jaime's arms rose to clasp his neck as she was swept off her feet and carried across the room and up the stairs as though she weighed no more than a newborn babe. She had time to form a blurred impression of a hallway with brown-and-beige striped wallpaper and a seascape painting before Karl took her through a doorway into a sunlit room with light wood paneling and the biggest bed she'd ever seen.

"Queen size, king size and your size," she murmured, unable to repress the laughter that bubbled forth. She was so full of love and joy that she felt she'd burst if she didn't express it somehow.

Karl grinned back at her as though he felt exactly the same way. His eyes seemed to absorb her into their warm blue depths, and her lips were drawn inevitably back to his.

Groping behind his back with one hand, Karl managed to keep his mouth on hers even as he caught the edge of the bedroom door and pushed it closed. But his hand slipped before he succeeded in securing the lock, and he broke their kiss with an exasperated exclamation. "Damn door!"

Jaime giggled at his almost comic impatience even though she felt the same urgent longing to be alone with him, the same overwhelming need to join her body to his again.

Lifting one hand, she stroked his dark red hair. "You know, this probably sounds very silly, but you were so angry the first time I saw you that I pictured you as a ferocious Viking warrior. Now here you are wearing that same expression and doing battle with a door!"

Karl turned his head and gave her his best glare. "You are an insolent wench! Do you know what ferocious Viking warriors do with insolent wenches? We carry them off to bed and ravish them until they scream for mercy."

Jaime smiled smugly as she reached down and locked the door. "Is that a promise or merely a threat?"

Karl crossed the room and lowered her carefully onto the mattress. "That's a well-documented historical fact. But since you still seem determined to conduct your own research, I'll give you my full cooperation."

He was surprised when Jaime rose to a kneeling position and began to unbutton his shirt. "On second thought," she told him, "maybe I'll ravish you."

Karl stood by the bed, more than willing to be victimized. He bit back a moan as Jaime's warm, wet kisses traced a path across his chest, and he was fully aroused by the time he felt her tugging at his belt.

When her hand closed around him, he shivered uncontrollably and whispered her name.

Jaime smiled up at him, glorying in his response. The fact that her touch could make Karl quiver, that she could hold that much strength and power captive with a brush of her fingertips, excited Jaime beyond anything she had ever experienced. She breathed in the musky odor of his arousal, then leaned forward to sample his salty, velvet-smooth flavor.

Karl shut his eyes and held her close against him. He was overcome by a pleasure that transcended the physical. Only a few short weeks ago, Jaime had been unwilling to trust him with even a small part of herself. Now she was offering all she had to give.

Unable to wait any longer, he lifted her face up and caressed her lips with his own. Then he joined her on the bed, pushing aside clothing until there was nothing left to keep them apart.

Jaime cried out his name as he entered her, exulting in his possession after weeks of lonely deprivation.

"I love you, Jaime," Karl whispered as he brought her closer and closer to fulfillment. "I love you."

Jaime clutched his shoulders, shuddering under him, her entire being responding to the man she held in her arms.

The sight, sound and feel of her climax pushed Karl over the edge of sensation. He lost all sense of place and time and self in Jaime's welcoming warmth.

For long moments afterward, he held her cradled in his arms, never wanting to release her, never wanting her to go away from him again. But with the return of rational thought had come the fear, the doubt. He needed to know how Jaime felt.

"Jaime?"

"Umm?"

"I have something to show you."

Jaime rubbed her nose against the crinkly hair on his chest, shifting in his embrace and stretching like a lazy, contented cat. "What?"

Reaching across her, Karl pulled open the drawer of the bedside table. He took out a gold band and handed it to Jaime.

She sat up to examine the intricately wrought floral pattern, the covers falling to her waist unnoticed. "It's beautiful!" she exclaimed.

Karl smiled, his eyes taking in the sight of Jaime in all her natural, unselfconscious glory. "*You're* beautiful."

But Jaime hardly heard him. She was examining the inside of the ring, puzzling over the indecipherable inscription.

"Here. You have to put the two of them together."

He dropped another ring into her hand. To Jaime it looked like an entirely different pattern, hearts and ribbons entwined. But when Karl snapped the two rings together, Jaime noticed with delight that a new pattern had been formed: two interlocking hands, bound together by ribbons and surrounded by flowers.

"How clever!" Jaime remarked. "Each ring has a complete pattern all by itself, but when you join them together a different, more complex pattern emerges. Nothing's lost, it just becomes part of a larger design."

Suddenly she understood. "That's what you've been trying to tell me all along, isn't it? That we could build a life together and each still retain our own identity, our own sense of self."

His eyes shining, Karl kissed her softly. "Yes. I was hoping you'd understand."

She lifted one hand to stroke his cheek, her eyes as brilliant as his. "I think I do—finally."

Karl pressed ahead, knowing that there would never be a better moment. "No matter what happens, I want you to keep these rings, Jaime. And I hope that someday you'll agree to wear them as my wife."

The familiar fear fought to claim her, but it was overbalanced by the love she felt for the man beside her. She had already made her choice when she'd left Miami, and she had reaffirmed it moments ago in his arms. But now she said the words for the first time.

"I love you, Karl. And I'd be proud to be your wife. Right here, right now."

Karl wanted to shout with joy. Instead he pulled Jaime to him and kissed her again. "All the time I was working on the rings, I was picturing this moment."

Jaime was deeply touched, and awed by his talent. "*You* made the rings? Oh, Karl!"

Karl was a little embarrassed by the intensity of her response. "Well, I had to do something with my free time this past month. I thought I'd go crazy waiting to find out whether or not you were coming to Seattle."

"But you were so patient, Karl. You didn't call or write. You gave me a chance to make up my own mind, to make my own choice. I think that was what finally made me believe that it could really work between us."

Karl smiled ruefully. "At the end there, I wasn't so patient. I thought about getting on a plane myself and coming after you."

"Being away from you made me a little crazy, too." She laughed at the picture in her mind. "I guess it wouldn't be so bad being carried off into the sunset by a Viking warrior who knows how to make beautiful rings—and beautiful love."

Karl threw the sheet aside and pulled Jaime down until she was lying naked beneath him. "It's almost sunset now."

"Wait!" Jaime demanded, one hand pushing against his chest. "I haven't read the inscription on the rings yet." She frowned as she tried to make out the unfamiliar lettering. "This doesn't make sense even with both rings joined together!"

Karl grinned as he slipped the thick band onto her finger. "It's Swedish."

"What does it mean?"

"Well," Karl said with a mischievous gleam in his eye, "a rough translation would be, 'I promise to love you forever.'"

Jaime looked up at him suspiciously. "How can I be sure of that?"

Her future husband claimed her lips with his and didn't stop until he'd kissed her breathless. Then he looked down into her flushed face and smiled. "You'll just have to trust me."

Epilogue

"It's hard to believe that it's been three years since I left Miami," Jaime said musingly.

Sharon hoisted a three-year-old Karla onto her lap and smiled at her friend across the big dining room table. "Well, it has been, and I've missed you! Thanks for inviting us to come to Seattle and stay with you. I know we're going to have a great time on this vacation."

"I'm already having a great time," Ted said between forkfuls of salmon. "This is delicious!"

Jaime looked at Karl, her pride obvious. "Even I've learned to tolerate salmon—the way my husband cooks it."

"I'm the one who taught him how!" Ivar declared.

"Oh, hush, and let Karl take the credit that's due him," Wilma admonished.

"Nag, nag, nag. All the woman does is nag."

Everyone else at the table hid smiles as the older couple continued their affectionate bickering. Ivar had grown a touch more confused over the years, but with his acceptance of that fact, and with Wilma's help, he was still able to live a full life in his own home.

"Your husband helps out a lot," Sharon observed as Karl disappeared into the kitchen.

Jaime smiled up at him as he reappeared seconds later carrying an apple cake. "With my job and my night classes, he's had to. But it was worth it. I finally have my master's degree—just in time."

Her hand drifted down to her stomach, fully rounded with pregnancy. It had occurred in spite of every precaution. Yet it seemed a natural, inevitable part of their deepening love—a love that left no room for fears or reservations. Jaime felt no regret—except for the weight she'd gained as a result.

She pushed away the piece of cake Karl tried to serve her. "If I eat anymore, I'll explode!"

"It looks good on you," Karl said with a meaningful glance at her full breasts.

Jaime tried to look reproachful, but ended up smiling instead. She was grateful when Sharon changed the subject.

"Did you find a job in substance-abuse counseling like you planned?"

"Yes, but after the baby comes, I'm cutting my hours down to Saturday and two evenings a week. Alex has promised to help me out by baby-sitting."

She smiled at her son who was seated next to her. He was seventeen now and only an inch or two shorter than Karl.

"He starts college in the fall," Karl added. "But we don't know if it's because he's really interested in a higher education, or if he's just going to keep Julie company."

"Come on, Dad," Alex said, trying to sound indifferent even as his face turned red. "You know I've always wanted to be an engineer."

Karl smiled, and Jaime rolled her eyes, wondering how her son could rewrite history so neatly. But neither doubted Alex's sincerity.

"I'm just glad you decided to go to college in Seattle," Karl told Alex with a wink. "I don't know how I'd run the company without you."

"I think you could manage," Alex responded. But he couldn't quite restrain the pleased smile that spread over his face in reaction to Karl's praise.

Sharon threw herself into the lull in the conversation. "Did I tell you that Maria called off the engagement? She decided the dermatologist was too dull for her."

"I thought she was dating an Argentinian business-man," Jaime said, confused.

Sharon shook her head. "He was the one before the der-matologist. Now she's going out with a race-car driver she met at the Miami Grand Prix."

Karl grinned. "Think she'll ever get married?"

"Why should she?" Ted said with a hint of envy in his voice. "She's having too much fun being single."

"Is Maria still with Catholic Services?" Jaime asked Sharon as they began to clear off the table.

"Yes. She keeps telling me that I should leave HRS and go over there to work with her."

Jaime hadn't been surprised to learn that—despite her threats to resign—Sharon had returned to work after six months of maternity leave.

"How is it going with HRS?" Jaime inquired curiously.

"There has been some reorganization, and I think it's helped. But basically it's the same old job—and we still don't get any respect for doing it."

Ted glanced up at his wife. "Stop complaining, honey. Compared to my job, yours is a piece of cake. And I told you before, if you don't like it, you can always quit."

Sharon looked at Jaime. "See what I mean?"

Jaime picked up a spoon and clanged it against a glass until all conversation stopped. "Everybody stand up."

A chorus of complaints and muttered objections reached her ears, but she only repeated her command.

When everyone was finally on their feet, Jaime reached over and picked up her own glass. "I'd like to make a toast.

To a lady who does the job because it's hers to do, and who gives it her best because her best is all she knows how to give. To Sharon."

Her eyes bright, Sharon smiled and drank deeply.

It was after eleven when Jaime and Karl stepped onto the porch for a breath of night air. The house was finally quiet, Karla had fallen asleep before eight, and even Alex had turned in early. Wilma and Ivar were on their way home, and Sharon and Ted had retired to the guest room.

Jaime sighed as she leaned back against Karl's warm frame. He kissed her cheek and slid both hands around to cradle her stomach. "Happy?" he asked.

"Yes, I'm happy. I wish everyone in the world could feel the way I feel right now."

"You don't regret the choice you made? Moving to Seattle, marrying me?"

"I love Seattle, I love my job. And most of all I love you."

The baby kicked against Karl's hands, commanding attention. "And you're not sorry about this determined little cuss?"

Jaime shook her head. "I don't think I could ever be sorry about bringing a child of yours into the world—even if I had ten children already." She felt the muscle in Karl's cheek move and knew he was smiling. "I didn't say I *intended* to have ten children, so don't you laugh at me!"

They stood watching the stars in companionable silence, Karl gently massaging Jaime's abdomen as the baby moved beneath his hands.

"Karl," she said after a while. "If it's a girl, can we name her Sarah?"

Karl's arms tightened around her. "I think that's a wonderful idea. And what about Lynn as a middle name?"

"Sarah Lynn Hallstrom," Jaime said, trying it out. "I like it. What made you think of Lynn?"

"It was my mother's name."

Jaime didn't say a word. She just snuggled closer, offer ing him all the love she had and a sympathetic ear.

Karl continued talking, his voice soft and filled with emotion. "When the memory of the day she left finally came back to me, I realized that my mother hadn't been the cold and unfeeling woman I'd been picturing all those years. She seemed just as desperate and scared as I was. Maybe I needed to block that fact out—to let my anger at her take over—in order to live with her desertion." He paused and then his words were a whisper on the still night air. "She was crying when she left, Jaime."

Jaime took one of his hands and drew it to her lips in a silent gesture of comfort. "Maybe you should try to find her," she suggested tentatively.

"A few years ago—right after we got married—I sent some letters, tried to trace her. But all I found were dead ends. I don't know why I didn't tell you about it then. Maybe I was afraid of looking foolish."

"I don't think it's foolish to want to know your mother's reasons for leaving, to want to discover what became of her."

"Wherever she is, I hope she's found the same peace that I have. The peace that comes with forgiveness and accep tance and love."

Jaime folded her arms over his. "I've found it, Karl. I was so wrong before. Leaning on you, letting you help me, let ting you share my responsibilities, didn't make me weaker. It made me stronger. Now I feel like there's nothing I can't do."

Karl nuzzled her ear. "Nothing?"

Jaime shifted against him. "I'm three days past my due date already."

Karl's kisses trailed down the side of her neck. "What did the doctor say about . . ."

Jaime laughed softly. "I didn't ask. I was afraid he'd tell me something I didn't want to hear."

She turned her lips into his kiss. When his mouth lifted from hers again, they were both aroused.

Smiling a smile as old as Eve, Jaime took his hand to lead him inside.

He hesitated in the doorway, touching her face with his free hand. "Jaime, are you sure you want to do this?"

Her eyes shining with love, Jaime pressed a kiss against his palm. "It would take a stronger man than you to hold me off, Karl Hallstrom."

With a groan, Karl pressed his lips to hers again.

Jaime clung to him tightly, returning the caress of his mouth. Before their marriage, she had loved him with a wild, desperate hope. Then she had lived with him and shared his life. Every time she'd reached out to him, he'd been there for her. Every day had seemed to bring a new depth of caring until she had come to love him with a deep, sweet surety that nothing could shake.

"I love you, Jaime."

"I love you, too."

"Ah, but do you trust me?"

Despite his teasing smile, Jaime saw the serious expression in his eyes. She framed his bearded face between her hands, her voice firm and sure against the quiet of the night. "Yes, I trust you. Completely, without reservation. How could I not? You taught me the meaning of the word."

Karl sighed and stroked her hair. "And you taught me the meaning of the word love."

"Then it was a fair exchange?"

Karl shook his head. "I got the best part of the bargain."

As her husband's lips came down on hers, Jaime just smiled and let him think so.

* * * * *

proudly presents
the long-awaited "prequel" volume of

★ LOVE AND GLORY ★

by
LINDSAY McKENNA
Dawn of Valor

In the summer of '89, Silhouette Special Edition premiered three novels celebrating America's men and women in uniform: LOVE AND GLORY, by bestselling author Lindsay McKenna. Featured were the proud Trayherns, a military family as bold and patriotic as the American flag—three siblings valiantly battling the threat of dishonor, determined to triumph . . . in love and glory.

Now, discover the roots of the Trayhern brand of courage, as parents Chase and Rachel relive their earliest heartstopping experiences of survival and indomitable love, in

Dawn of Valor, Silhouette Special Edition #649.

This February, experience the thrill of LOVE AND GLORY—from the very beginning!

DV-1

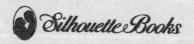
Silhouette Books

SILHOUETTE·INTIMATE·MOMENTS®

NORA ROBERTS
Night Shadow

People all over the city of Urbana were asking, Who was that masked man?

Assistant district attorney Deborah O'Roarke was the first to learn his secret identity . . . and her life would never be the same.

The stories of the lives and loves of the O'Roarke sisters began in January 1991 with NIGHT SHIFT, Silhouette Intimate Moments #365. And if you want to know more about Deborah and the man behind the mask, look for NIGHT SHADOW, Silhouette Intimate Moments #373, available in March at your favorite retail outlet.

NITE-1

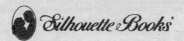 *Silhouette Books*

Take 4 bestselling love stories FREE

Plus get a FREE surprise gift!

SILHOUETTE·INTIMATE·MOMENTS

FEBRUARY FROLICS!

This February, we've got a special treat in store for you: four terrific books written by four brand-new authors! From sunny California to North Dakota's frozen plains, they'll whisk you away to a world of romance and adventure.

Look for

L.A. HEAT (IM #369) by Rebecca Daniels
AN OFFICER AND A GENTLEMAN (IM #370) by Rachel Lee
HUNTER'S WAY (IM #371) by Justine Davis
DANGEROUS BARGAIN (IM #372) by Kathryn Stewart

They're all part of February Frolics, coming to you from Silhouette Intimate Moments—where life is exciting and dreams do come true.

FF-1

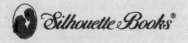

Silhouette romances are now available in stores at these convenient times each month.

Silhouette Desire
Silhouette Romance

These two series will be in stores on the 4th of every month.

Silhouette Intimate Moments
Silhouette Special Edition

New titles for these series will be in stores on the 16th of every month.

We hope this new schedule is convenient for you. With only two trips each month to your local bookseller, you will always be sure not to miss any of your favorite authors!

Happy reading!

Please note there may be slight variations in on-sale dates in your area due to differences in shipping and handling.